GUNSHOT TROUBLE

"Majors."

He turned, knowing the voice and what that voice meant. He saw Ben Maffitt's shape at the back end of the stable, half-merged with the gloom. Suddenly he understood that he had made the most fatal of all mistakes . . . he had underestimated a man.

Swinging back on his heels, Majors put a shot into the lantern and knocked out the light as Maffitt began to rock the stable with a steady roar of gunfire . . .

Ⓢ SIGNET BRAND WESTERN

SIGNET Brand Westerns You'll Enjoy

SUNDOWN JIM

Ernest Haycox

A SIGNET BOOK

NEW AMERICAN LIBRARY

TIMES MIRROR

PUBLISHER'S NOTE

This novel is a work of fiction. Names, characters, places, and incidents are either the product of the author's imagination or are used fictitiously, and any resemblance to actual persons, living or dead, events, or locales is entirely coincidental.

COPYRIGHT, 1937, 1938 BY ERNEST HAYCOX
COPYRIGHT © RENEWED 1965, 1966 BY JILL MARIE HAYCOX

All rights reserved

Published by arrangement with Mrs. Ernest Haycox

 SIGNET TRADEMARK REG. U.S. PAT. OFF. AND FOREIGN COUNTRIES
REGISTERED TRADEMARK—MARCA REGISTRADA
HECHO EN CHICAGO, U.S.A.

SIGNET, SIGNET CLASSICS, MENTOR, PLUME, MERIDIAN AND NAL BOOKS *are published by The New American Library, Inc., 1633 Broadway, New York, New York 10019*

FIRST SIGNET PRINTING, MARCH, 1981

1 2 3 4 5 6 7 8 9

PRINTED IN THE UNITED STATES OF AMERICA

Contents

SUNDOWN JIM

1

"I'm Still Alive"

WIND AND RAIN and summer's sun had turned the log stage station a silver gray. Coming up to the summit of Ute Pass, Jim Majors saw how small the station was against the massive background of rock and pine which, rising tier on tier, faded into the faraway snow-fields of the peak country. This was noon, with an overhead sun warming part of the small meadow, yet even then shadows from the surrounding cliffs crept toward the station, grayly staining the earth. Majors watered his sorrel gelding and went into the station for a meal, loitering over it because he had been a-saddle since five o'clock that morning.

When he came out a man crouched on his boot-heels against the house's sunny side.

Nothing had changed in the scene except the appearance of that man, yet this was change enough. Jim Majors' life had run through hard and dangerous channels and in him was a whetted sensitivity to the call of the wind, the breath of smoke in still air, the dim prints on dusty trails—and to the obscure shifts of men. And this was like a shouted warning.

He passed the man, and climbed into the saddle and rested that way while he rolled and lighted a cigarette, his glance turned eastward. But he wasn't sure, and he wanted to know; and he had a trick that he had used before in situations like this. One moment he was wholly idle, with his back to the station; the next moment he swiftly wheeled his horse and caught the man off guard. The fellow was a small, nondescript shape against the wall, but his eyes were wide and cool in the way they absorbed the details of Majors' appear-

1

ance—from the black edges of Majors' hair to the stars stitched into the sides of his boots. Majors showed the man a smile that was tough and long-lipped and narrow, and watched the other one's lids drop and shut out interest; whereupon Majors rode away.

The Pass meadow hung narrowly between the long rise from the west and the swift fall of the canyon to eastward. Back of him—and he chose to look around to see this—was a last view of the far desert out of which he had traveled; before him the road descended into a sunless gorge and curled about a huge rock wall. When he arrived at that turn, he looked back again, to observe that the little fellow was on his horse and riding toward a steep side trail into the timber. The news of his approach to Reservation, Majors realized, would precede him.

The stage road was a ledge hewn from the vertical face of this dark, damp cliff which reared higher toward the sky as he descended. Now and then it widened to permit the passage of wagons; and quickly narrowed again. A mile from the stage station, Ute Fork River came out of the northern heights and fell with a crystal glitter into the deepening canyon bed. Mist hung here like rain, wetting his clothes; afterwards he wound with the sharp loops of the road, the cliff to one side and the white-laced river rapids on the other. Down this narrow gateway he traveled, seeing the print of wheel and shod hoof in the soft dirt beneath; and at last, around the middle of the afternoon, the road fell out of the canyon, left the river's course and struck through a rugged, rolling country solidly covered with pines.

He had shown no particular interest through the canyon, but now his gray eyes searched the pines carefully and his ears caught all the stray sounds that ran through the drowsy, warm quiet of late Indian summer. There was this vigilance about him, even though he sat on the sorrel gelding with a loose-muscled slackness and even though his long lips held a remote smile. He was an inch over six feet and didn't show the bulkiness of his two hundred pounds. It was a distributed weight, lying in the muscles of his chest and upper arms, on the broad flats of his shoulders, in the girth of his legs. He had big bones. His fingers were long and blunt at the ends and a tuft of black hair grew behind each knuckle joint. His face was broad, his features boldly spaced and faintly irregular; the bridge of his nose showed a small break and on his

right temple lay the pale track of some old cut. These were
the scars that Jim Majors, at twenty-five, had to show for his
life. These scars, and the quickness of his eyes, and that remote and angular smiling. Behind such surface signs was a
toughness the years had beaten into him. Behind these signs
also were the weaknesses.

The dust-yellow road ran straightly between the close-
ranged trees and an overhead sun baked up a rank, resinous
smell. Cowbirds whirled in a swift dark cloud out of the trees
to the left of the road. Majors' shape held its indifference in
the saddle, but his glance ran over there, gray and sharp, and
it was no surprise to him when a man trotted from the trees
and fell into the road, a hundred yards ahead.

It was something out of a book whose pages he had well
learned, by disaster and by sweat. The man looked around
casually—too casually—and reined down until Majors came
abreast; and rode beside him. He was red-haired and ruddy
and freckled of skin, and young enough to show the glint of
laughter in his eyes. His glance touched Majors, its sharpness
only half-concealed.

"Tobacco?"

Jim Majors fetched out his tobacco sack and passed it
over. The other rider let his reins sag on the saddle horn and
rolled up a smoke, his teeth making a white flash when he
licked the cigarette together. He cupped a match between his
palms and bent a little, a net of crow-track wrinkles springing
around his eye corners. The edges of his hair were raw-red in
the sunlight. He had the huge fists of a good rope hand. In
those few moments, Majors knew, the redhead had gathered
all the information that was to be seen.

"Fine weather."

"Yeah."

"Stage is late today, ain't it?"

Majors said: "Didn't pass any."

The other one said, "Thanks for the tobacco," and gave
him the first direct glance. "My name is Brand. Brick Brand."

Majors drawled: "I didn't ask."

Brick Brand's eyes showed a more ironic amusement. "All
right," he said, and cut quickly out of the road, calling back,
"Thanks for the tobacco."

Majors watched him fade through the pines toward a country which rose and seemed to break into a yonder tangle of
gulch and draw. He murmured, "Number Two."

Meanwhile the road maintained its steady descent until, late in the afternoon, it led him to the brow of the foothills, wherefrom he saw a narrow valley turned amber and blue by sunlight's last hazy glow. Low ridges hemmed the valley on either side and a river—the Ute Fork—made a glittering, willow-fringed lane down its middle; ten miles away a line of bluffs rose apparently to box in valley and river alike. Below him a thousand feet he could see the housetops of Reservation.

At dusk he left the last hairpin turn of the road, crossed a branch of the Ute Fork by a covered bridge that ran the footfalls of his horse hollowly forward, and entered Reservation's main street.

He was a stranger here, yet this was like a hundred towns he had entered at dusk on many another night of his life. The street was a silver streak between low buildings whose square fronts and overhanging board awnings had long ago lost the shine of fresh paint. He passed a blacksmith shop, the smell of its forge fire hanging to the still air. Lights made a fogged shining out of dusty windows and locust trees formed an irregular line along the walks. Saddle horses stood here and there before hitch-racks and the wide mouth of a stable yawned at him, with a lantern swinging in its arch. Here he turned and dismounted, seeing two men tipped against the stable wall in their chairs. The lantern light showed the pale attention of their eyes.

He said, "Putting up," and took care of the horse and later went along the walk until he met the edge of another street running out of the shadows. On the four corners of the square this created were a saloon, a hotel, a feed store and an empty building. The hotel was across the dust and he could hear the clatter of dishes and the scrape of feet in its dining room. Yet he stood here a little longer, searching the town with that care he could not forget; searching the change in men's faces, for the lift and fall of voices, for the obscure shifts that now, as all along his past, he had trained himself to see. A group of riders loitered in the doorway of the saloon, illumined by its own thrown light. A half-dozen Indians crouched against the base of the hotel wall, entirely motionless. Behind him he heard one of the men in the stable say, in a quiet tone: "Good horse—strange brand." A long-shaped fellow with a cool face strolled out of the near-by dark and gave Majors a direct glance and passed on to the restaurant. His hat was cocked far back on his head, showing the edge of yellow hair. Up in a second-story window of the flimsy hotel a woman came to a window and looked into the street, her hands holding the curtains apart. Night air, crisp with the touch of coming winter, began to flow down the dark shoulder of the Silver Lode Range.

He crossed the street and entered the hotel's narrow lobby, wherein one man sat with a kind of huge gloom, half-turned from Majors. There was a raw pine desk and a stairway tacked without grace to one of the walls, and an arch through which Majors saw the dining room. He went over to the desk and picked up a pen, and wrote in the register "J. J. Majors," and waited until the man in the chair got up and came around the desk.

This one reversed the register with the steel point of a false arm, and studied the name, his lips faintly moving. He had a moon-round face and full, faintly flat features stained by the copper of Indian blood. His glance lifted and skimmed Majors and dropped. He said, "Take Number Four," and went back to the rocker.

The stairway swayed a little when Majors put his weight on it. On the dark upper landing he turned uncertainly in a narrow hall before finding an open door. He went in and lighted the lamp and saw nothing to distinguish this room from any other. Light flushed a yellow strip beneath the door of the opposite room and he heard a woman speak in a low, rapid voice, and heard, too, the brief answer of a man. Then both voices quit suddenly. Majors closed his door, judging that this was the woman who had been silhouetted in the window. He considered this dismal room, his lips lengthening, and walked to his window and looked down into Reservation's square—and at that moment saw a man quit the group by the saloon and cross to the stable.

His smile stretched out, thin and tough. There was never any change in this game. All the moves were according to a pattern, which was a pattern he had learned long ago. In a little while another move would be made—and he thought he knew what it would be. He got out of his coat and washed up in the bowl, and flattened his unruly hair and got into his coat again. For a moment he stood like this, his head tipped down so that the shadows in his eyes blackened. His features turned heavier than they had been. Afterwards he went to the bed and tucked in the trailing edges of the blankets, arranging them in a certain fashion to suit him. When he opened his door and stepped into the hall he heard the woman in the other room again break off from her talking. There was a long-drawn whisper, like a warning, and then somebody in there moved away from the door.

He descended the stairs, cut into the dining room, and took one of the vacant tables. A blackboard hung on the opposite wall, and somebody had written: "Menu—T-Bone and Mashed Potatoes—Apple Pie. Fifty Cents." Beneath it was this chalked notice: "If You Don't Like Our Grub Don't Eat Here!" Jim Majors laid both big arms on the table. His eyelids narrowed and faint wrinkles cracked the smooth surface of his forehead. There was a door behind him, leading directly to the street. In front of him a half-dozen men sat at one long table; in the corner was a smaller table, occupied by the yellow-haired fellow who had earlier passed him on the street. Majors caught that one's glance, so cool and so distantly bright. A half-breed waitress laid Majors' meal in front of him. When he was all through he put his half-dollar on the table and went directly to the street.

He stood with his back to the hotel wall, the shadows covering him while he tapered up a cigarette. A small wind, definitely cold, rolled off the mountains and the distant peaks cut their black spires out of the high sky. Supper hour's quietness had come and had gone and there were little messages running the street now that a man might miss unless he knew the voice of trouble. The tip of Majors' cigarette glowed against the solid disk of his face and grew dim and his eyes observed this street with the need to know what was happening. The Indians had gone. The blond man came from the hotel's dining room, his spurs dragging the walk. He passed Majors, cut over the dust and put a shoulder gently against the corner of the dark building. A hostler drove four harnessed horses from the stable and halted at the square's corner. Light poured brightly from the saloon and more men were gathered by its swinging door, bunched up and softly speaking. A half-dozen riders whirled in from the darkness and dropped down to join those others. Somebody said, "Hello, Ben." The group gave ground and a rider, with as square and solid a body as Jim Majors had ever seen, walked into the saloon, his personality towing everybody else behind him.

Little things were happening here, like straws blown before a wind. The blond man's head swung toward the saloon and came back and tipped up and Majors saw that he watched that second-story hotel room where the woman was—and where the hidden man was. The hotel man came out of his door and looked at the saloon a moment and turned; he hooked the steel point of his false arm around the door frame, hauling himself back into the lobby.

Majors threw his cigarette to the dust, watching the sparks spray as it struck. He shook his heavy shoulders together, walked diagonally across the square and entered the saloon.

Smoke and sound and the flash of light from a back bar mirror filled this place. Men crowded the poker tables all down the length of the room; men stood up to the bar, their bodies fitted comfortably over its edge. Somebody at one of the poker tables called "Ben!" and the rider with the square body wheeled from his drink, his glance striking out against Jim Majors. Black brilliance was in his eyes. His lips lay naturally away from big, broad teeth, which gave him an expression of grinning against the light's glare. Jim Majors' quick attention caught all this, even while he walked on to the bar—this, and the deep and square shape of a torso so extraordinary as to make the man's legs seem spindly by comparison.

Majors found a hole at the bar and waggled a finger for his drink. Talk made a steady, humming sound in the room. More riders shouldered in from the street and another voice said, "Hello, Ben." The barkeep came down to Jim Majors with bottle and glass, and waited there for the price of the drink, his hands automatically toweling the mahogany. Majors lifted a quarter from his pocket and held it until the barkeep's disinterested eyes rose.

Majors said: "Know a man named Ed Dale?"

He hadn't lifted his voice, yet this was like a snap of a trigger on an empty shell—a sound to reach men even through greater sound. The rider adjoining Majors made a slow half-turn and stared at him, but Majors had only a view of this from the extreme corner of his vision. He was watching the barkeep's eyelids lift and betray a streak of expression—and drop again. The barkeep took the quarter. He said, "Never did," and went down the bar. Majors poised his glass against the light, looking through the amber shine with his lips caught in that long, faint smile, remembering that there were stages in this game a man had to reach, one way or another. He felt and heard the effect of that question ripple outward, as though he had dropped a stone into water.

The talk checked down. Somebody at the end of the bar said, "Ed Dale?"

He drank his liquor at one breath, knowing the eyes of the room were turning to him; the feeling was that definite.

The barkeep came back and stopped, apparently waiting for the empty glass. But he said in his spare, even tone:—

"Lookin' for a man by that name?"

Majors said: "Tell him so, when you see him," and wheeled out of the saloon, leaving half-silence behind.

He stood on the corner to roll up a fresh cigarette, his breath running in and out with a deeper reach. Matchlight showed the fresh sparkle of his eyes and the tough, thinned-down edges of his lips. There was a stage running in from the valley side of town, making a racket in Reservation's quiet. Majors crossed the dust and took his stand by the hotel door, half-buried in the shadows again.

The blond man hadn't moved from the edge of the empty building.

The stage rolled up. Two passengers got out and made a run for the restaurant. The driver crawled down with a sack of mail and limped toward the hotel door. He was thin and old, with a silvered crescent of a mustache; and his bright blue eyes touched Jim Majors as he passed by, showing no expression. The waiting stableman hurried up to unhitch the four worn horses and to back in the fresh four he had been holding here.

Something here grew tighter and tighter; something here grew thin and odd. It was a feeling brushing across Jim Majors' senses, drawing his glance into all the apertures of this town. Men came out of the saloon, not talking and moving as though they had something to do. The square-bodied Ben shouldered through the doors, pointing silently here and there, which was an order that scattered those others along the street while he paced the dust and took a stand in the darkness beyond the horses. The hostler drove the old team away and the passengers came from the restaurant and stood by the stage door, waiting. All this was within the spread of five minutes.

The moments crawled on and a sense of something expected ran a cold breath along the street, colder than the wind rolling off the mountains. The square-bodied Ben made a

changeless stain in the shadows; and other men had gone on
to the corners of this square and had stopped. The blond
man's hat peak showed vaguely over the backs of the stage
wheelers. The driver's boots scratched across the hotel floor,
and afterwards he stepped through the door and stopped a
moment to freshen up a pipe. He had a limp mail-sack
tucked under one arm, which caused him to bend a little as
he ran the match across the pipe's surface.

Jim Majors lifted a hand to his cigarette—and when he
spoke it was with a summer softness, the motion of his lips
hidden behind his hand.

"Tell him I got here, and I'm still alive."

The passengers had climbed in. The driver walked on and
crawled up the wheels to his seat, tucking the mailbag under
it. He unwrapped the reins from the brake handle and for a
moment he was a gaunt, stooped shape against the night sky
while he adjusted those reins between his old fingers. He said:
"Gyp! Belle . . . ," and kicked off the brake.

The tall wheels were moving, but there was the smashing
fall of someone on the hotel's inner stairway and at once a
man rushed out through the dining room door, throwing himself at the stage with his body bent over as though in agony.

Coolness whipped through Majors and he flattened his
shape against the hotel wall; for he heard the square-bodied
Ben calling up in a voice that was solid and without pity:—

"Not tonight, Pete. Not tonight."

The fugitive had one hand on the opening stage door. He
raced with the stage, trying to lift himself inside, and he was
abreast Jim Majors—with the lunging of his wind loud in
Majors' ears—when a gun began to beat up echoes; the gun
of the square-bodied Ben. There were two shots. Majors
heard them strike into the fugitive. He saw the man stumble,
still gripping the stage door, still trying to pull abreast. But
his legs all at once quit lifting and for a brief moment the
desperateness of his will caused the stage to drag him on a
yard or more before he let go and fell into the dust.

The stage gathered speed, rocking toward the covered
bridge and the hairpin turns of the foothills. A woman cried
out and rushed from the hotel, passing Majors. Dust rose up
and made all this vague to him for the moment. The smell of
powder drifted into his nostrils. He saw her drop and try to
lift the dead man's head into her lap. She was repeating his
name in a wild, crying voice, her white shirtwaist rocking

across this dismal semidark. He heard her say: "Ben Maffitt—someday—someday. . . !" That was all. She was crying
again in a way that turned Jim Majors cold.

Ben Maffitt walked slowly across the street toward the
saloon. The blond one, Majors observed, hadn't stirred from
his long-held spot by the corner of the empty building. And
at that moment a new bunch of riders were galloping into
town from the hillside.

2

Katherine Barr

NOBODY in this town made any gesture toward the dead man or toward the girl who crouched in the smoky dust and cried out her heart; and this was a brutal indifference Jim Majors didn't understand until his glance crossed the street again and discovered Ben Maffitt bulked in the saloon's doorway. Maffitt waited there with his silence, so sure, so arrogant.

This was the story of the town completely told. A thousand nights could add nothing to what Jim Majors knew at that exact moment. If there was any pity in Reservation it cringed away from Ben Maffitt's presence; if there was any decency on this street, it remained shamefully silent. The newly-arrived riders rounded in at the saloon, but he saw them only as a massed blur on the corner of the scene. For it was Maffitt he watched, studying the man's motionless shoulders and arms with the premonition of trouble to come. Anger burned rankly in him, and the cool game he intended to play here became impossible. The crying of that forlorn girl destroyed the set of his judgment, and, even though he knew he opened up every risk he should now be avoiding, he couldn't stop the swing of that temper. It was a weakness for which he had more than once been punished, as the scars on his face showed; nevertheless he walked into the dust, as far as the kneeling girl, and spoke to her.

"I'll take you back to the room."

He stood patiently by, the details of this roundabout scene vivid on his senses. The new riders made a still group on the street, not dismounting. He had an incomplete view of the tall blond man still posted by the edge of the empty building.

11

Maffitt's crowd showed their scattered and indistinct shapes in the surrounding dark and Maffitt remained as solid as a stone image in the glow of the saloon's doorway. Maffitt watched him and the blond man watched him—and every eye in the town was turned his way. It was an impact he could feel.

Nobody spoke. The girl's crying was a fading, hopeless note in a silence that got heavier; when he spoke again his own voice, gentle as it was, ran solidly through the dark for the whole town to hear.

"Come up."

But he knew she couldn't rise, and so he reached down and lifted her and turned her against his chest. She murmured, "Don't let him stay there," and nothing held her upright except the pressure of his arm. Meanwhile in his ears was the sound of somebody crossing from the group of riders just arrived in town. He changed the position of his arm around the girl and turned her head.

It was another girl, dressed in a man's riding clothes, her shape turned slim and tall by the half-shadows lying in the center of this square. She walked with a swinging step and all he could distinctly see at the moment was a surface of black hair and features sharpened by the sight before her. She stopped, her glance touching the dead man and rising afterwards to the girl half-collapsed in Jim Majors' arms.

She said: "Tony, why are you here?" Her voice was strong, evenly rounding off the words. It carried an authority that scraped against Majors; it churned up his temper.

He said: "This is a hell of a time to ask questions."

Her chin lifted, moving her cheeks into cleaner light. She had been looking at Tony, never seeing him. Now she saw him, and anger visibly colored her judgment and her lips made a long part across white teeth.

One of the mounted figures by the saloon called to Majors in a grating voice: "Keep your voice down, pilgrim," and spurred on. Majors saw the shape of the man weave in the saddle as he came, old and stiffly tall, with a narrow face further brought to point by a white goatee. He had a rawhide quirt half-lifted in his hand, and when he halted he shook it at Majors. "Keep your voice down."

The slim girl said: "Dad, never mind."

All the town watched through the cold shadows. Majors said to the girl Tony, "I'll take you to the room." But the heaviness of her body remained constant and he thought he had to carry her. Time ran slow and thin, the threat of the old man above him and the tall girl's eyes emptying anger on him, and all the yonder men carefully listening. His mouth was a long streak across the weather-bronze of his skin, narrowed to that edged, tough half-smile.

Tony pulled away from him and murmured, "It's all right." He turned her and walked back to the hotel with her.

The hotel man stepped aside from the doorway, the steel hook of his arm flashing in the light. Majors followed the girl up the loose stairs, going into her room. Dust yellowed her white shirtwaist and tears caked dust against her face, and her eyes were half-open, showing him a glance dim and wild. She sat loose-shouldered on the edge of her bed. He removed his hat and stood uncertainly at the door, making his guesses about her. She wasn't very old and she had a shapeliness and a prettiness that a good many men had probably observed.

"Don't let him stay out there."

He said: "I'll take care of that. Your husband?"

Her head rolled on the pillow. "No." But the question had seemed to break through her despair. "I guess you must be new here."

"Sure. Why?"

"Nobody else would ask me that question. Don't let him stay there. He was—" She rose from the bed and turned her back to him in the far corner of the room, wiping her cheeks. She said dully: "Guess I must look pretty bad. Well, that's the way things happen to me. I liked him. He was a boy and he got mixed up the wrong way. That's all. I liked him. He was trying to get out of the country." She came about, fear slowly thawing from her face. "I hope I live long enough to see Ben Maffitt die like that!"

Someone came up the stairs with a light, quick step. Majors said, "This Ben Maffitt—"

A voice called through the doorway: "Maybe you're too curious."

Spinning on his heels, Majors saw the dark-haired girl there, her eyes considering him without friendliness. He had a clear picture of her then. She wasn't as tall as the street's darkness had made her seem. The riding trousers had helped to create that illusion, shaping her in a slim, boy-figured fashion. She wore a man's shirt open at the neck; it fell carelessly away from her throat and showed the smooth, ivory shading of her skin. He had gathered the impression that her features

were sharp, but this too was an illusion dispelled by the
room's light. Her lips were long and her eyes wide-spaced
and colored by a gray that had no bottom; and the strongest
impression she left with him was of a temper that could
swing to the extremes of laughter, and softness, and anger.
There was, he thought, this capacity for emotion in her.

She broke his thoughts with her curt question. "Are you
through looking at me?"

He could be soft and he could be blunt. He matched her
temper now. "Don't be so proud. I see nothing to justify it."

Her eyes showed him a fresh outrage. But Tony, in the
corner, was crying again in an exhausted tone. It turned the
dark-headed girl across the room. Majors watched the way
she went over to Tony and put her arms around the girl.

She said, so gently: "Tony—Tony. I'm sorry you've been
hurt. I'm so sorry."

The roughness went out of Jim Majors. This girl held Tony
against her breasts and her lips were broad and maternal and
she was saying: "Cry, if it will help, Tony."

Majors swung from the room, but he turned again to have
a final look, not quite knowing why. There was a difference
between these two that any man could see and it added something to the dark-haired girl's character that she should be
here comforting this Tony whose life, he guessed, was pretty
much of common record in the town. The dark girl's eyes
lifted and met his smileless glance, and held it, with a faint
expression of curiosity. He made a burly, heavy-boned shape
in the doorway, the scars on his face definitely toughening its
expression. He said, "Maybe I was wrong," and went to his
own room.

He had left the door open and the light on—and he saw
the edge of the bed quilts hanging straight down, though he
had tucked them in before leaving. A small smile struck
across his lips again, harder than before; and he blew out the
light and shut the door, descending to the lobby.

The hotelkeeper swung himself in a rocker, the steel-
hooked arm hanging idly down. He rolled his head toward
Majors, using no extra effort. Breathing made an unusual
sound in his heavy chest. There was a layer of fat under his
chin and his round, copper-stained face showed a gray, surly
composure; as though he believed in nothing.

Majors remained by the street door, tapering up a cigarette
while he considered the crowd rolling around the yonder

saloon. Apparently Maffitt had entered the saloon, but the old man with the white goatee stood on the walk and other riders made a half-circle around him. The night was colder and blacker than it had been. They had taken the dead man from the square. Shadows shifted along the base of the empty building opposite; a cigarette glowed and died there, to tell him that all his hope of playing a quiet game was gone. They were watching him, they were weighing him, and they would never get him out of their minds. For this was a country that hated strangers and a country filled with men who looked over their shoulders at a past they had run from and couldn't forget.

The hotelkeeper's voice rustled like dry sheets of paper rubbed together. "How was the Sundown country when you left it?"

The question held all the shock of a bullet fired at his ear. Majors had his back to the hotelkeeper and he remained that way, but his lids crept nearer together and his lips ran thin; and the last thought of ease went out of him. He said, over his shoulder, "I don't know you."

"I wondered about that. I lived in the Yellow Hills five years ago—and I heard of a J. J. Majors." Afterwards a heavier tone weighted down the hotel man's talk. "Sundown Jim. Sure."

"Who's the man with the white chin-whiskers?"

"Pedee Barr. It's his daughter Katherine upstairs. You'd better be right. If you ain't right . . ."

"You'll never find anything under my bed, friend."

"It wasn't me that looked," said the hotel man. "But I guess you knew the kind of country you was ridin' into. Better never be anything under your bed—and nothin' pinned on your vest."

"We'll wait and see who's curious enough to have a look at my vest."

"It won't be a long wait."

Jim Majors saw the high, stiff frame of Pedee Barr wheel through the saloon door. He had wanted to play it quiet for a while, but that would never be possible now; and at once a weight in his mind tipped the other way, throwing him back to habits and impulses he liked better. It was time to make a break, to roll up a little lightning and find out where it struck. He had a trick that always betrayed this kind of decision; he pulled his shoulders forward and threw down his cigarette, expelling the smoke through his nostrils in a long sweep of breath. Light struck the solid irregularity of his features and the scar on his temple showed white, and he was smiling again, the powder color of his eyes brighter than before. When he crossed the square he noted that the blond man had disappeared.

He shouldered through the doors, a strong draft of smoke and sound running against him. Certain things he wanted to see—and instantly saw. Pedee Barr stood in a corner of the saloon, his goateed face narrow and small-boned and strictly unsmiling. The men around him, Majors judged, were his own men; and when Pedee Barr's glance lifted and came over to him, full of a proud man's intolerance, Majors noted how all those others swung about to copy the gesture. Ben Maffitt sat before a poker table at the room's other end, the chair turned to permit his wide chest more freedom. His hat clung to the extreme back of his head and a clump of coal-colored hair fell down across his brow. He had a cigar clenched between his big teeth and his interest was only half-captured by the game.

Majors caught his slanting, sly glance; it was a manner of indifference not quite hiding the catlike alertness of his interest. Majors went on to the bar, using his shoulders to make himself a place. The men on each side gave way to this pressure, their glances bracketing him cheerlessly. He recognized one of them as the rider who had been up at the summit stage station.

Majors laid his arms on the bar, waiting his turn. He felt a growing pressure in the place; it was like a steady force on his shoulder blades. He made a circle on the bar with one forefinger, watching the pale imprint show on the scarred hardwood surface, and he was carefully laying away in his head the thing he had learned, which was that Ben Maffitt and this Pedee Barr were friendly enough to share the shelter of this saloon. It was one piece of a puzzle to be shaped against other pieces when the time came.

He got his bottle and glass and poured a drink.

Behind him a man said: "Heard you asked about Ed Dale."

Jim Majors put his fingers around the bottle when the barkeep came back to get it. He said: "Leave it here," and turned and saw Brick Brand. The edges of Brand's hair burned a pure red in the light. He had a self-assurance gleaming like humor in pale blue eyes.

"You know Ed Dale?" said Majors.

The redhead considered Majors blandly. "Where was he from?"

Majors said, "Maybe same place I'm from."

"Why you think he's in this country?"

"He came in one side and he didn't come out the other. So he's here."

"It's a big country. Might be any one of a dozen places."

Majors looked at the redhead's poker expression. He said: "If you don't know him what the hell you bothering me for?"

The redhead's eyes grew rounder. But there were other things here to trap Major's attention. The talk had fallen away so that all the room could hear this. Men watched him. Pedee Barr's head was craned forward and he had cupped a hand behind his left ear to catch the cool run of those words. Ben Maffitt swung his body in the chair and his glance slanted over the room, very keen.

The redhead's grin came back, like a warning; he was, Majors judged carefully, a tougher man than he appeared. The silence tightened and the redhead drawled: "Your time ain't so valuable, mister. Maybe you're a friend of Ed Dale's. Maybe you just want to find him and pay back the five dollars you owe, or maybe you got a letter for him from his grandmother. Then again, maybe you don't know Ed Dale at all, except what you learned from a reward notice."

Majors said: "He had a fresh bullet-mark on his right hip and a picture of a girl in his coat pocket."

His attention was half on the redhead and half on Ben Maffitt. His answer was like added weight to a silence already heavily strained. Maffitt's head rose another inch and his stare was direct now, all indifference gone. Majors had the full effect of the man's black eyes. And then there was a little by-play that gave the scene away. The redhead looked back at Maffitt and when he returned his attention to Majors he wasn't smiling.

He murmured, "That's different," and put one hand forward and in a quick motion threw back the lapels of Majors' coat.

Majors made no gesture to stop that. But he knew he had reached the end of an alley. All the men in the saloon waited and watched, and the tension in here was something that couldn't last. What he did now would make him or it would break him, for that was the kind of crowd he faced and this was the kind of country he was in. He was a big, idle shape backed against the bar, his heavy elbows hooked over its edge, and his solid shoulders negligently drooped. His lips ran a rolling half-smile across the heavy irregularity of his cheeks. It wasn't that he meant to smile, but he was remembering how changeless were the rules of this game. The incidents of his life kept repeating themselves, move for move, fight for fight, scar for scar.

He said: "Pull the coat together, like you found it, Brick."

The redhead was smart enough to know trouble when he saw it, and he saw it now. His answer was to take one backward step and stop there, stiffly placed.

"No," he drawled, "I guess not."

Majors pushed himself away from the bar, gently speaking. "All right, Red. This is a treat on me."

The redhead raised both arms, but he never got them fully lifted. Majors was away from the bar before he had finished speaking. He caught the redhead's jaw with a straight jab that made a pulpy echo in the room, like the flat of a cleaver against meat. Brand's face tilted toward the ceiling and he hit out with his fists and struck nothing. Majors shot a blow into the man's stomach, doubling him up. The redhead fell against Majors and tried to hang on. There was another man coming up from the corner of the room, yelling: "Boot him, Red, boot him!" Majors threw Brand backward and measured him and hit him twice on the face and sent him to the floor. Brand lay there, supporting himself on his arms, his breath caught in his throat.

The second man rushed on, whirling his arms in windmill style. He struck Majors and got his arms around the latter's neck and jammed his knees into Majors' crotch. It was barroom fighting, wicked and punishing. He jabbed his thumbs into Majors' ears and stamped on his feet and tried to swing his weight to catch Majors in a strangle grip.

Majors wheeled and carried this man in a complete circle, meanwhile watching Brand try to come up from the floor. All the faces in this room were pulled into lines of strict, savage attention; these men were ringed around him, a wolf glitter in their eyes.

Brand was half-upright. Majors waited for the other man's head to duck in again, and reached up and slugged him in the temple. He felt the fellow's grip loosen, which was his opportunity. He jumped aside and caught the man from behind, shoulders and crotch, and lifted him off the floor; he swung him face downward, forward and backward for momentum, and threw him through the saloon doorway.

Everybody heard that crash on the yonder walk—that and the wild howl that followed.

Red was on his feet, blood dripping from the corner of his mouth. There was a gap between his teeth, and his eyes didn't quite see Majors, who stood there and waited. The redhead said, between breathing: "That's all!"

Majors stepped back into the center of the room. He wasn't looking at Brand. He had turned away from the man and it was this indifference the men in the saloon saw; this indifference and the hardness of that smile which remained so constant on his lips. The scar on his temple showed white in the lamplight and his hair fell across his forehead; and the depth of his breathing lifted and lowered his chest. He had his eyes on Ben Maffitt then, and in them was bright eagerness.

He waited like that, measuring Maffitt—as though inviting him to speak. Then he said: "Brick, come around here and pull my coat together."

The silence got close and dangerous. Ben Maffitt, motionless in his chair, showed the room no expression, though Major knew the room waited for Maffitt to speak.

Majors repeated softly, "Come around, Brick, or I'll bust every rib you own."

Red came around. Pain had begun to punish him and he held a hand across his lips and mumbled through his broken teeth: "You got to rub it in?"

Majors said: "Just teachin' a dog to mind."

Red reached out and pulled at the lapels of Majors' coat; and he wheeled and charged out of the saloon.

Majors went to the bar and helped himself to another drink. His back was to the crowd, but he could see the reflections of all those men in the bar mirror. Nobody moved and nobody spoke. He paid for his drink and wheeled, and for a moment Ben Maffitt's eyes considered him with a tremendous interest. But there was no other expression on the man's cheeks and he made no move; and so Majors walked across the floor and through the swinging doors.

Brand crouched over the other man, who lay flat on his

back. Brand stared up at Majors. He said: "You busted his arm."

Majors said, "Too bad," and crossed to the hotel. But he wasn't thinking of those two. He was thinking of Ben Maffitt who had never stirred, never spoken. Maffitt could have taken up the fight, or he could have put more men into that fight. But he hadn't. Majors remembered the sharpness of his eyes—and the underlying slyness. This man was a schemer before he was a killer, and so twice as dangerous.

Majors filed that in the back of his head, and walked up the stairs. No light showed from the girl Tony's room, and there wasn't any talk in there. A faint odor of tobacco smoke lay in the hall's blackness. Majors caught the heel of his boot in a knothole and stumbled against his own door. Suddenly he halted here, kicked open the door, and drew swiftly aside. Smoke was ranker in the room, and then a match burst against the dark and by its glow he saw the ruddy face of the blond man.

The match went out. The blond man said:—

"Come in and shut that door."

3

House in the Pines

MAJORS stepped into the room. He kicked the door shut with his heel and stood against it.

The blond man pulled the cigarette from his mouth. He said:—

"You had a hell of a lot of nerve walkin' into that saloon. You got away with it—but don't let it make you too proud."

Majors drawled: "You been watching the girl's room for an hour. Why?"

"It was Pete Riley. I wondered if he'd make it out of town. He didn't."

"What was he up against?"

The blond man took another drag on the cigarette. Its glow lightened the pale surfaces of his eyes and showed the ironic stretch of his lips. Silence went on a little while. Then the blond man said: "Same thing you're up against, though I may be mistaken. My name is Buff Sultan. I run a ranch down the East Fork. Me and my sister." Afterwards he added one gently hinting sentence. "Maybe I'm mistaken about you."

Majors said: "You came here to ask me a question. Go ahead and ask it."

Buff Sultan's chuckle came softly out of him. "All right. . . . You want help?"

"What kind of help?"

"Never mind. You're here for a reason. There's only two reasons: you're running away from something, or you're lookin' for somebody. You want help?"

"I don't pick my help blindfolded."

21

"No?" said Buff Sultan, a slow amusement in his voice. "That's something you'll learn. If you stick here you'll be glad to get help from anybody, no questions asked. Maybe we can make a trade. My help for your help."

"I'll listen," said Majors. He crossed to the window, hearing sudden sounds fill the street.

Pedee Barr was in the saddle down there, with the other men of his party swinging up. Katherine Barr came from the general store and went to her horse. The rest of the group turned to leave Reservation, but she held her horse a moment longer in its place, her glance very definitely seeking something on the street; and the impatient swing of her shoulders told Majors once more of a temper strong in all its reactions. Ben Maffitt walked from the saloon and stopped in the doorway, the light of which made a black block of his body. He did a strange thing then. He removed his hat and looked over to Katherine Barr, saying nothing and making no motion. Majors' interest whipped alive; he tipped his head nearer the window. Katherine Barr turned her horse and stared at Ben Maffitt, but though Majors watched this scene closely he saw her make no sign at all. Nothing, apparently, passed between them. A moment later she whirled the pony into the darkness, following her father. Ben Maffitt turned to watch her ride away.

Majors' voice was sudden-sharp. "What's between the Barrs and this Maffitt?"

Buff Sultan's answer crept dryly across the room. "I guess I made a mistake about you. You're quicker than I judged. You're wonderin' about the Barrs and about Maffitt. You're wonderin' about me. Listen: The longer you stay the more you'll wonder. You'll never get it untangled. If I was you I wouldn't try. Just pick your side, and let it go like that."

"Which side?" said Majors.

Buff Sultan rose from the chair. He crossed to the door, placing his feet carefully on the rickety floor. He was a vague shape over there.

He said, more cautiously than before: "I guess I found out what I came here to find. Don't trust anybody—and don't trust me, for I'm just as apt to knife you as the next man. That's the kind of a country you're in, which I think you know by now."

"It wasn't what you came to say," said Majors.

"Changed my mind," answered Buff Sultan, a touch of

hurry in his voice. He opened the door a notch, watched the hall a moment, and slipped out. Majors heard him go down the unstable stairway.

Posted again at the window of this lightless room, Majors found Ben Maffitt still by the saloon, lost in thoughts which held him perfectly still. Two or three minutes afterwards, Buff Sultan came from the hotel, crossed the street to a horse racked in front of the empty building. He wheeled around, leaving town on the opposite side. Ben Maffitt's hatbrim rose, a sign of his interest in the departing Sultan. A man came from another angle of the street, went over to Maffitt and spoke a few words. Maffitt nodded.

Majors turned from the window, not bothering to light the lamp. He propped a chair under the doorknob, hauled the bed to the room's least exposed corner—making a great racket—and turned in for the night.

At breakfast time he noticed Tony waiting on table. She put the meal before him and stood by a moment. She said, "Thanks for last night," and there was the hint of softness in the round surfaces of her lips. It mildly surprised him to discover that she was a pretty girl, all her features even and composed. Her eyes were quite dark. The tragedy of the previous night was somewhere in the background of her mind, more or less like a quality of wistfulness or of fatalism, as though she had put the whole episode behind her because there was nothing else she could do. But it was the way she looked at him, quietly and personally and with a faint warmth, that caught his attention.

He said, "That's all right."

She moved her shoulders gracefully. "I liked Pete. I knew his folks. I wanted to see him get away."

She made an impression, and later he watched that balanced swing of her body as she walked back to the kitchen; and he kept her in his mind while he ate.

Afterwards, on the street, eased against the hotel wall, he filled his pipe and had a better look at a Reservation flooded by the fresh and tawny light of a late fall morning.

Morning's quiet controlled the two almost empty streets. Other frame buildings and other stores, hidden by the previous night's shadows, ran back from the square, a meat market, a saddle shop, a barber shop, a print shop bearing on its false front the sign: UTE BASIN WEEKLY ROUNDUP. A doctor's shingle showed itself above the doorway of a narrow little house adjoining the print shop. Up the street which led to the bridge was a larger building with grilled windows on its second floor. Now and then somebody strolled casually into view. The hotelkeeper came from the lobby and went toward the meat market, his steel hook glittering in the sun. A barkeep was swabbing out the saloon, and when Majors noted that saloon's name, he filed it away in his mind for what it might mean. The name was OLD DIXIE. Fifteen years after Lee's surrender, somebody in Reservation still nursed his unreconstructed politics.

A freshness in this whipped through him and revived a faint eagerness to be on the move. He was a man quick to feel the moods of the outer world, and quick to answer them; he was a man whose strength and weakness lay in a strong love of action, because it was action that satisfied his hungry muscles and restless nerves. He went over the square and stopped at the stable a moment, coming before a frail-seeming little hostler who wore a derby hat and a pair of striped pants held up by yellow suspenders.

Majors jiggled a fresh match across the bowl of his pipe, meeting the hostler's inquisitive glance. Majors said: "I'll be going out in a little while."

The hostler leaned on his pitchfork. "You got a nice horse." And then he put out a hopeful question: "Not a valley horse?"

"Not this valley," returned Majors.

The hostler waited for additional information that didn't come. He shrugged his small shoulders. "Ev'body in this dam' country is full of mysteriousness."

A stubby man whirled around one of the corners of the square and came on rapidly; whereupon the hostler laid his pitchfork aside and moved into the semidarkness of the stable, catching a set of single harness off a peg as he traveled.

The stubby man reached the stable arch and stopped there, swinging a black satchel against his knees. His round cheeks were pink and shining from his morning's shave. He stared at Majors in an extraordinarily direct manner, and said: "You're the new man? Majors?"

"That's right."

The short man called down the stable,—"Hurry up, Henry,"—and swung back to Majors. He said bluntly:

"That's a hell of a vile-smelling pipe you're smoking. Ever have throat trouble?"

Henry drove a buggy up to the arch. The short man tossed in his bag and climbed to the seat. "No," drawled Majors.

"Nicotine never did any man any good. Better quit while you're young." He called to Henry: "Going to the Hole. Back by noon." He drove the buggy out of the stable, made a fast, dust-ripping turn at the hotel corner, and disappeared.

"That's Doc Showers," said Henry. "A mighty good man on busted bones and gunshot troubles."

Majors grinned. "That all?"

One of Henry's suspenders slid off his sloping shoulders; he snapped it back with a thumb. "That's about all we got in this dam' country. You want I should saddle the gelding?"

"Yes," said Majors, and walked across the yellow, heavy dust toward the bridge. The building with the grilled windows put one wall to the street and one to the shallow river running along Reservation's back side. In this town it was obviously the latest addition, the newness of paint not yet dissolved by sun and wind. The date printed below the bell tower was 1877. When Majors came to the doorway he stopped a moment to light his pipe again—and from the edge of his vision he saw what he had thought he would see. A man stood at the saloon corner watching him, Henry looked on from the stable, and the hotelkeeper was a silent shape beyond the square.

Majors' smile made an intractable crease along his lips when he moved into the building and came before the soles of two boots draped up on a flat desk. Behind the desk, lying back as far as the chair would safely tilt, sat a man lean and weathered and yet clearly no older than Majors, with sandcolored hair and a pair of taciturn eyes in which watchfulness seemed permanently imbedded.

He said in the slowest, most indifferent of voices: "Wondered when you'd be getting this far down the street."

For a moment Majors said nothing. There was, in this room, something sudden and unexpected; as though he had rounded a corner and found the passage blocked. Something as definite as that. It was like a pressure placed against him; it was an antagonism silent and very strong. He could see that the man was braced against him—and had been that way for a long while. Prepared for trouble, expecting it, and waiting now for it to break . . . These were the quick impressions Majors received. Then he said:—

"My name is Majors."

"Already found it out. Guess you know mine."

"No," said Majors. "Not yet."

The man showed disbelief in the narrows of his amber-stained eyes. "Charley Chavis," he said. There was a copper badge with four ball points on it, pinned to his vest.

"Glad to know you," Majors returned. He was absorbing this Charley Chavis with a mind that was quick and exacting and troubled by a hint of something which didn't show. There was a center to this Chavis completely covered by reserve, a hidden disposition, a state of mind guarded deliberately.

Chavis said: "So what can I do for you?"

He was waiting, he was braced against something. Majors' lips showed a lengthening smile and he shook his head; it was not possible for him to know how heavy and tough a shape he made in this room, the scar on his cheekbone like a signal of character.

He said: "Nothing. Nothing at all. I may be here awhile, so I was just looking around."

"It's your custom," observed Chavis with the same heavy irony, "to waltz into strange towns and throw men out of saloons? Just for fun? Or was you tryin' to tell something to somebody in the Old Dixie?"

Majors suddenly asked: "A lot of Southerners around here?"

The marshal delayed his answer, as though weighing the question for what it might mean. Finally he said in a reluctant way: "Yes."

"The Barr family Southern?"

Charley Chavis glumly nodded.

"Where do those folks live?"

Reluctance increasingly weighted the marshal's speech. He was turning surly—and somewhat nervous. "Up the head of the Ute's south branch."

Majors followed this with a quiet-spoken question. "Why did Maffitt kill Pete Riley?"

Charley Chavis hauled his feet from the desk and got up. "Go find your own damn answers! You come here and you don't tell me anything, so why should I tell you anything? You been pryin' around here ever since you hit town! We all know that. If you got some business, I'll listen. If you ain't—don't count on me for anything."

The sludge in Majors' pipe began to fry. He tapped the bowl and refilled and lighted it, his motions easy and slow. Nothing disturbed his cheeks; but his impressions were all strong and accurate as he watched the cast of Charley Chavis' close-set eyes. This town marshal was disturbed and defiant—and using anger to cover something like fear. Here was a man he would never be able to trust. Majors was very certain about that lack of loyalty in Chavis, that guarded secrecy of motive which would never rise to daylight.

He said, gently, "Won't trouble you," and wheeled from the marshal's office, crossing directly to the sorrel gelding. After he climbed to the saddle, he paused long enough to ask the shriveled Henry a few questions which he knew would be public information the moment he left Reservation.

He pointed eastward. "What's down that way, Henry?"

"The Sultans and the Ketchums and Gray Oldroyd," said Henry—and added eagerly: "You goin' that way? . . . And yonder in the Hole—which is the little valley beyond—you'll find Dobe Hyde's outfit."

Majors pointed southward. "What's there?"

Henry looked at him, a native shrewdness showing. "You don't know? Well, at the end of that valley, where the south branch of the Ute Fork falls outa the mountains, you'll find the Barrs, friend. That far as you figure to go?"

Majors said gently: "Anything beyond?"

"Well," said Henry, "there's a pretty broad trail you could take, on up into the rough country. That would be the Pocket."

"What's in the Pocket, Henry?"

Henry, talkative as he was, folded his lean lips together and turned back into the stable.

Majors swung left at the square, heading toward the eastern valley. Behind him was a town that covertly watched him. He knew that much from the quick side-glances as he passed along; and he knew it from the feeling in the small of his shoulders. Reservation dwindled to a few scattered houses and a few corrals, and then he curved over beside the meandering shallows of the Ute Fork's east branch and followed the dusty road down the narrow valley's middle.

Low, pine-sloped hills, perhaps five miles apart, formed the walls of the valley; and about ten miles ahead was a low line

of buttes which seemed to shut the valley off. The sun lifted
in the east, red from autumn's haze, half its heat gone;
cowbirds swirled in thick flights from the river willows. It
was, he saw, a pretty little land locked away from the world.
Cattle country strictly, though no livestock showed along the
flat stretch; the beef would still be on summer graze up in the
timber. A few miles from Reservation a narrower road
turned to the left, crossed a bridge and struck for the
northern ridge. Over there, sitting somewhat above the valley,
was a house. At this junction a star route mailbox bore the
name of Oldroyd.

Farther on, half down the length of the valley, another
road took off to the right, marked by an arch with an elkhorn
mounted on it. The mailbox here said: "Judas Ketchum."
The Ketchum house was a white square at the base of the
right-hand ridge. Majors rode alternately at a walk and gallop, the smell of the earth pleasantly rising to his nostrils and
the sweet, half-crisp air filling his big chest. There was an
ease and a rhythm in his muscles and his senses lifted to a
satisfying world. This was the action he had to have, this yellow dust running beneath him and the steady jar of the sorrel's stride traveling along his solid frame. Sunlight drew his
lids nearer together until faint wrinkles cut a crisscross pattern at the edge of his temples.

But if he sat slack in the saddle, his glance registered the
details of this valley with an intent care, as though there was
a story here he had to know. Ahead of him the river turned
gradually to the south, and the valley began to pinch in and
he saw the sharp break in the oncoming cliff wall where the
river broke through; and down there three men sat on their
horses, grouped together in some kind of parley.

It was, he told himself, a long talk or a long wait; for he
covered a good mile before he reached them, to see directly
that one of these men was the blond Buff Sultan. They had
squared around to face him—this Sultan, and a youngster of
about nineteen with a square face, and a man old enough to
be the youngster's father and with the same kind of features.
Jim Majors pulled up, observing the etiquette of the situation.
Buff Sultan's blond cheeks showed him no recognition, which
was all Majors needed for his own cue.

He said to them generally: "Good day for ridin'. Where
does this road go?"

The oldest one said with a reserved courtesy, "Into Dobe Hyde's valley."

"Get to Fort Custer this way?"

"A pretty long ride. Looking for a job?"

Majors considered this older man until the other said: "You saw the road down there with the elkhorn arch?"

"Ketchum?"

"That's me. A job?"

Majors took time out to load his pipe. Ketchum slid a glance to Buff Sultan, who made the faintest of nods. They had, Majors guessed, been discussing him while he approached. This was the kind of country it was—so tight and so self-contained that one stranger sent a definite current of disturbance to the extreme end of the valley. It told him something. Trouble had hardened them all, it had set them all into camps. He had felt it in Reservation, and he could feel it now—a resistance that pushed against him, that closed tightly around him.

He said, "No, I think I'll be riding," and left them like that. He guessed it was the Sultan house he saw a quarter-mile in from the main road. Half a mile on, he reached a canyon with straight walls and width enough to let only the river and this narrow road pass through it. Semidarkness lay here for a distance of several hundred yards, or until the canyon widened and the road fell between the shoulders of a broken hill country. And at once, seeing a trail lift into that ridge he had skirted all the way from Reservation, he took it and soon found himself closed about by timber, climbing steadily.

He had spent all the years of his active life in the open, this Jim Majors; and it was a part of his long training that he could travel now with the country perfectly outlined in his head, its directions plain and the character of the land immediately clear. He had that compass sense. At noon, from a high bare knob, he could see, behind him, the round pocket which he judged to be Dobe Hyde's valley. Before him the stringers of the broken country, dark with timber, undulated like heavy sea swells westward until they rolled against the sharply climbing shoulders of the general range. Somewhere between this spot and that great mountain mass lay the meadows of the Ute Fork's south branch, where the Barrs lived. He pushed along the trail into strong shadows and into deep silence, and an hour or so later came upon a stumpy clearing wherein sat a frame house, sagging badly at peak and flank, silvered by weather, its broken windows staring at him sightlessly.

Curiosity led him to it. He dismounted at the low front porch where grass sprouted between the warped boards. Looking into the front room he could see that stray cattle had made a shelter of this place and had scrubbed themselves against the door's edges. A stairway ran up along one side of the room. A fireplace showed the black ashes of a fairly recent flame. Without warning steps sounded in the depths of this house and then a woman, a girl in her early twenties, appeared at an inner door.

She saw him and stopped with a shocked intake of breath, and that shock completely changed the expression of her face. Astonishment gripped her so completely that for the space of a small moment she could neither speak nor move. During that interval he saw fear come freshly to her eyes.

4

The Posted Notice

THE WAYS of Majors' life had trained his senses to be critical
and exacting; so now he stood here and gathered the impressions that came to him. She must have ridden to this isolated spot, yet her horse wasn't to be seen in the clearing,
which meant that she had probably left it out of sight in the
timber. On her face at first had been a faint touch of eagerness, as though she waited for someone. In its place now was
a genuine fear which told him how dangerous she thought
this situation was.

She was a moderately tall girl, with corn-yellow hair and
features which reached out for light and showed the swift
changes of her mind. Her shoulders unconsciously straightened opposing him, and her hands were tightly closed.
Breathing disturbed her breasts and color ran freshly across
her cheeks. He could stand there, mind thoroughly on guard,
and yet appreciate the supple lines of her body. She was, he
thought, in that first maturity which follows girlhood; and all
this while he watched the fear fade from her glance, as
though she had calculated him and had come to her own decision. She had a quickness of mind that he appreciated, and
the ability to be cool under strain.

He said: "Sorry to disturb you."

Her answer was deliberately meant to show him no great
interest. "The country is free for anybody to ride in, I suppose."

It made him smile. "Sure. Free for me and for you—and
for the other man you expected."

31

He saw a part of her fear rise again. She said: "Which way did you come?"

He pointed eastward. "That way."

"I haven't seen you before."

"New here."

Her lips softened, which added to his information. Having identified himself, he presented no great danger to her. She was almost serene in her composure and her face lightened and grew prettier and she watched him with a more direct interest. She was a well-shaped girl, her features quick to express her thoughts; and laughter and the love of life seemed to lie impatiently behind her eyes and her lips, waiting for release.

He said, "I'm on the right trail to the Barrs?"

She said, "Yes," and her glance went beyond him into the still, bright meadow. She was poised as though listening, as though waiting. "Do you know them?"

"No." He reached for his pipe, black head bowing as he filled it, his lips making a long, brief-smiling line. She expected someone—and the run of the moments began to trouble her.

He murmured: "Place looks pretty old. Didn't know this country was settled so long ago."

"The house? It was built in '60."

He was mildly surprised. "Don't see how it could get so run-down that soon."

She said: "Look at the window on your left. Below it, in the wall."

He had to step back to catch a view—observing that as he retreated from the doorway she followed until she was on the edge of the porch. The panes of the windows had been broken out, the sash had been beaten in. He saw what she meant, then. Below the window the faded wall bore the punctured mark of gunfire.

She said: "You don't know about that?"

"As I said, I'm a stranger to the country." He lighted his pipe, a feeling running along his back that was too strong to disregard. These were the details which guided his life, obscure sounds in the stray wind, fugitive impressions upon the earth, the shift of men's voices and the dim currents of warning that traveled their invisible channels to touch his senses. He never quite understood why it should be this way with him, but he had learned long ago that by obeying these im-

palpable signals he had survived the hard back years, and
that when he disregarded them trouble came to him. He
didn't immediately turn, yet he knew that somebody hidden
in the depths of the pines watched him now. He said in the
same slow, music-making voice:—

"Better be on the travel."

All this while she had been studying him, her lips thoughtfully joined. She came to some quick decision and said:
"Wait. Are you riding for the Barrs?"

"No," he answered. "No."

"I wish you hadn't seen me here."

His admiration for this girl increased. It was the quickness
of her judgment that appealed to him, the deliberate way she
came to the point. He looked at her. "I haven't seen you
here."

"All right. That's a favor. You might as well know my
name, which is Edith Sultan. If you stay you'll find it out
anyhow."

He lifted his hat and made a quick turn toward the sorrel
near by. One swift sweep of the line of trees showed him
nothing. But a signal continued to flow from that direction,
touching his nerves and pressing against his muscles. He got
quickly into the saddle and trotted toward the farther mouth
of the mill trail, not looking back. The trees closed around
him presently and the forest shade closed down; and in the
still air lay the scent of dust. Studying the soft earth he observed the print of a rider recently come this way.

For an hour he rode the covert trail, up and down the rolling contours of the broken land, outwardly idle but inwardly
alive. The feel of this land was odd to him. Somewhere was a
line as definite as a chalk strip that separated the men of the
country, affecting their judgment and their actions powerfully. He could pull certain scenes and incidents from his
head to establish that point: as the fated Pete Riley spinning
into the dust at the crash of Ben Maffitt's gun, the laconic
talk of Buff Sultan in the hotel room, and Charley Chavis'
poorly concealed irritability, and the bullet holes in the wall
of the deserted house behind him. Above this—and the key
to all the subtle actions of men—seemed to lie the pressure of
something out of the past. Majors had dealt with the violent
treacheries of men long enough to make a guess as to that
key. It would be, he thought, a hatred begotten of some old
quarrel that kept growing with the years.

So thinking, he came out of the timber around two o'clock of this bright fall afternoon, and found himself at the rim of a narrow valley lying north and south with the base of that rugged mountain range which hoisted itself, one rocky tier upon another, toward snow-pointed peaks distant in a bright blue sky. Ute Fork's south branch largely occupied this narrow valley, the sun catching up the froth of its occasional rocky shallows. A road skirted the river; and river and road disappeared around a bend in the farther south where hills seemed to squeeze the valley thin.

He cut down the rim, reached the road, and followed it around that bend. Cattle grazed the narrow meadows and the heavy pines descended in dark masses from the Silver Lode Range; the valley's walls, to either side, grew higher. The road went definitely upward until, at the end of a good hour's travel, he skirted one more bend and saw a house and its scattered sheds and corrals backed against the valley's end. White ribbons of quick water marked where the south branch of the Ute Fork tumbled out of the range.

It was a ranch walled in on three sides, facing the narrow valley. A bridge crossed the river, and fed a trail which faded into the climbing timber. A dog rushed at him, and he could see men stirring around the corrals; and one man rose from the house porch and waited for him to ride up. When he reached the yard and wheeled, waiting for an invitation to dismount, he recognized the narrow-shaped Pedee Barr.

Majors said: "Afternoon," and indicated his leisure by folding both hands over the horn.

Pedee Barr's eyes were black and altogether unfriendly. His lips made an old man's bloodless line above the white goatee and the muscles of his jaws showed a stubborn bunching. He was, Majors immediately understood, a Southerner with an ancient pride that ran up and down his back like a steel rod; hot-tempered and thoroughly intolerant when angered. But he had a courtesy that made him say, with a reluctant Southern drawl:—

"You are on my land, sir. I did not invite you here. But since you are here, step down and have a chair."

Majors said, "Thanks," and swung from the saddle, strolling to the porch. The open door presented him a vista all back to the rear yard. Women talked somewhere in the depths of the house and the sound of an ax rang out from the yonder corrals in flat-ringing echoes. He took his survey briefly, but he knew Pedee Barr's ink-dark eyes were observing that display of interest. The old man said: "Sit down."

Majors settled himself in a rocker. This box-sided valley unrolled before him a half-mile or so before bending from sight. A little breeze scoured through the open hallway, fanning the back of his neck. Pedee Barr took a seat, producing a cheroot which he rolled between his lips, without a light.

A man rode from the timber on the far side of the Ute Fork and came on across the narrow bridge, the footfalls of the horse rolling very clear through the afternoon's drowse.

Majors said: "Where would that trail lead?"

Pedee Barr drawled: "I could not say."

The rider crossed the yard, his head swung to study Majors. He was tall and sharp-faced and quite dark of skin, with enough of a resemblance to old Pedee Barr to be a son. The old man's cigar dipped between his lips and the young one passed around the corner of the house; there had been a signal between the two.

Majors was a loose shape in the rocker; he was idly smiling. "No settlement of any kind up that way?"

Pedee Barr stared directly at Majors. "I must tell you, sir, that you will find no answers to your questions here. If it is what you came for, you might as well return to Reservation."

That pressure of suspicion and hidden motive which had rubbed him since his first hour in the country grew greater, as though this spot was one of its sources. The sound of the ax stopped, and the talking of the women, and afterwards someone came through the hall with a light, quick step.

Pedee Barr got up promptly. Following suit, Jim Majors turned to find Katherine Barr pausing in the doorway.

Pedee Barr said: "I believe you have an apology to offer my daughter for the ungentlemanly character of your speech in Reservation last night."

Majors spoke directly to the girl, the half-smile remaining on his solid lips. "If you consider an apology in order, I freely make it."

Pedee Barr spoke with a cold, rising tone. "I hear no direct apology, sir. Either make it or tell me that you refuse to make it."

Katherine Barr said: "He has made it, Father."

She was in a gray dress that matched and deepened the gray of her eyes and turned her hair a more shining black. She stood idly against the doorsill, seeming tall to him again;

it was an illusion made by the way she carried her head, by the way she held her shoulders. He noticed once more the ivory shading of her skin and the turn of her lips. She had a pride that, like her father's, could sweep her violently and set up its blaze in her eyes. There was, Majors thought, that tremendous capacity for emotion in this girl, though her expression was almost severe now. The lines of the dress cut an accurate outline upward from her hips, showing the half fullness of her breasts; and something in his glance at that moment freshened her color.

She said, to Pedee Barr: "Have you asked him to stay for supper?"

Pedee Barr murmured: "I have not asked him," in a thinly final way.

Katherine Barr looked back at Majors. There was a break in her expression, a minute embarrassment. These were the times, Majors thought, when the hidden color of the girl's personality broke through the repose of her face—these times when she was disturbed or angered.

He said: "It is not my desire to intrude."

Men came silently around the corner of the house, causing Majors to swing on his heels. They stopped at the steps, four of them, loosely grouped together.

Pedee Barr said: "This is my son Fay Barr—and this is my son Ring. I regret my third son, Dan, is not here for you to meet. These others are Creed and Will Barr."

Majors could distinguish little difference between Fay and Ring Barr, except that Fay was the younger of the pair. They had the same lank build, the same dark narrowness of face, and their eyes held the same close distrust that was characteristic of their father. Pedee Barr was speaking again, to Jim Majors.

"I have my own ideas why you came here. I want you to remember these boys. It is entirely your business what you do, but if you set yourself against us, expect no charity from me or from them. I want you to understand that. There will never be another warning. Now, if you have nothing else to detain you . . ."

Majors clapped on his hat and went out to the sorrel, climbing up. He had his look at this group, at the metal-darkness of their faces, at old Pedee standing so stiff and domineering above them, and at Katherine Barr, who looked his way as though trying to read what he thought. He lifted his hat to her and his sudden grin appeared, long and ironic. He pointed at the trail leading across the bridge into the heights of the range.

"If Ben Maffitt comes out of the Pocket in the next day or so, you might say I'd like a word with him."

There was no change in Pedee's features.

Majors swung away, and had reached the gate when the girl's voice stopped him.

"Wait!"

He pulled around. Pedee Barr said, "Come back, Katherine," but the girl ran on, stopping by Majors' horse.

She looked up. "Tell Tony I'd like to do something for her. Tell her that." Then her voice dropped. "I want to talk to you, sometime. But don't come into this valley again."

"The road's free," pointed out Majors.

She gave him a direct look. "It may be. But you've already talked to Buff Sultan. We know that."

Pedee Barr called her name more imperiously and she turned away. Majors put his horse to a trot and presently passed around the bend. Sunlight held the sky, but it had gone from the valley and the bite of winter lay in the shadows. At the next bend he saw a rider slide off the rim at the same point at which he had earlier entered this little valley, and come galloping forward.

A hundred yards away the rider drew in to a walk; and thus they came abreast. It was, Majors guessed, the third son, Dan Barr. The family resemblance was on the youngster's face, though he had a broader spread between his eyes and less sultriness in them. Abreast Majors, Dan Barr said "Howdy," and after Majors had answered the youngster flung his pony into a gallop and went by.

At one point in the valley Majors took note of a well-used trail shooting off from the road to the river, crossing at a gravel ford and angling instantly into the high timber. He made note of it, meanwhile considering the Barr family with a practical interest; and so came to Reservation at suppertime's dusk.

Instead of going directly to the stable he dropped off in front of the print shop and went in.

It was a single room with a counter, behind which stood the cases and hand press and accumulated junk of a printer's business; a man, prematurely gray and sallowed by his trade, turned reluctantly from the cases. After he got closer to the lamplight Majors discovered he was younger than the shadows made him out. He presented Majors with a thoroughly weary, disillusioned expression.

Majors reached into his pocket and took out a single folded sheet of paper. He said: "I'll wait while you print this up."

The man said, "I was about to close shop."

"Won't take a minute," Majors suggested, and turned behind the counter. The printer lifted his shoulders and let them fall; he walked to the case. Majors handed him the paper and stood back, watching the printer's expression slowly change. The man's glance slanted angularly at him, bright and wise and old.

"That lets the cat out. You sure you want it printed?"

"Go ahead," ordered Majors. He fished for his pipe and packed it, and stood there smoking while the printer's hand moved swiftly along the case. Riders trotted past the office and a supper-triangle began to bang. The printer locked up the type and ran an ink roller over it and pressed out a copy, handing it to Majors.

"How many you want?"

"One's enough."

"More than enough," agreed the printer dryly.

"What's the cost?"

"I guess that's all right," said the printer. "I'm sorry for you."

Majors left the office, riding to the stable; afterwards he crossed to the jail. He met Charley Chavis at the doorway and waved him back. "Talk to you a minute," he said.

Chavis turned into the room.

"Listen," he said, "I don't want any part in your business. I just found out you talked to Buff Sultan last night."

"News spreads."

"You dam' right," said Charley Chavis with unusual vehemence.

"How fast you figure this will spread?" asked Majors, and handed the marshal the printed sheet.

The marshal's glance hit the printing and bounced back to Majors. He stepped away from Majors, shaking his head. He moved his hands nervously. He said: "No, not me. What the hell you come here for? That's what I thought this morning." Anger got into his talk, vehement and complaining. "You got no business shovin' into this place. Who the hell asked you to come here? I didn't. Nobody in the town did. Well, why then?"

There was an election picture of Charley Chavis on the office wall. Majors went over and took out the tacks that held it, then pulled the printed sheet from Chavis' loose fingers and went to the street. He thumbed the notice onto a bulletin board beside the door, called to Chavis, "I'll use your office now and then, Charley," and strolled down the streeet.

When he got to the hotel he looked behind him to see Charley Chavis standing before the notice, reading it. A man came out of the saloon, walking rapidly that waay.

The notice had on it this information:—

REWARD

The United States Government will pay $500 for information concerning any of the undersigned men, all of whom are wanted for bank robbery, train robbery, mail stage holdups or for violation or other Federal statutes. These men last known to be in the Pocket country of the Silver Lode Range:—

> ED DALE
> THORPE CAROW, *alias* SALT RIVER TOD
> WILLY LEE BREEN
> YANCEY STOWBRICK
> HARRY M'GILLIVRY

Communicate with U. S. Marshal Jeff D. White at Territorial Capitol, or to the undersigned, in Reservation.

J. J. Majors, *Deputy United States Marshal*

5

⊷•◉•⊶

Dobe Hyde

MAJORS went to his room and washed up and returned to the lobby. Night's full darkness rolled off the shoulders of the Silver Lode Range and a little wind, definitely cold, began to stir in the street. The lights of the Old Dixie made a mellow gush across the square, outlining now and then a townsman casually strolling by. The supper-triangle began to ring again from the dining room door, beating into this hour's deep silence. Last night the town had been alive; tonight it seemed empty.

Majors crossed the square and entered the saloon. A pair of men sat idly at one of the poker tables and the printer had his belly to the bar, drinking in gloomy silence. He threw a swift side glance at the arriving Majors and afterwards turned half-away, which was, Majors understood, a clear signal of his desire to keep out of trouble. The barkeep saw Majors' lifted finger and slid a bottle and a glass along the counter. Majors had his drink and stood there, hearing a chair scrape behind him.

Presently a voice said: "The drink is on the house, captain."

Majors turned. One of the men at the poker table had risen and come forward. He was short and soft-fleshed, dressed in a black serge suit and a white shirt with a string tie. A diamond ring flashed on the little finger of his left hand and his black hair lay oiled and flattened to his head. There was a close attention in his eyes, but no depth of expression.

He said, "My name's Cal Soder."

Majors shook hands with him. There was no strength to

40

Soder's grip; only a cold brief pressure and a swift with-drawal. The barkeep slid another glass along the bar. Soder poured a short drink and murmured, "You're welcome in my place any time, captain," and downed the drink with a quick tip of his head. The printer had turned to look at this scene and the barkeep rested by, both hands on the bar's surface. The remaining man at the poker table showed Majors a thin, impassive countenance.

Majors nodded. "Thanks."

Soder said: "I run a clean place here and want no trouble. I ask no questions and treat my customers like gentlemen. It is my wish that you won't find it necessary to use this saloon for fighting."

Majors grinned. "We'll both wish that."

"No," said Soder, insistence coming to his talk. "It is more than a wish, captain. It is something I ask. I make no excep-tions, even for law officers."

Majors quit smiling. His heavy head lifted a notch and the gray surface of his eyes showed a smokier color. "You had better drop that information to Ben Maffitt."

The saloonman said calmly: "Make no mistake about Cal Soder, captain. I have run my business in some lively towns and I have handled tougher peace officers than I think you are. Maffitt will be a customer of mine long after you're gone. I do a lot of business with boys from the Pocket and find them all genteel customers. Don't come in here for trou-ble, captain. I will not have it."

Majors said dryly, "I'll let that remark go by, Soder."

Soder shrugged his shoulders. There was no heat or added sharpness in his voice, but definiteness was increasingly there. "I want it to be clear to you."

Majors put a hand into his pocket and drew out a quarter and laid it on the bar, whereupon Soder said, "The drink was on me, as I believe I said."

"No," murmured Majors, "I guess not."

But he was careful to watch the faint signals in the back of this saloonman's eyes, suddenly knowing him to be danger-ous.

Soder's mouth changed minutely. He said, "Not civil of you, captain; but it's your business. You're strange here—and you're young, and you need friends, which you are never likely to have in Reservation. I watched you in action last night and thought you had more grit than good sense. It was the wrong play to make, and I can tell you now that you'll either be dead or out of this valley in sixty days."

"Maybe," said Majors, "and maybe not"—and closely watched the little devils of a remote temper dance deep down in Soder's obscure eyes.

Soder shrugged his shoulders. "I saw Tom Smith with his head chopped off, in Abilene. I saw Wild Bill lyin' dead on a barroom floor in Deadwood, four years ago. They were smarter men than you, captain. And this is a tougher camp than those places were. I give you the warning for what it's worth—and not out of friendliness, either. I do not like you, and no merchant in town likes you. You come here and make business bad for us by keeping the boys scared away. That's part of our trade you're botherin'. We're not askin' the Territory or the Government to come in here and stir up trouble. We'll run our business like we want, regardless." He gave Majors a stiff, straight glance and added evenly: "There's more to this business than you can handle, and there's more than one way to skin a cat."

Having said this, he turned and went back to the poker table.

The printer stood with both elbows hanging to the bar, his head moodily slumped over. The barkeep hadn't stirred. Soder loosened himself indifferently on the far chair and faced the thin-cheeked gambler. A pair of riders ran past the saloon, the hoofs of their horses lifting muffled sound from the street's thick dust. Majors took out his pipe and tapped it on the bar hard enough to jerk at the printer's nerves; the printer looked around at him, eyes obscurely bitter. Majors returned the pipe to his pocket and left the saloon.

He had his supper and went up to his room. He drew the blinds and lighted the lamp and stood a moment filling his pipe. After he got it drawing well, he laid himself full length on the bed, his boots hanging over its end, and stared at the ceiling.

There was no clear pattern to this business, which was the way old Jeff White had warned him it would be. He had come up from the Sundown country, summoned by Jeff, who had been his chief for five years. He could remember Jeff's grin and the way that veteran man-hunter tugged at the ends of his tawny mustache—which had been a portent of something.

Old Jeff had said: "You been leadin' a sedentary life lately, Jim."

And he had answered: "Nothin' much to report, for a fact."

Whereupon Jeff White's bright blue glance had gone through him like a high-powered bullet. "Well, kid, in two hours you'll be on your way to the Ute Fork country, across the Silver Lode."

"A man?" he had asked, and could remember that old Jeff had quit smiling. Old Jeff had taken time to light up a cigar, his hands long and white and beginning to take on the transparency of age. At seventy, Jeff White was a legend, but once he had been unbeatable at the draw when he had to draw—which was seldom, for Jeff White's fame rested on his smartness.

He said now: "Well, there's half a dozen men around Reservation I'd like to have. But it ain't the men so much, as the country. That town is bad. It protects anybody who's on the dodge. There's some ranches strung along the Ute water, but as far as I can get it, they ain't much better than the tough ones. The dam' country is ready to blow up over a quarrel that goes back ten or fifteen years and I guess one set of ranchers is usin' the toughs to help out. There's a marshal at Reservation. Don't trust him. Last sheriff was bushwhacked seven months ago. What we got is a scope of land turnin' into an outlaw strip. I don't want any war to get started and I don't want all the outlaws in the West to run there for shelter. I'll give you warrants for some of the boys wanted on federal charges. That's your excuse. But the real thing I'm after is to open that country up."

"A large order."

Old Jeff had looked at him and had said candidly: "I lost Joe Mossman there last year."

Majors remembered asking: "How far can I go, Jeff?"

Jeff White's eyes could get agate-hard. They had, then.

"You're the kind of a scrapper that can be pretty tough, Jim. I've seen you work. The sky's the limit. I'll ask no questions. Just clean it up in your own way. There's things a man with a star ain't supposed to do, which you know as well as I do. But I'll never ask you whether you stuck on the right side of the line or not. That's the mistake I made with the last boy. I told him to be fair. I ain't telling you that. If I did you wouldn't last."

He had walked away from old Jeff's office with this last advice: "Try to find out what the politics of the situation is before you show your hand. Don't trust a living soul. Well—there's one man you can rely on. If you've got to get word through, old Sam Rhett who runs the stage will do, but don't let anybody else know about that." Afterwards he had added: "Maybe you'll come through. It will depend on some qualities you've got—good and bad both—which I see better than you do."

So he was here; and at the end of his first twenty-four hours it was plain to him that even old Jeff didn't know how wicked the situation was. In every man's mind lay either a hatred or a fear, rising from some source he couldn't yet discover. There was no neutral party in the country. Running over the list of the people he had so far met he realized that not one of them was free. Not one.

Somebody came up the stairs and walked to the rear of the hall. Riders were trotting into town.

Majors remained slack-muscled on the bed, piecing his stray bits of information together.

The Barrs were openly hostile and had some arrangement with Ben Maffitt and the other outlaws of the Pocket. Buff Sultan had come here to hint at a bargain he would make—and then decided not to make it. The saloonman, Cal Soder, had expressed the antagonism of the town, and the sorrel-headed marshal wasn't to be trusted at all. It made a kind of tight circle, and though Majors' mind prowled around the outer edge of that circle carefully he found no break through which he might force his way.

It didn't surprise him, for he knew how men acted in times like this. They would go on with their fighting, but they would draw farther back into secrecy, either afraid of the star he wore or despising it. They would use him for their own purposes if they could; and if they couldn't use him they'd try to get rid of him.

There was this gray realism in Majors' head. The years had hardened him; the years had ground into him a sense of men's treacheries. He had taken enough punishment in his time to be able to return that punishment without pity, and it was one of his weaknesses that, knowing so little of the soft side of life, he was skeptical of its existence.

He hoisted himself from the bed, refilling his pipe while he ran his calculations out to the end. So far he could find no

break and no place from which to start working. What he
had to do was wait for a break, or make one; and he had a
hatred of waiting. Maybe it was better to make a break. He
had enough warrants in his pocket and maybe it was the
proper play—to ride into the hills until he found a man he
wanted, and drag him out, and see who answered that challenge.

Somebody else trotted into town. Lifting the edge of a window blind, he saw Katherine Barr swing in at the general
store adjoining the empty building and get down. She stood
on the walk a moment, her glance searching the street and
presently turning toward the hotel. Afterwards she went into
the store.

He left the room and walked down the stairs. The hotel
man sat in his chair talking to someone Majors hadn't seen
before. Both of them looked around at him.

The hotel man said, "That's Majors, Dobe."

The other one got up spryly and stuck out a hand. He said,
"I'm Dobe Hyde. Heard you was here."

He was short and baldheaded with a pair of pale gray eyes
as bright and cold as a magpie's recessed deeply in a round
face. He wore a suit of clothes that didn't fit him and a wool
shirt stiffened by sweat and dust. There was dirt grimed into
the creases of his skin and he carried cattle smell strongly
with him. His small, rosebud mouth made a single vivid dot
against the steel-gray stubble of his whiskers.

Majors took the extended hand.

"Pay me a visit," said Dobe Hyde. "If you calculate to stay
here long."

Majors recognized the indirect question, and directly answered it, "I intend to stay."

Dobe Hyde's glance came out bright and slanting. "Fine.
Country could stand a little law."

The hotel man put in his dry statement. "Who for, Dobe?"

Dobe Hyde grinned, his dry skin seeming to crack at the
effort. He was all slyness and smartness, even in his humor.
He reached over and dug the hotel man's ribs with the blunt
end of his thumb. "A joke on old Dobe, hey? Listen, Broderick, I'll abide by law as soon as anybody else will."

Broderick grunted: "That will be a long time, Dobe."

Dobe Hyde let go a short shrill bleat of laughter. "As soon
as any. Not before and not after." He had been looking at
Broderick, but his glance came surreptitiously around, as

though to catch Majors off guard, as though to trap something that might have shown in Majors' face.

He said: "Come over and see me. You hear it said I'm pretty hard and pretty close. Maybe so—maybe so. I learn well and I don't forget. Come over and have a meal on me."

The hotel man slid in his ironic remark: "He'll serve you beef, Majors—but it won't be his beef."

Dobe Hyde cackled. "Never was a hand to disregard the custom of the country, Broderick."

All this while he had never directly faced Majors and never directly looked at him; all his glances had been thrown from one side of his face or the other; and all had been quick and bright and brief. Suddenly he slapped Broderick on the back and, saying no more to Majors, went out of the lobby at a loose shuffle. Majors observed him get on a white horse badly in need of grooming and go down the street at a trot which showed him as the poorest of riders.

So Majors watched Dobe Hyde leave town. Nor was he the only one to take heed of the little man, for during the few minutes in which Dobe had talked with Majors, Charley Chavis stood in the heavy shadows across the square and kept a close eye on the scene in the lobby. Chavis waited until Dobe Hyde was entirely out of Reservation and then cut back to his horse standing in the livery stable, rode around the town, and caught the silhouette of Dobe Hyde in the road leading down to the Ute's east branch. Charley Chavis dropped back at a safer distance and settled to the pursuit.

Meanwhile Majors remained in his tracks, his eyes thoughtfully considering the hotel man. He said in a speculative tone: "Broderick? Was that the name? James Broderick?"

The hotel man's big shape was wholly sagged in the rocker. He stared through the window, away from Majors. He said, "Yeah," reluctantly.

"Your name reminds me of something, though I never met you in the Sundown country. You stayed back in the Yellow Hills."

Jack Broderick's huge shoulders settled deeper into the chair. "I guess," he murmured, "you know me now."

"No," said Majors quietly; "I'm doing you a favor. I don't know you."

Broderick's moon-shaped face came about. "Why?"

"Put it down in the book, Broderick. A favor—for a favor. I'll ask for my favor later." Broderick started to speak, but

Majors went rapidly from the lobby, remembering something. At that moment Katherine Barr walked from the store with a package under her arm and started across the street. She saw him, and for a brief interval he felt the quick search of her eyes, even in the semidark; afterwards she went on to the restaurant. Majors walked to the stable, saddled the big gelding, and left Reservation by the road which led to the Barr ranch. Beyond town a short distance he stopped and drew aside into the black shadows of a pine tree. He waited half an hour before Katherine Barr came along, riding alone.

He said, "Wait," and cut across the road.

She advanced until she was beside him.

"I think," he said, "you had something to tell me."

"Maybe," she answered. "Maybe I did."

There was a thin cut of a moon in the low sky, silver-pale and shedding almost no light along the earth. The near-by shoulders of the Silver Lode created a massive darkness that lay over them. He could see her shoulders swing and he could catch the vague outline of her features. But there was something quick and alive and stormy in this girl and it came out to stir him now, though he didn't know why.

"I'm sorry my father suggested the apology. It wasn't necessary."

"Let it stand."

She remained silent for a moment. The river was near by, the wash of water over its shallow gravel bed a low rumor in the dark. Wind rolled down from the peaks, steady and cold.

She said: "I should like to be friendly, but I can see no chance of that. Do you know what all this means?"

"No," he said; "not yet."

She said, "Perhaps you will. You leave the impression of being able to take care of yourself. But I wonder who you'll get the story from."

"Make a difference?"

"Yes," she answered. "It makes all the difference. There are only two sides in the valley. Your information has to come from one of those sides. Whichever side tells you the story, your judgment will be colored."

"One side right and one side wrong?" he suggested.

She delayed her talk again. When she did answer it was in a slower, quieter voice.

"I have not said that. I belong to one side. I believe in my people. I do not say we are wholly right, but right or wrong, that's where I must be."

"I'll listen," he said.

But she said "No!" in a voice instantly aroused, and he knew then how deeply she felt. The wild, partisan instinct of her family governed her life also. She added: "You must find out for yourself. I was told, in the store, what you were. That's what I thought yesterday—and so did my father. It is impossible for me to trust you, or for anybody to trust you. Do you see why? Because, whatever you try to do, it will be for one side and against the other. You may not mean it that way, but nevertheless you cannot make a single move in the valley without taking part in our quarrel. That's why we can't trust you. And if you are wise you'll trust nobody either."

He said, "I came here to get certain known outlaws. What's that got to do with a quarrel?"

She said, "You'll see."

"You want that quarrel settled?" he asked her.

Once more the same swift suspicion was in her talk. "It never will be settled. Maybe you think we ought to be open-minded. Maybe you think I ought to be generous enough to forgive. But my oldest brother was killed three years ago in this fight and I know who did it—and never, never will I forgive that!"

He said quietly: "I guess it is a good thing the Lord made some women with gentleness in 'em—like the girl Tony. I like her better."

Her indrawn breath cut a thin echo in the night. He might, he thought, as well have hit her with his hand. Her shoulders swung and she slapped him across the face, full force. She was outraged. "Don't you suppose I feel sorry for her? It's a tragedy—but how could I help that? How could anybody help it?"

He said distinctly, unfavorably: "You are less a woman than I thought. Good night."

There was a distant rumor of a traveler, coming out of the depths of the canyon. Katherine Barr murmured: "That will be one of my brothers. He'd shoot you if he found you with me."

"Or he might get shot," said Majors briefly. The Barr pride and the Barr assurance raked him the wrong way; it made him rough with his talk. "Your family is a little brash."

"You'll regret that!"

"I have found," he told her, more gently, "that life is largely a matter of regret. Which is about the extent of my wisdom." He had backed his horse into the coagulated darkness beneath the pine tree, waiting there. Katherine Barr went on at a walk. Thirty yards down the road he heard the oncoming horseman draw suddenly up.

"Katherine? You'll catch the devil for traveling to town alone!"

Katherine Barr said: "Never mind, Ring."

Afterwards their voices faded in the distance.

Majors returned to town, put away the horse and went up to his room. He sat down on the bed's edge; and was like that, scowling over the bowl of his pipe, when somebody knocked softly on the door and opened it without invitation. Tony was there. She hesitated a moment, watching his expression with the faint break of a smile softening her cheeks; and presently she stepped in and shut the door.

He said: "Tony, you're a little sudden."

It took away her smile and he could see the change in her pliable lips. She said, almost humbly, "Don't you ever get tired or lonely? I do."

He said: "Sit down, Tony. I'd like to ask a couple of questions."

She came over and dropped to the edge of the bed. She was smiling again, her expression frank and soft—and personal. There was a sweetness in this girl that a hard-earned knowledge of the world had not destroyed. It was something that still remained, giving a faint fragrance and desirability to her.

Dobe Hyde rode into the Sultan yard and called across the dark, "Hey, Buff!"—and waited until the front room light went out and the door opened. Sultan was just inside the threshold, making no target. Dobe Hyde said, "It's me, Buff. It's Dobe Hyde. Come here."

Buff Sultan walked down the steps. The light came on again in the room, and Edith Sultan appeared a moment before closing the door.

Dobe Hyde said: "Listen. That new feller is a deputy marshal. Who y' suppose got him here?"

Sultan said: "Don't know."

"Well, he's after some of Ben Maffitt's bunch. I took a good look at him. He ain't any fool."

"No," said Sultan. "He's tough."

"Well, now . . ." drawled Dobe Hyde in his piping voice, and let it go at that for a moment. Afterwards he said: "Supposin' he gits some of those boys and makes it hot for the Pocket bunch? Kind of takes away old Pedee Barr's support, don't it? You see what I see, Buff?"

"Maybe," said Buff Sultan cautiously. "Maybe I do."

"Sure you do. Well, you and me ain't never done no business together before. I been a feller to play on my own hand strictly. But maybe we can work somethin' out on this. Come over and see me in the mornin'." He turned back to the main road.

Buff Sultan hadn't spoken and old Dobe finally threw his shrill voice behind him. "Think you'll come?"

"Maybe," said Buff, and returned to the house.

Edith Sultan said, "What did he want?"

Her brother shook his head. "Not sure. Mysterious. Wants me to drop over and see him tomorrow."

"You be careful with that old pirate."

"Sure—sure," agreed Buff. But then he said, "Where you going?"

His sister had put on an old riding hat and was on her way to the door. She turned at his question, a slim, thoroughly alert girl with the lamplight heightening the color of her cheeks and catching the laughter of her eyes. Her lips showed him a pursed smile. Buff grumbled: "Hell of a time to be ridin', Edie."

Still smiling at him, she went out. He stood in the middle of the room, scowling over her departure, hearing her ride down the road to Reservation.

Posted in the thoroughly black background, Charley Chavis saw that meeting of Buff Sultan and Dobe Hyde. He also saw Edith Sultan later leave the ranch and cut over toward the ridge, fading into the night. Whereupon, with this much knowledge gained, he turned back to Reservation.

6

***

The Break

MAJORS got up from the bed, leaving Tony to sit passively there. Her glance followed him around the room. Over in a corner he came about and stopped. "You pretty fond of this Pete Riley?"

The girl shrugged her shoulders. "I guess I liked him a lot. Well, he was nice to me. That's more than most people are. A girl like me gets used to almost anything. Anything but kindness."

"Why'd Maffitt kill him, Tony?"

"Well, he won a lot of money from Maffitt. That's when he was with the bunch up in the Pocket. He came down here and decided to get out of the country, but Maffitt followed him. It was the money—and I guess Maffitt thought Pete knew too much about what was going on."

Majors said: "What's going on, Tony?"

She looked at him for quite a while, soberly and sadly, "You're just pumping me. That's all you're interested in."

"Tony," he said, "you want to see Pete Riley's death squared?"

"Why should I care what happens to people? Nobody cares what happens to me. Listen: This is a selfish town, a cruel town, and why should you worry if these men kill each other off? All I want is just a little something for myself. Just a little something."

She watched him, seeing how quietly he listened. Her cheeks were rose-colored and her shoulders rested back against the head of the bed, loosening the full lines of her throat and breasts. That small, obscure smile appeared, and

51

gradually faded. Finally she shrugged away whatever she
might have been thinking and spoke in a thoroughly indifferent voice. "Oh, I'll tell you. I like you—and when I like a
man I'm a fool. Listen. I was brought up here. My folks had
the first ranch on this side of the Silver Lode Range. I saw
everybody come in. The Sultans and the Ketchums and the
Oldroyds and then Dobe Hyde. And the Barrs. It was the
Barrs who changed everything."

She stopped, her pliant features going dark from the things
she was remembering.

"Dad's place was back up in the broken country, halfway
between the two branches of the Ute. I lived there until I was
ten. It's deserted now. All broken down."

Majors at once recalled the house wherein he had seen
Edith Sultan. "I know the place," he told Tony.

"We lived there until I was ten," repeated Tony. Her eyes
were round and bright with the memories of that time. "Then
the Barrs came in. They were Southerners and they never
quit fighting the war. Everybody else in the country was
Northern. Well, they took part of Dad's range, and he was
too good-natured to kick about it. It was all free range. Most
of it still is, around here. Old man Barr kept writing for his
relatives to come up, and pretty soon he had a lot of them
here. Then he pushed his cows nearer our place. Dad had to
fight or give in. So there was a fight, and they killed him. The
Sultans and the Ketchums and the Oldroyds rode against the
Barrs after that. Katherine and her brothers were all kids, but
there was one older brother, Clay, who got killed, and one of
the Ketchum boys got killed. And so did old man Sultan—
Buff and Edith's dad. I went to live with the Oldroyds until I
was eighteen."

He could see how the years had broken her spirt and left
her with an indifference and an obscure smile that meant
nothing. She added: "The Barrs took our place and the fighting died down. All of us kids grew up. But nobody's ever forgotten anything and the hate's still here just as strong as it
ever was." She paused and afterwards gave him a quiet bit of
advice. "You're a fool to get into it. Let them do their own
quarreling."

"'What about Ben Maffitt?"

"Maffitt handles the outlaws that drift into the Pocket. You
can figúre Ben is on the Barr side. They've got an understanding. The Barrs know they're hated by everybody else, so

they keep friendly with Ben Maffitt's bunch. If another fight starts, Ben Maffitt will side with the Barrs. That's the only thing that keeps Buff Sultan and the rest from starting in again. But someday it'll start, and it won't stop till one side is ruined. Well, let them do it! That's the fear we've all lived under ever since I've been old enough to remember anything."

He said, "Thanks, Tony."

She rose and went to the door, but turned there and looked at him with her head lifted and the lamplight fully shining on her eyes. Her breathing quickened and her lips held a small, faint smile again. She murmured, "All right," but she didn't open the door.

He came over. He said, "I guess you've had a tough time."

Her shoulders lifted and fell, expressively. "I know men. You're pretty proud. You don't know what it is to be helpless and alone. I do. I've been hurt so much that there isn't much left—not even hatred. People could be happy if they wanted to be. But they won't, and you won't. Why?"

She left the room without waiting for his answer, closing the door quietly. Yet something remained behind, something soft and gentle and appealing. It clung to his mind long after she had gone, disturbing him, cutting across his alert speculation. She was a warmth that touched him.

Below him was the sound of the arriving stage. A man's voice, rather strident and angered, reached him. "Where's that deputy marshal?"

He cut out of the room immediately and went down to find the old stage-driver, Sam Rhett, standing in the lobby's center. Reservation's citizens were crowding in here, and the saloonman, Cal Soder, was at the doorway taciturnly watching.

Broderick said: "What's the bad news, Sam?"

Rhett's eyes, a hard pale blue, swung to Majors.

He said: "They stopped me on the hill. I had four mail-sacks. They only took one—the lightest one."

Majors said: "Where?"

"At the bend where the road leaves the Ute canyon. There was three of them." The driver looked at the gathered crowd and showed them an old man's stubborn contempt. Cal Soder chewed a dry cigar between his teeth, his attention narrowly pinned to the scene. The hotel man was in the background. Rhett spoke to Majors again, "One of the boys seemed proud.

He told me to tell you the sack would be up in the Pocket if you wanted it."

Majors' black hair lay ruffled along the edge of his forehead. He seemed sleepy. The scar on his cheekbone showed whitely and his solid lips made a long line across the darkness of his skin. He knew what this was. It was a break. It was Ben Maffitt's challenge, which he could take or leave alone. But he knew he had to take it. The whole thing had been framed in a way to make it clear to him. Nobody said anything, but they were watching with that indirect closeness of men weighing him for his value.

He said: "Maybe I better go get it."

"That's your say-so," drawled the driver. "I'm half an hour late." He turned and made his way through the crowd, and presently he had lashed his fresh horses into a gallop, leaving Reservation behind. The crowd withdrew from the lobby, leaving Majors there with the false-armed Broderick.

Broderick's asthmatic breathing rasped the dead stillness. He turned, putting his back to Majors, and was in this attitude when he spoke over his shoulder, not turning his head and scarcely moving his lips.

"I guess you got your call, Sundown."

"Maybe," said Majors.

"I kind of wondered, last night, why you made that ruckus in the saloon. Seemed a little proud and foolish at the time. But maybe it was to get a call."

"Maybe," drawled Majors.

"Well," said Broderick, "you got your call now."

"A little bit soon."

The hotel man's voice was as near a tone of curiosity as he had so far permitted it to be. "Somethin' else I don't quite understand. You come here and you ask a lot of questions, which is the mark of a tenderfoot. But you ain't a tenderfoot, and you knew you wouldn't get any answers. You knew it would get you pegged either as a fool or as a man lookin' for trouble."

"I'm no hand to play a waiting game, Broderick. If trouble had to come, just as well it comes soon."

"You got it," grunted Broderick and sat himself heavily down upon the rocker.

Majors strolled to the street and stood a moment, having his look at this quiet town. Two men shouldered into the saloon. A woman came from the general store, hesitated, and walked rapidly away from the square. Cal Soder remained in front of his saloon and a little noise came from the dining room kitchen, so still was the night air. Doc Showers hurried out of the stable, his short-paced steps going *chop-chop-chop* on the boards of the walk; he turned at the corner and presently disappeared into his office. A light presently gushed from the window. Majors rolled to the stable at an indolent pace. Henry was there, but Majors saddled the gelding himself. By the pale light of the lantern hanging down from the arch he could see curiosity place an almost intolerable strain on Henry's cheeks. He trotted by the hostler without comment, turning toward the bridge. When he crossed it the pacing of his horse lifted long, rolling echoes. Five minutes later, from the heights above Reservation, he saw the town dimly huddled in the black flats. Then he hit the stage road at a straightforward gallop, steadily climbing.

Majors had scarcely crossed the bridge when a man cut out of the saloon and took to his horse standing at the rack. He spoke to Soder. "He got up the hill?"

"Yeah," said Soder, whereupon the man headed out of town on that road which led to the Barrs'—and to the Pocket.

It was, as Majors remembered, about ten miles from Reservation to the entrance of the Ute's upper canyon. Riding at a comfortable pace, he knew he made a mark for whoever might be waiting in the trees beside this road, but it was one of the chances of the game he had to take—and the blackness was a stout shelter, thick and solid. Wind minutely rustled the pine tops and he could hear, so still was the night, the far-off reverberation of the Ute's water slamming over its rocky channel.

It was entirely clear to him what Ben Maffitt had meant by the holdup. By stealing a single mailbag which could hold nothing of value, Maffitt was publicly declaring his challenge; and Majors knew that in accepting the challenge he was playing the game according to the rules Maffitt had laid down.

Yet even as he recognized the risk, Majors was actually relieved to have this break come, to have this open excuse for moving into action. For he knew the kind of men that lived in these hills. They were the same kind of men from whom he had learned, in other years and other places, the hard lessons of survival. However much the people of the country might hate him and work against him, they had a respect for the quick draw, the instant answer. Boxed up and inactive in Reservation, the prestige of his star would have dropped to nothing.

Certain things he definitely knew. There was no peace or possibility of peace between the factions; no trust, no moderation, no least hint of reasonableness. The quarrel went too deep and it went back too far, and pride and trickery had tangled them all in a pattern that couldn't be untangled. There were, apparently, no neutral parties. And he stood alone.

He had no illusions as to old Jeff White's reasons for sending him here. Jeff had said: "I've seen you work—and you can be tough. Certain things a man with a star can rightfully do, and certain things he can't rightfully do. But I'll never ask you if you stuck to the right side. You clean out that country." Having failed in every reasonable method, old Jeff had given him a free hand.

The smell of the night was keen in his nostrils and the sounds of the night came sharply to his ears, and thus as he rode alone he understood that there was but one answer—if there was any answer—to the problem: to work on the greed and the pride and the angers of the people involved; to put a pressure here and watch for a break; to lay a bait there and wait for a man who would take it; to drop the acid of doubt and suspicion on a man and divorce him from his old loyalties, and so to break up the factions and leave every group uncertain and ridden by doubt and at last weakened by fear. It was, Majors had long ago learned, the one thing everybody understood. Fear.

This was his line of thought as he pushed on up the road. He sat idle on the leather, his senses keen to what the night would tell him, but his mind free. There were no rewards to this business—and always there was the thought of a sudden end. It left him with a sense of isolation and a growing loneliness. The decisions of his life had been hard decisions and the instruments he had to use often had been brutal, even though the final effect had been justice. He had his scars. He could look back on the trail and remember a few friends. But the consciousness of his job was a heavy weight and the fine balance of right and wrong was always in his mind, more real than any outward reward or punishment. Yet with all this,

one thing kept him going. A sense of fidelity to the star he
wore, a feeling of pride, very deep and without voice, in the
ultimate ends of his job.

There was, farther along the night, and considerably
higher, a sudden increase in the cold wind flowing downslope
and by this signal he knew that he had arrived near the
mouth of the Ute's canyon. Dust smell, very faint, came with
the ruffling wind, a signal that somebody had been by this
way. The Pocket country lay over to his left. Turning out of
the road, he left the vague starlight behind him and entered
the blindfolding darkness of the pines. There was no knowing
where a trail lay, but of this he was indifferent, having other
considerations in mind. Presently, less than a half-mile from
the road, he dropped out of the saddle, groped around for a
few dead pine branches and built up a small fire.

That little amber-orange cone of light was as startling in
the velvet density of the night as the crash of a rifle shot. He
stood back beyond the reach of its glow for a little while,
watching the flame draw upward to its spiraled point. The
ground was a tinder-dry carpet of pine needles along which
the fire spread slowly and he risked something to duck into
the light and gouge a channel around the fire to prevent its
farther creep. Afterwards he waited a good ten minutes until
the light faded back to a ruby char against the earth. Skunk
smell drifted with the small breeze; his horse was gently fiddling. In the saddle again he rode steadily south, feeling the
country rise and break beneath him. By this blind traveling
he crossed three small canyons and came to what appeared to
be the edge of a deeper cut. At this point, well into the broken country, he picketed the horse, wrapped the saddle blanket around him and dropped into a shallow, cat-napping
slumber.

He was up at the first signal of dawn. The stars were cold
and brilliant in the sky; faint pulses of light began to dilute
the coal blackness of the earth. Before him and directly below him lay the deep slash of another canyon, wherein fog
sluggishly rolled. He found a clear way of descent, the fog
pressing damp and heavy against him. There was a creek at
the bottom of this defile and another canyon leading away
like the downstroke of the letter T. This he followed until
better light showed him that he was on a definitely traveled
path. Immediately he put the gelding to work, angling up
from the canyon and reaching timber again. At six o'clock

the world was all clear, sunlight crackling through the east.
At seven, the trailless and rough stretch of timber gave way
before a small meadow.

Trees ran along its three sides; on the fourth it seemed to
drop away to lower ground. There was no sign of a house
and no apparent break in the timber on the other sides,
though he saw that the meadow had been cropped down by
livestock. Here and there were the remnants of a rail fence;
and in the windless air was the clinging smell of woodsmoke.

He skirted the meadow until he reached the trees to one
side of it; and so worked his way forward carefully. He
crossed a trail and viewed the roofless relic of a log cabin. A
hundred yards onward the trees gave out again, and so did
the high land, breaking downward into a bowl-like depression
through which a heavy creek ran rapidly, passing out at a
narrow gate between a solid rock wall. At the edge of the
creek, and well backed-up against the side of the bowl, stood
a frame house and a corral. Smoke spiraled from the house's
chimney. A man strolled along the yard, headed for the corral.

And at that moment a bullet's slug struck at his pony's feet
with a brief *thwut,* and the echo of a hidden gun, delayed by
distance, began to roll its metal echo all across the bowl. The
man in the yonder yard made a complete circle, his face rising and whirling in swift inspection. Two other men rushed
from the house—and the man originally in the yard pointed
upward to Majors. That was all Majors took time to see.
When the second echo of the rifle rushed across the stillness
of these high hills, he had backed into the adjacent timber.

He dropped from the horse, hauled his rifle from its boot
and went out toward the rim of the bowl again on his belly, a
small stringer of earth protecting him from the marksman,
who seemed to be somewhere on his left.

This, he realized, was Ben Maffitt's place—the Pocket.

7

The Mail-sack

IT WAS LESS than two hundred yards downward and forward
to the house. The echo of the second shot from the lookout
posted on the yonder rocky heights had not quite died, and
the three men in the yard were motionless when he lined his
sights on the ground in front of them and let go.

The bullet, kicking up its dust, broke the three out of their
tracks. The two nearest the house wheeled and ran for the
door. The third man rushed toward the corral, whereupon
Majors put a bullet in front of him, near the corral's gate.
That little snakehead of dust was a powerful persuader. The
man pushed his hands against the air and stopped and turned,
and for a moment remained rigidly still. The lookout kept
slamming his bullets into the roll of ground beside Majors.
Lying under its shelter, Majors felt the small clots of kicked-
up earth spray the back of his neck. Suddenly, head bowed,
the man below raced for the house and got inside.

From his position Majors viewed three sides of the house.
On the back side timber came down from the hills to within
fifty feet of the place—and part of this open distance he also
commanded. The lookout's position was, as near as he could
judge, on top of the rocks at the gate of the Pocket, and that
was a good four hundred yards to his left.

When the lookout's first burst of firing stopped, Majors
ventured one quick look over the roll of earth; he saw
nothing.

But the windows of the house—three downstairs and one
above—gave the men inside a good chance at him; and so,
digging his elbows into the earth, he settled methodically to

59

the job of driving them back. He started at the left-hand window and worked over to the right, putting a shot through each. He slid fresh shells into the gun, hit the upper window, and went to work on the lower windows again. Those were ten- or twelve-inch panes, the distance was under two hundred yards on a bright, windless morning, and he had a pocket full of cartridges. Sunlight set up a flash on each pane and when that flash disappeared he knew he had shattered the glass. This was a slanting fire that reached through and covered only part of the front rooms, but he knew from a lack of answering fire that he had driven them away from the windows. The lookout took up the fight again, all these shots cracking the stillness of the hills, rolling long echoes back and forth across the bowl. He finished the windows, laid two bullets through the door, and lifted his sights over the roof of the house, waiting for somebody to show up in the back yard.

He had them boxed, but it wasn't smart to suppose that all of Maffitt's men were down there. Some of them were undoubtedly riding the timber and all this racket was honey to draw bees, which made him think of his own exposed position. Meanwhile, to keep the game going, he sent a bullet at the house's tin chimney and considered the solid timber closing down on the right edge of the meadow. He had pretty well announced his own location to the world, and the back of his shoulders began to itch and grow chilly, which was a sign that he had stuck here too long. Laying a pair of shots through the shattered windows to subdue the curiosity of those men, he backed into the trees, got aboard the gelding, and galloped straight west.

The ground fell quickly into a definite trail. He swung into the trail and followed it until he saw the floor of the Pocket directly ahead; he turned aside then and ran off into the trees. Thus circling the Pocket, with the sense of wasting minutes pushing him hard, he came to the creek at a rather bad place and spent two or three minutes finding a crossing. Afterwards, the stiff pitch of the surrounding hills slowed him and it was a good ten minutes before he could have the gelding and run downslope, where he came once more to the end of the timber—this time on the back side of the house.

Less than a hundred feet in front of him stood an open door. Through one window of a rear room he could see men grouped together. He counted five of them.

The lookout's gun now and then threw its flattened voice

across the Pocket. Crowded behind a pine's trunk, Majors brought up his Spencer, laying its sights on the doorway.

The situation grew riskier. Somewhere riders, hearing all the commotion, would be moving in. On the strength of that belief he had changed his position. Yet he stood now in more open timber, with his back uncomfortably exposed to anyone who might come down the hill and discover him.

Maffitt's men made a loose group in the kitchen; one of them came to a window, lighting a cigarette, not showing much concern. The rest of them weren't moving around much. The lookout's gun, after a prolonged silence, crashed the morning's stillness again. Majors thought about that aimless shooting, with a quick, prying interest, and he thought he knew its reason. The lookout was waiting for somebody in the timber behind him. When he turned his attention to the house again he found one of Maffitt's men in the doorway.

It was the redheaded Brick Brand. Brand stepped out of the house and came on a dozen paces or so. The scars of the saloon fight showed like black patches on his face; his lips were considerably swollen. He held a cigarette in his fingers, now and then taking a quick drag and removing it. He squatted down, sighting over the corral toward the rock cliff at the lower end of the Pocket where the lookout was. Afterwards straightening, he moved toward the edge of the house, in the direction of the corral. In another moment he had stopped. He tossed down the cigarette and balanced himself on his heels and apparently debated making a run for the corral.

A second man came to the doorway and called: "Never mind that, Brick."

The redhead turned back. He said: "To hell with it. He ain't broad enough around the belt to bluff me."

" 'Sall right. Stand pat. He'll bump into some fun before long."

The redhead shrugged his shoulders and took a step toward the door. Majors lifted his gun beside the tree and centered Brick Brand's chest with the sight notch.

"Freeze right there. Both of you boys."

The redhead had one foot advanced. He stopped in that awkward position. His head whipped around and the swiftness of the gesture threw him off balance; he teetered and took another step; then he held himself rigid, staring at the muzzle of Majors' gun. The man in the doorway, having advanced beyond the sill, could not quickly hook back into the room, and so Majors' command rooted him. There had been some talk and motion in the kitchen. It stopped at once.

Majors called: "You in the doorway. Tell one of the boys to toss out that mail-sack."

Brick Brand's eyes were round, winkless. He grumbled, "What the hell——?"

The other man, not venturing a motion, barked out his thoroughly outraged opinion. "You're a complete dam' fool, Majors. This ain't the end of the party. Not none. We . . ."

"The mail-sack, son."

Both of them held their positions, but the feel of this situation got tighter and tighter. They were playing for a break. Brand turned his head, an inch at a time, looked at the man in the doorway, and slowly brought his glance back to Majors. Something definitely passed between them.

The man in the doorway said: "You got your chance to slide out. Better. There ain't always trees to hide behind. Ever think . . . ?"

Majors laid a shot near that one's feet; dust jumped upward and the man flinched and jerked his head aside. All those inside the room faded against the floor. Majors could see this through the window. He heard them hit the boards.

The fellow at the doorway called over his shoulder: "Throw out that dam' sack, Ed."

Somebody walked deeper into the house. Brick Brand's shoulders settled and by that sign Majors knew he had quit hoping for a break. The mail-sack sailed through the doorway and struck the man who stood there.

Majors called: "Unbuckle your belt, Brick, and drop it. Go pick up the sack. Bring it here."

Brand's fingers slid to the front of his belt, moving carefully. Up on the heights behind Majors a crow's brusque alarm rang out.

Brand dropped his belt and crossed to the mail-sack. He retrieved it, walking foward.

Suddenly he stopped. "To hell with it. You ain't tough enough to shoot your turkey cold."

The crow's voice was a message that bothered Majors. Something was going on behind him, and the moments began to drag wickedly across his nerves. He ground down an impulse to look behind him. He said: "Maybe not. But I can put a couple of bullets through your knees and leave you crawlin' on your hands the rest of your life. God dam' you, come up here on the run!"

Brand jumped forward like a scolded dog. When he came to the trees his breath was reaching deeply into his lungs. He walked on until he was only the space of an arm from Majors' gun. He stared at Majors' face and grunted, "Take it easy—take it easy."

Majors backed away. "Keep in front of me, Brick," he snapped, and took time to whip one glance behind him. He saw nothing, yet trouble was like a rank smell on his senses. Pacing backward, with Brand marching obediently on, he came to his horse and stepped into the saddle.

He said, "Throw it, Red," and caught the sack with one hand. He still saw, through the little alley between trees, the motionless shape of the other fellow at the doorway, with the rest of the crowd bunched behind, waiting for the break.

Brand pulled both hands slowly above his hips. He said, "You dam' Sioux, there ain't anybody in the world that tough. You'll see."

"What?"

"No," grumbled the redhead. "I ain't askin' trouble. Why come here and stir up all this? Everything was fine. You wait. Ain't no one man alive that can make this play stick."'

"On the run, Brick," ordered Majors. The redhead turned, rushing downgrade in long leaps.

Immediately Majors put his horse around and shot into the trail leading up and away from the Pocket. At the first bend he wheeled in the saddle to see men pour out of the house toward the corral.

He pushed the gelding to its limit, not just then bothering to get off the trail. It ran in quick climbing circles back to the green heights above the Pocket and leveled away for a distance, and finally ran downgrade. That way, eastward, lay the Barr ranch and Reservation; and when the next straight stretch of the trail showed him he was dropping between the walls of a canyon, he abandoned the trail and swung south through a still more rugged country. Later in the day, having circled south of the Barrs, he found himself somewhere in that area where the deserted house stood. Cutting this side of it, for a more direct shoot to Reservation, he found a road—and a man in it.

The man heard him trotting up and turned, showing Majors a bland, slow-dispositioned face and a pair of long, humorous lips. He was in his early twenties, gawky of shape and motion. Lashed behind his saddle was a quarter of venison.

Majors said, "Howdy," and dropped to a walk.

The bland young fellow's eyes took in the mailbag and considered Majors with a more direct interest. He said thoughtfully: "So you did."

"What?"

The other one's eyebrows, bleached white, shifted; a grin moved across his lips. "Aw," he said, "I was just talkin' to myself. Guess I ought to be a sheepherder. Gettin' a little colder, ain't it?"

Majors said, "So long," and galloped ahead.

At noon he dropped into Reservation, put up the horse, and walked to the hotel with the mail-sack over his shoulder.

He found Broderick slouched down in the customary lobby rocker. He laid the sack on the counter.

"Leave it there until the stage comes in."

"That why you want it left there?"

Majors said: "No, I want the town to see it." He cut into the dining room and had a meal; afterward, in his room, he stretched out for a short sleep.

Three quarters of an hour later Matt Oldroyd—who was the indolent young fellow Majors had passed on the trail—came into Reservation and stopped behind the hotel. He unlashed the quarter of venison and lugged it into the kitchen and grinned at Tony, who sat alone, eating a delayed dinner. She looked up at him, her expression suddenly smooth and reserved and faintly startled. Oldroyd's grin died and he made an awkward shape above her. Nothing was said for a while, yet there was something between them, stronger than the silence; the girl's cheeks showed color and the surprise faded behind a stolid expression. Matt Oldroyd stared down at his boots.

He said in a tone that held a heavy regret: "There's always things a man may be sorry for, Tony."

She sat with her legs tucked beneath the chair, composed and indifferent. There was that old sense of fatalism in her voice, as though nothing much mattered. "Oh, well, Matt . . ."

"Ain't seen you since last summer. How you been?"

She looked squarely at him. "How would you think?"

He said, humbly: "Don't, Tony. Don't."

"How's your mother?"

"Fine."

She looked away from him. "Tell her I send my love."

Matt Oldroyd put his hands in his pockets and walked around the kitchen, his sandy head bowed over. He was a soft-speaking man, slow of motion and taking life pretty much as it came.

But when he got to the far corner of the kitchen he squared himself around and looked at her again. "Tony, maybe I'm a little late in sayin' this. I—"

She said quickly and with a flash of pride, "You don't owe me anything. I'm old enough to know what I should do and what I shouldn't do. If I do the wrong thing, I won't blame anybody else for it."

He shrugged his shoulders and let it go like that, coming back to the quarter of venison on the table. He reached for a butcher knife and a meat saw, and cut off two slices.

"You always liked this. One's for you. One's for that new fellow—Majors. He get back to town with his mailbag?"

"It's out in the lobby."

Matt Oldroyd's interest sharpened his features. "Yeah? He wants everybody to see he brought it back?" He stood there, thinking about that, shaking his head a little. "No doubt he's tough. It's to be seen in the man. But he's got no friends here."

Tony stood up. "No. They'll use him, and they'll trick him—and they'll kill him!"

Matt Oldroyd watched her expressive features take on a rare energy. He had seldom seen her like this. It narrowed his glance; it made him say dryly, "Like him, uh?"

"If I were a man, Matt, I'd be on his side. I hate this country and almost everybody in it. The men around here are just animals. Not one soul trusts anybody. There isn't any pity, there isn't any peace. Nothing but treachery! He knows that by now. He knows he's alone. I can see that in his eyes and in the way he talks. But he'll stay. And he'll be killed."

She came before him, the flame of her anger making her prettier, giving her eyes a luminous shining. She was a woman, suddenly, that Matt Oldroyd didn't know, with depths he had never suspected. And yet her anger was soon gone, giving way to that sense of futility beaten into her by the ways of life. She looked down, and spoke indifferently, "Oh, well, I guess I've always asked too much."

Oldroyd gathered up the quarter of venison, far more stirred than his easygoing face showed. "Maybe," he said. "Maybe." She brought up her eyes and for a moment they faced each other with a common memory pulling them silently together by its recollections. It made her say, very gently: "I never held anything against you, Matt. And you owe me nothing."

Matt went out, lashed the venison behind the saddle, and rode around to the square. He had Tony in his mind, but he was also thinking of Jim Majors, whom he had liked at first glance. There were secrets in this basin dangerous to disturb, and hidden arrangements so uneasily balanced that a man blundering into them would set off the fuse to the whole powder-magazine underlying the country. Majors might be tough, but toughness wasn't enough.

Matt had pulled in the pony to consider the emptiness of Reservation's two streets. He was smart enough to understand that the mailbag was Majors' declaration of intention and he also knew Ben Maffitt wouldn't let the challenge lie. It was a matter of survival. Probably Majors knew that—and maybe Majors deliberately wanted to bring on a showdown. Matt couldn't see any hope for the deputy marshal's survival in such a showdown, but there was in him a strong admiration for the big, heavy-boned stranger—an admiration that pulled strangely at his sympathies and upset the easy run of his thoughts. It was as though some compulsion got into him. He went out of Reservation by the east fork road at a quick clip.

8

The Way of a Woman's Mind

WHEN MAJORS opened his fight against the house in the
Pocket, Ben Maffitt was breaking a cold camp some ten miles
to the south of the Barr range. At nine in the morning he
reached the Barrs' and with the familiarity of a visitor well
known, went in to have breakfast. Old Pedee came into the
dining room and sat with him; the boys were working over a
bunch of fresh horses in the corral and Katherine was upstairs. Maffitt, not showing his interest, nevertheless listened
to her light steps tapping along the second-story hall.

"Any news?" old Pedee asked.

Maffitt shook his head. Mrs. Purdy, who was cook and
housekeeper for the Barrs, brought him another cup of coffee.
Maffitt's lips shaped up a grin, showing the heaviness of his
teeth. He pulled a cigarette from his mouth and, in laying it
on a near-by plate, let its ashes fall on the tablecloth. He
hauled his vast shoulders around and stared at her, the grin
broadening. Mrs. Purdy showed him the sharp hostility of her
eyes. Dropping the ashes had been deliberate on his part; he
liked to bait this woman who hated him so much.

He had an ironic sense of humor, this Ben Maffitt, and sly,
sharp perceptions. There were no illusions in him. The Barrs
needed him for the power he could swing against the opposing factions in the valley. Those factions grew stronger as the
years went along and the old-time Barr supremacy became
less certain, needing whatever support it could get. This was
why Pedee Barr had made his peace with the outlaws in the
Pocket.

Maffitt knew the Barrs disliked the familiarity he used

67

toward them. They trafficked with the devil and still wanted the devil to keep his place. It was a situation that amused his taciturn fancy and caused him to·frequent the ranch, to eat and to sit on the front porch and to assume a deliberate manner of equality. It struck at their pride and it made them uneasy. Looking at Pedee, he could catch that feeling behind the arrogant cheeks of the old Southerner.

Pedee said: "You're on risky ground when you have your boys lift mail-sacks from stages.

"I did not particularly like it."

"You want that Majors to stick around here?"

"Let him alone. He can do nothing. His hands are tied."

"I disagree. He's not a man to fool with. I sized him up in Reservation. I know men and I know him. Take a look at his eyes sometime." Maffitt pulled himself around in the chair, not smiling now. "A lone wolf with the smell of smoke on him. That first deputy Jeff White sent over here figured the star he wore would be plenty of protection. This Majors knows better. The star means nothin' to him. He sleeps light and his mind runs faster than yours or mine—and if he was an outlaw he'd be fifty miles in front of a posse all the time, laughin' at them. We're up again a fellow that likes to hunt and knows how."

Pedee Barr said: "I do not understand why you took the mail-sack."

Ben Maffitt's square, sun-blackened face showed slyness again. "He's got a weakness—and I'm playin' on it. He'll come after that mailbag."

Pedee Barr shook his head. "I do not like it."

"Be smart, Pedee. If we don't stop him what happens to us? Buff Sultan and Dobe Hyde were watchin' this thing close."

Pedee Barr rose up at that. There was something iron-hard in this man, a pride that would not bend and a fixity of opinion that could never be disturbed. "I ask nothing of this country except to be let alone."

Ben Maffitt grinned. His tone had no sympathy. "Sure. After you get what you want, you're willing to quit fighting. But how did you get your land in the first place, Pedee?"

Pedee's black eyes flared. "This land was free."

"So it was," countered Ben Maffitt. "But other men were on it first, includin' Tony Black's father."

Pedee Barr called out: "Never mind—never mind!"

Maffitt got up. "Wait a minute, Pedee," he said. "Don't use that horsewhip manner on me. I'm old enough not to fool myself, and so are you. Dog eat dog. You ate your dog, askin' no favors and givin' no sympathy. Now there's other dogs waitin' to eat you."

Pedee Barr said: "I do not ask your advice."

Maffitt's face showed the wisdom of a wild, brutal life. "If I pull out my support you're finished."

The bridge at the crossing of the Ute began to boom up sound, and Katherine Barr's steps made rapid echoes down the stairway. There was a group of riders in the yard, with a man calling: "Ben's here, ain't he? This is his horse."

Maffitt went out of the kitchen and along the hall, ahead of Pedee and ahead of Katherine Barr who had come down the stairway. Four of his crowd sat in their saddles beyond the porch, waiting for him. Brick Brand spoke instantly:

"Where the hell you been, Maffitt? Seen Majors come this way?"

Old Pedee and Katherine were beside Maffitt; and Barr's three sons came around the side of the house with the two older Barr relatives. Maffitt was saying: "He got to the Pocket—and you didn't stop him?"

"No," said Brand. "No, we didn't stop him."

Ben Maffitt stood with his big-thewed legs apart, bracing his two hundred pounds on the porch. Blood flushed the sides of his neck, below his flat ears. "You saw him?"

"Plain enough," answered Brand, dryness rustling his talk. "Plain enough and close enough. He put twenty shots through the windows of the house—and took the mail-sack."

Maffitt's eyes were bright and round-sprung. The silence continued. Then that long, considering slyness began to creep into the angled edges of his features.

"So we're the suckers," he said, and looked at Pedee Barr. "I told you he had the smell of smoke on him. It won't do to wait. And we won't wait." He turned his attention on the riders again. "Go on back to the Pocket. Tonight's the time we'll ride into Reservation."

For a moment nobody moved. They were all watching his heavy lips stretch away from his teeth, as though he were squinting against a hard sun. But there was no sun against his eyes; and he wasn't smiling.

He said, "Better ride," and watched his crowd break way. The Barr family didn't stir, and when Ben turned to Pedee and saw Katherine near by he removed his hat and his expression softened. He said to Pedee Barr: "He'll hang that mailbag up in Reservation like a scalp. Well, it's my scalp. I saw this comin'. One of us is top dog. Him or me. If I let it go another day I'm licked and so are you, Pedee. You understand?"

"No," said Pedee Barr. "No, I don't."

Maffitt's grin was long and gray. "When a man takes up the gun, Pedee, he can't ever put it down. You took it up and there's the smell of powder on you and that smell drifts with the wind for all the wolves to catch. Long as you live they'll be prowlin' up this valley, waitin' for a kill."

Old Pedee Barr said: "I want nothing started, Ben. Let him alone."

Maffitt answered, "Man that lights fires has got to burn his fingers," and looked at Katherine Barr, as though he wanted her to speak, as though he waited for a smile. But she had said nothing and there was nothing in her eyes that helped him. So, without saying more, he went to his horse and trotted across the Ute bridge, soon vanishing.

Katherine Barr watched him go; and turned to see how dark was her father's face. His pride would never let him unbend and never let him admit error; nor was there in him any capacity to express gentleness or sympathy or laughter. A good deal of the Barr steel was in her own makeup, and much of the capacity for sudden fury. That part of her character she had long ago recognized and had often regretted, much as a woman might look in her mirror and feel a deep sadness for some irregularity of features. Yet, strong as was that turbulent run of family blood, she could look at her father now with a detachment and a sense of difference.

There was a strain of imagination in her and a wild depth of feeling that she had let none of them see. Not that any of them had been much interested in knowing what her mind or heart was like. She could not recall anything other than a uniform sternness from her father—neither gentle nor ungentle. It was a quality of self-absorption in him and in all her brothers, excepting only Dan. In Dan, the youngest and the most lighthearted, she could catch the slash of that same imaginativeness. It put her apart from them—and it made her lonely. Her mother had died long before, and so now she was isolated in a house full of men who had little interest in anything except their own private thoughts.

She said: "Will he go to town tonight?"

Her father made a pushing gesture with his hand, setting the question aside. He said to the boys in the yard: "Get the rest of the crew here. I want to say something."

She said, "Dad, don't let—"

He gave her the briefest of glances. "Never mind, Katherine."

She went inside and up the stairs, hearing the men talking below. From the window of her room the valley lay sunlit and tawny and the quick water of the Ute made a bright glitter. The long slopes of the Silver Lode were deep, dull green and a white cloud sailed alone in the far sky and the air coming through the window held the scent of autumn and of smoke.

Her father's manner was always severe, but its added severity now was clearly an indication of a strain he felt. She could guess that Ben Maffitt had laid that strain on him. Standing by the window, buoyed up by the freshness of the day, she remembered how Maffitt had removed his hat and turned to watch her. His eyes were not pleasant eyes, even when he tried to be humble. There was always the stain of basic brutality in them and the gray shine of an animal wisdom gained through his career. The truth was, she was afraid of Ben Maffitt, her instincts clearly telling her that this man wanted her and would, if he set his mind to it, deliberately involve the Barrs in greater trouble to gain his end. Nobody knew what thoughts lay in his head or what schemes he nourished.

She had never liked the idea of her family seeking support from him and had said so, though her protest meant nothing to her father, who was no man to take advice from a woman. Now she thought she detected in him a faint uneasiness, and that, in turn, destroyed her own sense of security. The situation was out of his hands.

And so she found herself considering Jim Majors, not only as a possible source of help, but in the way a woman would think of a man when her curiosity and her interest had been aroused. He made a vivid image before her—so solid and so alert, the irregularity of his features so thoroughly masculine. The small smile, she thought, was a kind of signal of his character. It showed the world a serene indifference, yet in it too was a sadness that seemed to imply that he had lost contact with the world and could depend on nobody but himself.

At his age—which she thought was well under thirty—he had learned too much of the cruelties of men. He had fought too much, he had too often played his chances out to the thin end. That gambler's fatalism was in him definitely. Maffitt, she guessed, was an open book to Majors; and he could match Maffitt's animal wisdom and Maffitt's pure violence. This was why Maffitt meant to go in to Reservation tonight. Maffitt was worried.

At noon she went down to the dining room with all this in her mind. In addition to her father and three brothers there were two other men at the table, Creed Barr and Will Barr. Once, more Barrs had lived here. Some of them had died, some of them had returned South. The family resemblance ran true in all of them in its darkness and narrow-jawed face construction, in its distant flame of partisanship. To the world Katherine was a thorough-going Barr. Yet in her own mind was a doubt and a growing uneasiness; and a kind of irritation at the moody silence at this table. Only Dan showed any break from that traditional mold. He looked at her now, a secret smile in his glance. Fairer and franker than the rest of her family, he was the one brother with whom she felt any definite tie.

After dinner she waited until the men had scattered out, Creed and Will riding southward toward the end of the Barr range, the others working up the horses in the corral. Around two o'clock Dan Barr went over to the tool shed to repair a mower. She crossed to the shed, feeling her father's glance reaching toward her from the corral. Dan saw all this and smiled, lowering his head over the mower.

She said: "What was Dad telling you?"

"To keep out of Reservation."

"That all?"

"I guess he's worried. We're puttin' a guard on the south end, by the last line cabin. And he wants us to keep away from the Pocket crowd."

She said, "It's too late for that. Maffitt walks in and out of the house as though he owned it."

"Man that plays with a skunk will smell like one." Dan looked at the sun and quit working on the mower. "Guess I'll take a ride."

"Saddle up for me, too."

Dan strolled to the stable. Katherine remained in the shed, watching her father turn and keep Dan under observation.

That unusual alertness suddenly troubled her, quickening the run of her blood, but when Dan brought out the two horses she walked out and swung into the saddle. They had both turned to circle the house when Pedee Barr said, "Just a minute," and came before them.

"Where you going?"

"A ride," said Dan, smoothly. He was smiling down at Pedee, seemingly amused.

"Stay away from Reservation," Pedee. "Stay strictly on your own range."

Neither answered and at once Pedee's face showed its narrowing length, its quick, intolerant temper. "I will not stand the sulks from either of you two. Speak out or unsaddle your horses. There's plenty here to keep you busy."

Dan said, gently: "Maybe you forgot something. Katie is twenty-one years old. I'm twenty-two. That's answer enough."

She had seen her father like this before, inner violence freezing him to a thin, stiff shape. He said, "Get down!" Katherine saw the ease and the laughter leave her brother's eyes. He who always took life so smoothly had changed in the space of one quick minute. "No," he said. "I guess not."

Pedee Barr called to Ring and Fay who, propped up on the top corral bars, were watching. "Come over here."

The two older brothers obeyed, their spurs dragging the dust. They came slowly and showed astonishment, and stopped near by.

Pedee Barr's lips barely opened when he spoke to them. "Take Katherine and Dan off those horses."

Fay said, puzzled: "They ain't paralyzed, are they?"

"Do as I say!" ground out Pedee Barr. "It does not matter to me how old you may be. I intend to make you mind."

Dan laughed outright at the somber, uncertain expression of his brothers. But his answer was short and quite flat in tone.

"I guess this better be settled now. Either of you fellows lay hand on me or Katie and I'll kick the ever-livin' lights out of you."

"Wait a minute, kid," warned Ring. "You're a small touch proud." He started forward, ruffled by Dan's challenge.

Katherine broke in. "Ring—be careful!"

Ring stopped, thoroughly puzzled. "Well, what in hell is everybody so sore about?"

Fay meanwhile had been watching Katherine's face. He

came to a quick decision and turned, touching Ring's arm. "Leave 'em alone."

Pedee reached up and caught the cheek straps of both bridles. Something on his face at the moment rather terrified Katherine—an expression that denied them recognition. They were strangers who had crossed his will and the affront seemed to make him forget they were his children. He said in suppressed fury: "Get off. Get off and go to the house."

Dan lifted his reins. He looked down at his father, paler than he had been.

"Sir," he said, "if you don't step aside I'll run you down."

Nobody moved and nobody spoke. Ring and Fay were shocked still, and Katherine was locked with her brother in a monstrous duel with her father's will. All this had struck out of a clear day, rising from nothing in the space of a few minutes. It was a blackness of temper that, lying latent in all of them, rushed up now and unsteadied their reason. Katherine's heart struck her chest in hard, quick beats and each drawn breath grew more and more painful. She wanted to step down from the saddle and surrender, but something in her prevented it—something that was pride, or that was a memory of affection her father had never offered. And in this interval she realized with a fatal clarity that this was the Barr family, unlovely and intolerant, as the rest of the valley saw it.

At once her father dropped his hands and turned, going at a rush toward the corrals. He yelled: "Where's a whip? Fay—where's your rawhide?"

Fay jumped at Pedee Barr and held him. He looked over at Katherine and Dan and called: "Get out of here—go on!"

Dan said: "Let him go. I want to see what kind of a man I've got for a father."

But Katherine murmured "Come on," and spurred from the yard, Dan reluctantly coming behind. They dropped into the valley and followed the road, saying nothing at all for a half-mile.

Dan let his reins fall to curl up a cigarette. Katherine noticed his hands were quite unsteady, and this was what made her speak.

9

The Meeting in the Pines

"WHY? Why did we do that?"

He said: "I guess I got to thinkin' of Mother. I got to thinkin' that she had thirty years of that."

Katherine said: "We are hated by everybody in this country, aren't we?"

He shot back, "Why not?"

"No. We're not that wrong, Dan."

He said, quietly emphasizing his words: "No more wrong than Dobe Hyde or Buff Sultan—or the rest of the valley. We got our land the way they did. When the fight comes I'll stick with Dad, and so will you. But that doesn't change the mistake the Barrs made when they came here."

Below the second bend he cut out of the valley, up to the bench. Katherine followed, but she was quick to notice the odd side-glance he gave her.

He said casually: "Where you going?"

"Oh, just for a ride."

He said nothing more until they were well into the timbered ridge that ran its course toward Dobe Hyde's valley; then he stopped, flushing. "I'll go the rest of this way alone, Katie."

She knew her brother pretty well. "A girl?"

"A girl."

"I've never seen you with her."

He shrugged his shoulders. "From the looks of things I guess you never will." That was all he seemed willing to say.

Wheeling about, he ran down the wooded trail and around a far curve. She held in her horse awhile, watching that trail and tremendously disturbed by the note of pessimism in the voice of her favorite brother. He had always been so cheerful and so gay that his present temper definitely discouraged her. Things, she realized, were worse than she had ever permitted herself to believe.

She rode directly through the timber to an overgrown military road which, long before the establishment of the Silver Lode stage route, had been Reservation's only connection with the world. Buffalo had first traced it. The fur brigade had come this way, and Indian war parties had stamped the trail more plainly on the earth. It was the route used by men going up to the Montana mines and after that the freighters and the army men had followed it. It had been but ten years since Custer had passed this way, his yellow hair shining in the sun and his face full of laughter at a future mercifully hidden from him. In this dust was the story of the West; in the silent depths of these pines lay memory of rifle fire and warriors singing and the dry squeal of wagon axles. It was very vivid to her, because so recent. In this lonely land the pattern remained untouched. Jim Bridger had once stopped at the Barr house. Wild Bill had paused there on his way to Deadwood; she could still remember the ease of his voice and the almost feminine fairness of his face. This had been only four years ago.

She thought of these things as she rode, bearing toward a high point of the ridge from which she knew she could sight Reservation and the country surrounding it. Long riding had made her thoroughly familiar with the region. The truth was Katherine Barr had a profound responsiveness to the breadth and wildness and loneliness of the land. Over on the rim of the world lay the East and its towns and once, as a child, she had seen Chicago. It had left no impression and no desire to return.

Ahead of her the road reached its summit, falling off into the valley where Reservation lay. She reached this summit, seeing the town's housetops below her; she turned from the road to put herself beyond sight of anyone who might be traveling by. Threading the trees this way, she came into a small clearing and found Jim Majors there.

He stood beside his horse, turned toward her; and she could tell by the lift of his shoulders that he had been closely listening to the approach of her horse. His expression lightened and lost that rather tough and lonely look that she had noticed in it before. He removed his hat, showing a smile. It was apparent that he had come here to watch the town; there was a space between the trees through which he could observe Reservation's main street and the roads which came out of the two valleys.

She remembered their last meeting. But she said, "I really wanted to see you," and got down. It struck her then that his smile held a definite sadness, though of this he probably wasn't aware.

His actions and his surface mannerisms were blunt and deliberately hard, as though he neither cared for people nor trusted them. But in his smile she read a different story. This physically rugged, jet-haired man had depths of feeling hard to penetrate.

She said: "I suppose you've found out most of the story by now."

"Most of it."

She wasn't quite prepared for so direct an answer. It disturbed her. Unaccountably it put her on the defensive.

"You didn't learn it from the Barrs. So it had to come from people who hate us."

"I suppose."

"Is it fair to judge us from that?"

He said: "When a man draws water out of a muddy well he has to let it stand in the bucket. I learned that a long time ago. I'm not judging the Barrs."

"Sooner or later you'll have to do it."

"Maybe," he said. He looked toward the town. A pair of riders came down the valley of the Ute Fork's east branch, roiling up dust behind them. It was in the middle of the afternoon, with the sun already dropping below the Silver Lode peaks. She could see how carefully he weighed those two riders; how their approach toward town did something to his thinking.

He said, casually: "Your people coming in tonight?"

"That's why I wanted to see you. Maffitt is coming in."

"I expected so."

"Why?"

He spoke with a trace of humor. "I raised his bet and he's got to call. This game never changes much. Same thing over and over. Your folks coming, too?"

She said, frankly, "I don't know."

He watched her, his under lip pursed over the upper. His eyes were gray as powder. They searched her for things she hadn't put into the answer; they weighed her expression. It was an endless watchfulness she had noticed in him before and which was more apparent now.

She said: "Maffitt means to kill you, of course. You know it. He'll bring four or five men down from the Pocket. You have no help in town. How—"

He said: "In a hurry?"

"No."

"Well, there's a grandstand seat. Let's sit and watch the town fill up."

He went to the edge of the ridge and turned, waiting for her. She made no motion for a minute but her mind was evenly divided between agreement and refusal. She had no business being here, yet her interest in him was quick and personal, stirred by that half-smiling indifference he showed her. It told her so little and covered so much; and it was a momentary thought of her father's violent rage that made her decision. She went over and sat down near him. He settled against one of the pines, letting his heavy muscles go idle. He pulled out his pipe and packed it and got the smoke drawing to suit him. They had a clear view of the town.

He said: "Maffitt will come. I think your people will also come. So will Dobe Hyde and Sultan—and the rest of the people. They'll all be there when the ball opens."

Her feelings were more and more involved. "How do you know?"

"The mail-sack is in the lobby. Everybody knew about that within a couple hours. Everybody knows Maffitt will pay me a visit. The rest of the country will be on hand. They want to see what happens to me—or to Maffitt. A lot depends on that."

He was, she recognized, governed by indifference; actually he seemed beyond caring. When his glance went out to the town his lids came nearer together and a net of wrinkles sprang around the eye corners. His wide chest lifted and fell to an undisturbed breathing. Katherine Barr watched him with an attention she could not help, his personality definitely swaying her judgment.

"How much," she murmured, "depends on it?"

He looked at her thoughtfully. "Your family hangs by a

thread in this country—every other rider scheming against you. Maffitt is the thread. If he should by any chance die, the rest of this country will be knocking on the Barr door tomorrow evening. I guess you know that."

She said, "Yes," in an out-pushed voice. "Is that what you want?"

His head turned again and, following his glance, she saw another rider breaking across the valley of the east fork toward Reservation, a small and almost stationary shape in the distance. It was then four o'clock or beyond, with shadows beginning to deepen in the timber.

She repeated: "Is that what you want—to break my family? Do you think we are that bad—or that the poeple on the east fork are any better?"

He said briefly, "Haven't decided."

"You will have to decide."

"Yes."

Her strong and self-assertive pride lifted. She straightened and her lips opened to speak for her family, to tell him how the years of hatred had hung over her. Yet none of that came out. For he was looking at her with a wistful wisdom that seemed to absorb everything. She had the feeling that he completely understood. It was one of the strangest moments of her life, to sit here and feel her anger die and to feel a rising apprehension for this big man's own safety. She saw him—so vividly—standing in Reservation's street with Maffitt and Maffitt's men turning the corner of the Old Dixie. She saw light crossing the street, but all these men were in the shadows and then the scene in her mind ran into the shadows and she could see no farther.

Majors watched the lift of her chin, the quick transition of light and dark in her eyes. Her lips parted and came together again, even and red along the ivory smoothness of her skin. She sat crosslegged on the ground with her supple fingers laced together. The riding clothes she wore showed the womanly lines of her body, its grace and vigor, and for him there was a powerful hint of the fire within. It revived his acute hungers.

He said: "It will do me no good to tell you this. You are very close to being beautiful."

She showed him an actually startled expression, her eyes widening. Color ran across her cheeks richly and her body bent toward him, so intent was her curiosity. She was

smiling, that lightness breaking through the pride that held
her expression so steady. She rose and spoke in a disturbed
voice.

"What is beauty, Jim?"

He came to his feet, his words quick and rough. "It's what
a man sees—and what a man feels. A fire in the night. How
can a man say it, Katherine? Spring wind after winter. Something in a woman's eyes and in her lips. Or in the turn of her
body. Something to make him go out and kill if he has to.
There is no way of saying it. It just is—when a man sees it."

She murmured: "That's enough for me to hear."

He checked himself, forcing the indifference back to his
face. A heavy ball of dust lifted halfway down the east fork
valley, which would be more riders making for town. The
valley remained clear and sunless but shadows were piling up
layer on layer in the timber. He said dryly: "More people.
Nothing ever changes."

She came over until she might have touched him with her
hand. He could not know it, but his talk had swayed her like
heavy wind. The restrained fury in his words had reached
into her, releasing a hundred swift half thoughts, setting off
the rich riot of her own imagination. She had never heard a
man speak like this before, nor had known that anyone could
reach to these violent depths of expressiveness. For these
were things she had often thought and felt in her own solitary
riding—and she had never believed she would find them in
another.

She said: "Does it have to be tonight, Jim? Does it have to
be either you or Ben Maffitt?"

"We'll soon know about that."

He had taken the pipe from his mouth. He had put his
hands behind him. The faint scent of her hair lifted to him.
Her shoulders made a straight line and her lips were faintly
pursed, with sweetness in them for a man. And the heat of
something rash and timeless and thoughtless brushed them
both. It moved him on his feet and drew his muscles together.
Poised this way, he pushed aside his desire to reach out and
pull her forward, and for the rest of his life he regretted that
opportunity wasted, forever afterwards wondering how it
might have been if he had obeyed his wishes. She looked up
at him, her lips edged with a smile. She said: "Good night,
Jim," and whirled over to her horse. A moment later she galloped out of the clearing.

He got into his own saddle and trotted down the side of the ridge into town. Dobe Hyde and three other riders were at this moment wheeling in from the east fork road. Buff Sultan was at the corner of the Old Dixie with Ketchum. Other men he didn't know were heading for the restaurant, and Charley Chavis stood in the doorway of the jail office.

Majors stabled the gelding and went directly to the hotel, passing Edith Sultan in the lobby. She looked at him with a certain interest, but he saw that she didn't mean to recognize him; so he went up the stairs, washed, and came down for dinner.

Tony, presently, brought him the venison steak and explained it. Majors said: "Matt Oldroyd? Not a bad-looking fellow."

Tony said, "Yes," but she wasn't cheerful. She bent down to say something to him, but Cal Soder came in and Tony straightened without speaking and went back to the kitchen. Dobe Hyde and his three companions stamped into the dining room. Some other rider entered town at a steady pace. Lights began to break the gray twilight, and when Majors finished his meal and went upstairs darkness had rolled completely across Reservation. This was as it had been on the night of his first appearance, the town slowly filling and shapes scattered along the shadowy niches of the walks.

As Jim was standing by his window, evenly drawing pipe smoke through his nostrils, he saw Ben Maffitt appear with four riders behind him.

10

━━━━━◆◉◆━━━━━

Turn of the Hour

FROM THE room's window Majors watched the town slowly
fill. Ben Maffitt and his men rolled into Soder's place and
Charley Chavis came quickly down the street and also entered the saloon, like a hound called to heel. Buff Sultan
lounged against the corner of the empty building. Dobe Hyde
and Ketchum were still in the dining room below. Pedee Barr
hadn't yet appeared, though Majors was certain he'd soon
come. For there was the smell of a kill in the sharp air and
that scent would draw them all. This was the hard knowledge
he had learned from the long years past: the signals of coming death were as clear to men as to animals.

In a little while he would go down and take his stand on
the street. The game ran that way, its rules compelling them
all, no matter what they wished or what they felt. Pride made
men strong and pride led men to their ruin; it was their
strength and their folly. Now and then, along the back trail,
Majors could remember a few great ones who understood the
meaning of life, their senses sharply savoring the wind's keen
edge, the far blue shadowing of the horizons, the great silence
of the hills and the deep, deep glitter of the stars by night.
They were the laughing ones, the great ones—full of youth
and venture. But most men lived in twilight, coming doggedly
to their ends without ever knowing what they had missed.

It was near stage time when Pedee Barr, flanked by his two
older sons, trotted out of the dark and stopped by the saloon.
Majors dallied by the window a little longer, in no sense certain how it was to be for him when he walked the street. Old
Jeff White had said: "I have lost one fine boy over there and

82

it is time the country was cleaned out, however it has to be done." Well, there were soft ways and hard ways and this was the hard way. The country lay even-balanced on the edge of trouble, Ben Maffitt supplying the weight that kept the scales level. This was why he had deliberately brought on the present showdown; if he destroyed the big outlaw's power he also destroyed the deadlock.

For if Maffitt went down the people along the east fork would rise against the Barrs to finish a fight fifeten years old. He had told Katherine Barr that he was not judging the rightness or wrongness of her family; he had omitted to tell her that in all these ancient grudges the original right and the original wrong ceased to be important, violence piling up on violence until nobody was right. His job was to put an end to it so that a man might ride these roads without need of a gun. Somebody had to lose and somebody had to win. If his methods were hard, like the pain of a knife cutting dead flesh from live, he could not help it. It was this knowledge that painted its shadows in Majors' eyes and laid its silence upon his tongue and stamped that brand of loneliness across his solid face.

Dobe Hyde left the restaurant and stopped by Buff Sultan on the opposite corner and presently came back to the hotel's side. Chavis left the saloon, returning to the jail doorway up by the bridge. Half a dozen men stood in the livery stable's mouth; and a man slipped out of the saloon's back entrance and vanished into an adjoining alley. At the same time Ben Maffitt came from the Old Dixie's front door, a pair of men walking with him, and took station on that corner. The hostler drove four fresh horses from the stable; out on the east fork road rose the sound of the fast-running stage.

Majors swung from the window, the picture complete in his mind. Always at times like this there was a change in him he could never describe. He had stood there watching the street with an interest that was quick and yet half-detached; and now the ease began to leave him and the detachment fell away and he was controlled by a stream of thought that ran through his head sharp and swift. His senses were keener and it was the little things that began to register, the crack of a board in the lobby below, the memory of the man who had ducked into the alley, the way Dobe Hyde had briefly stopped to speak to Buff Sultan. Controlled by a growing excitement, he turned downstairs.

The dining room was empty, but two men stood in the doorway and faced the street. The mail-sack remained on the lobby desk. Broderick sat shoulder-deep in the usual rocker, his steel-hooked arm hanging down. A pair of small, prematurely aged riders stood in a corner of the room and when he looked at them their eyes turned scrupulously aside. When he stepped from the lobby they would be behind him, commanding his back; for a moment he thought of this, and presently dismissed the thought. Edith Sultan remained by the desk, her expression strangely set. The stage was just then rolling into town.

He moved over and picked up the mail-sack. Edith Sultan's lips, so full and soft, stirred, and he thought she meant to speak. He had that moment to admire the poise of her head and the bright shine of her hair and the impression of laughter lying so free and reckless somewhere within. Afterwards he walked to the lobby's door to meet old Sam Rhett, coming in with Reservation's mail-sack.

Majors said: "I'll take that, Sam. And here's the one you lost up in the hills."

He spoke without a lift of tone, yet his talk had weight enough to carry across the square. He knew Ben Maffitt, hugely shaped against the light of the saloon's door, heard it distinctly; he knew that Charley Chavis, standing by the bridge two hundred feet away, heard it. The silence in this town was like that.

Sam Rhett handed over his mail-sack and took the one Majors offered without change of expression.

He said noncommittally: "So you went and got it? A funny thing. Nothin' of value in it."

Majors murmured: "We don't know what it's worth—yet." He knew Sam waited for whatever message he might carry over the Silver Lode to Jeff White. But there was nothing to tell and nothing, Majors knew, that Sam's old eyes couldn't see. He said: "Weather's uncertain, Sam. Better be on your way."

The stage-driver turned and crawled up to the high seat. The hostler hadn't finished hooking up the fresh team and Sam took this time to light his pipe and to let his old eyes scan this town as it was. When the hostler handed up the reins Sam laced them slowly between his fingers; he remained motionless, lost in hard calculation. Presently he looked down on Majors and spoke quite gently, "So-long, kid"—and kicked off the brake and cursed the horses into a dead run. The stage swayed around the corner, ripping up high sheets of dust, raced over the bridge with a huge booming of planks and vanished in the darkness beyond.

Majors had been in the doorway. He stepped down now and crossed the walk and stopped at the edge of the square. Maffitt was forty feet away, diagonally across the square and boldly outlined in the saloon's glow. The two men with him had spread away from Maffitt's elbows, one of them grinning through his bruised lips. This was Brick Brand again, with the memory of the morning in his grin—and the thought of what was to come in the grin too. Sultan was at the corner of the deserted building. Dobe Hyde had faded. Charley Chavis remained, as before, in front of the jail—far enough away to be out of the shooting. There was a knot of men still by the stable, and solitary shapes scattered in the half-shadows of the street, and the feel of other men in the heavy darkness beyond.

All this while he waited for Ben Maffitt to speak or swing into motion. Yet the big man made no sign and the silence got thin and the moments began to drag out; and then Majors, keyed to a higher and higher pitch of attention, began to think of the man who, going out of the saloon's back door, had ducked into the alley. Maffitt, he guessed, was playing this game indirectly again. There was that slyness in the heavy-shouldered outlaw, a slyness that rose not from fear but from a wish to pile on pressure until his opponents broke.

Majors stepped into the dust, pacing it at even strides. He skirted Buff Sultan at the corner of the empty building and kept on toward the knot of men at the livery stable, putting Maffitt on his left rear. He didn't know any of the men by the stable, nor did he care much about them. They stirred as he came up, and he brushed a man at either elbow as he went by. Behind them, he wheeled suddenly and said: "Go on—get out of here."

The group shifted; faces whipped around, making a sallow show in this gloom. He thought he had to speak again but someone murmured, "Sure," and the whole bunch rolled over the walk and started down the street. All this while Jim watched the alley across the way, and now saw a man run out of it and travel back toward the saloon.

There wasn't anybody left in the stable. Majors trotted to the rear door, and on into the blanket-thick shadows lying around the back of the town. He moved fast, running toward the river. When he reached it, he dropped down to the gravelly bank, cut under the bridge, and came up beside the jail. He continued on to the rear of the jail, and then saw light shining down a narrow space between some buildings. When he had threaded that narrow space, he found himself in the street, near the print shop. He had made a quick half-circle of the town, and stood now behind Maffitt.

Maffitt and all those others were turned away from him; they were still watching the stable.

There were no lights in this part of town and so, moving softly, he crossed the street and walked along the edge of the building fronts until he had reached the dark corner of the square, by the feed store. The saloon and the hotel were on opposite corners; and Buff Sultan now was on the diagonal corner by the empty building. Directly ahead of Majors, not more than five yards away, two men stood in thorough quiet, unaware of his presence. Ben Maffitt's men . . .

All the town's attention went single-mindedly toward that stable, and everybody waited; and Majors, backed against the wall of the feed store, let the situation ride. Suddenly Maffitt stepped out from his corner and looked up to where Charley Chavis was, and afterward he raised his other hand, making a signal. The two men near Majors at once crossed the street and took station near the hotel.

It was at this exact moment that Doc Showers drove his buggy out of the night and turned into the square, his lips making impatient sounds at the horse.

Somebody called: "Doc, for God's sake get out of here!"

Showers stopped his horse, his stocky torso turning in the seat. "What?"

"No—no, Go on! Go on!"

"Dammit," exploded the doctor, "make up your mind." He cheeped at the horse and rolled into the stable. Ben Maffitt abruptly slapped a hand hard against his thigh, which was a sound loud enough to cause Buff Sultan to whip around. Maffitt was signalling up the street with his hand again. And then Majors said:—

"Wrong spot, Ben."

This was the moment when he had to admire Maffitt. In the full silence of this street and in the half-darkness, he could see men wheeling and he could see their faces swing to search him out. All this was on the edge of his vision, for his attention clung to Maffitt, whose body was a motionless hulk against the saloon lights. It was this coolness, this calmness under tearing strain that Majors observed with a growing respect. The redhead, Brick Brand, stepped away from Maffitt and came to the edge of the walk; the other man who had been with Maffitt all this while suddenly cut around the big outlaw and moved into the open square. He was thirty feet away and facing Majors when he stopped, angular and loose of joint and long-armed. He carried his head forward, searching the shadows until he saw Majors; and when he saw Majors his body straightened and his elbows rose gently—and stopped.

Not until all this shifting had taken place did Maffitt turn and spot Majors. Time ran on and there were little things happening along the street that Majors caught vaguely. Sultan had straightened against the vacant building. Dobe Hyde walked from the hotel and stood directly behind the two men Maffitt had silently ordered over there.

This was the way it was when Maffitt spoke:—

"Hello, Majors."

It seemed to be a signal, for the angular fellow in the middle of the square stirred in his tracks and began to talk.

"Listen. You lookin' for Ed Dale. I'm Ed Dale."

Majors said: "All right. You're the man I want."

"You can come and get me. I'll be right here."

"No," said Majors. "Drop your belt and walk this way."

"Not any, mister. Not any."

He could remember, Majors could, past scenes such as this one, when time narrowed down and the moments were like slowing pulsebeats. The talk was about done and they had arranged themselves as they wanted. He could expect a shot from Brick Brand and one from Ed Dale; and the two men over by the hotel were waiting to rake him with a side fire.

Maffitt called in a loud voice, "Look, Majors!"—seeking to draw his attention away from Ed Dale, whose elbow faded backward as he pulled his gun.

There are sights that cut an unforgettable pattern in a man's mind and this was one of them—Ed Dale's body crooking over from the effort of his draw, his feet planted wide apart in the dust; and that was how he was when Majors' bullet hit him.

The echo of the shot rocketed through the streets, and Ed Dale teetered on his heels and then seemed to grow rigid.

Other things were swiftly happening. Dobe Hyde's voice rose shrilly from the hotel porch. "Not this time, fellers!" And Maffitt's arm swung over and hit Brick Brand hard enough to throw the redhead off-balance. He said, "Hold it."

Ed Dale's knees buckled, and he faded down against the dust, a dead man already forgotten.

Majors whipped a glance over to the hotel and saw why those two Maffitt men there had not fired. Dobe Hyde stood behind them, repeating his warning: "Don't do nothin', fellers." And Maffitt had checked Brick Brand. The sense of change rushed over the square. Maffitt had turned and his head was tipped up, and Majors, following the big outlaw's glance, saw Matt Oldroyd in the upper window of the unused building, holding a rifle dead against Maffitt.

This was directly above Buff Sultan. Buff Sultan walked away from the building so that he could look up at Oldroyd. His blond head whirled around and he was at once grinning. "What's holdin' you back, Ben?"

Pedee Barr and his two sons walked from the saloon and stopped directly behind Maffitt.

Majors held his spot, watching men change. There was a violence here that ripped the covering off these people and showed the fire and the hatred inside; that showed unmercifully what they were. He could see some of them grow and he could see some of them shrivel; it was all here.

Dobe Hyde's voice drilled the quiet with its passionate, shrill demand. "Matt! You got the gun on him! Drill the son-of-a-slut!"

There was no answer from Matt Oldroyd. Ketchum wheeled out of the untenanted building to whisper to Buff Sultan, whose grin remained ineffaceably on his florid cheeks. It was a real amusement, dry and full of irony; he was enjoying this grim joke. Maffitt's other men were still. Brick Brand laid his back to the saloon wall and waited coolly for whatever was to come. This Majors saw in a quick glance. But it was to the Barrs he paid his silent respects. They had come deliberately out of the saloon into this situation, to stand here and back up Ben Maffitt, who remained heavy and solid and slyly indifferent. They were loyal to whatever bargain they had made with the outlaw. And nothing, it seemed, could reach through Maffitt's physical courage. He had no mercy in him, no loyalty and no conscience. Yet he stood like a rock, giving not an inch, massively indifferent.

Buff Sultan's grin was greater and greater. "Well, Ben," he called. Dobe Hyde cried out: "By God, you won't get another chance like this! Drop him, Matt! Or I will!"

Majors walked away from the wall of the feed store, into the half light of the square. He said, "Keep still, Dobe," and felt the whole weight of this town's interest swing around. There was a tension here he wanted to break.

Dobe Hyde called: "Hell's afire, don't you know where your bread's buttered? There's the man that—"

Majors said, "Shut up."

He knew now that Matt wouldn't shoot. The kid had a steady hand. It was Dobe Hyde's insistent yelling that fed this hot fire. Sultan's grin faded completely and he showed Majors a puzzled face, as though the game were going wrong. Ketchum moved a step away from Sultan, speaking briefly: "Be careful, Majors. We're friends of yours. Not Maffitt."

"I want to see you fellows in the hotel. That includes Barr and Maffitt."

"There ain't a room big enough—" began Dobe Hyde violently, and stopped. For Majors walked across the square to him, brushing Maffitt's two men aside. He grabbed Hyde by the shirt front and the crotch, and lifted him and threw him into the lobby. He followed in. Dobe Hyde landed on his feet and rushed forward, full of impulsive rage. He struck out at Majors and missed. Majors swung the flat of his hand against the cowman's chest and knocked him down. It made quite a bit of noise, particularly the high-pitched bawl Dobe Hyde let go. Boots began to rattle along the walks. Turning quickly, Majors watched Ketchum and Sultan come into the lobby, neither of them pleased. Dobe Hyde got up, rubbing a hand along his leg. He had lost his hat and one single wisp of gray hair stood upright on the forepart of an otherwise bald head. Rage sparkled in his agate-colored eyes and wind pumped in and out of his chest; he stood uncertainly by the lobby table, too tangled in his emotions to say anything at the moment.

Sultan drawled: "That's workin' against the grain, Majors. I think it was a foolish thing to do. We got you out of that trap."

"Stand aside, Buff," said Majors.

Buff Sultan looked behind him and stepped away from the door. Maffitt and Pedee Barr walked in.

11

◆━━◎━━◆

Ultimatum

MAJORS settled his shoulders against the stairway post and pulled out his pipe, and let the moments go by while he packed and lighted it. Everybody watched him. The girl Tony, crouched in the upper hall, looked directly down on his head. Edith Sultan had crowded over to a corner of the lobby. Broderick was near her, wholly without expression. As for the others, he could see how little they trusted each other —and how little they trusted him. This room was actually too small to hold all the condensed hostility flowing out of them. It was, he supposed, the first time any of the principal actors in the valley quarrel had been brought together; and all that held them here was curiosity.

Charley Chavis came in and Cal Soder stepped up from the walk, meaning to enter.

Majors said: "Nobody asked you, Soder. Get out."

Soder's face, though trained to reveal nothing, could not hide his sudden shock; and Maffitt shook his shoulders, as though not pleased. Buff Sultan seemed to smell the possibilities of trouble, for he looked behind him quite carefully. But Soder turned without comment and went away. From his position Majors had a view of the square. Doc Showers walked to the dead Ed Dale, squatted a moment and strolled away. There were other men—Maffitt's partners—grouped around Dale. Matt Oldroyd appeared at the lobby door and remained there. He grinned at Majors.

Dobe Hyde burst out: "A man helps you squeeze out of a tight hole—and you belt him down. By God, next time you can die!"

"That's right," put in Buff Sultan. "We came in here to back you up. It was a fool play. Say what you figure to say. I don't stay in the same room with a Barr any longer than I got to."

Majors held the pipe evenly between his teeth, eyes half closed against the rolling smoke. He let his muscles go slack. The tension of the fight was wearing off and weariness spilled through his big frame. He knew these men. He knew them perfectly, and because of that he spoke with no softness.

"I'm obliged for the help; but that wasn't why you came in. You boys are grinding your own axes. Now that you've done me a favor you figure I'll turn the grindstone. I'm taking no sides in this."

Dobe Hyde said in his high voice, "Is that all you got to say?"

"No," said Majors, "it isn't. You see how it goes. There's a dead man out in the street. Tomorrow maybe there's another. Who'll it be? Maybe one of you fellows. Think it over. We could settle this fight right here, for once and all. The country is big enough for everybody."

Broderick lifted his head and stared at Majors, one deep crease crossing his forehead; and then they were all watching him as though they didn't believe what they'd heard, or as though he had said something which made no sense. He reached for a match and looked up at Tony. She sat on the top step, her hands folded across her knees and her body bent. The girl's features were sober and sweet and controlled by some remote dreaming that showed its faint glow in her eyes.

He brought his attention back to the room—back to Sultan who was speaking.

"You're a funny cuss. One minute I figure you smart as a fox. Then you do some fool thing or say some fool thing that don't make sense."

"Sure," agreed Majors. "But maybe this makes sense. Who's the next dead man? I know what you're thinking, Buff. It's the same thing Hyde is thinking. When this man Maffitt is chased out you've got a clean crack at the Barrs. That's what you're waiting for. Tonight, you figure the time's soon coming. Maffitt looks weaker now than he did half an hour ago. So you're full of courage."

Ben Maffitt looked at him, passive and intent. Majors knew the wildness behind that man's low forehead, yet even then he could admire him. But there was another story to be read in Pedee Barr, who had never opened his mouth since the beginning: somewhere in the arrogant narrow face was the first break of doubt—the faintest stain of uncertainty.

"You're through?" asked Sultan.

"So you're proud," mused Jim Majors. "But suppose Dobe Hyde makes a deal with Ben Maffitt and turns against you as well as against the Barrs?"

Dobe Hyde opened his mouth wide, and shut it.

Sultan's florid cheeks took on extra color and he stared over at Dobe Hyde. "You can answer that one, Dobe," he suggested.

Dobe shook his head.

Then Ketchum spoke up. "Why, what in hell are you tryin' to start?"

"I have seen it done," commented Majors. He pointed at Dobe Hyde. "Or suppose Ketchum and Sultan make a deal with Maffitt—and leave you out cold? There ain't a nickel's worth of trust in the whole bunch. Dog eat dog. I've seen it happen before."

Silence came on again. Majors exhaled pipe smoke and watched it curl up against the light. His lips made a half-smile and he hooked an arm over the stair post, placing his weight there. He knew these men. They would remember what he had said. They would turn it over in their minds, and its effect would bite deeper, burning up whatever trust they had.

"So," he murmured again, "who's the next dead man?"

Sultan growled, "You're a hell of a man to be wearin' a star. Come on, Ketchum." He wheeled from the lobby, Ketchum following. Dobe Hyde reached down for his hat on the floor. "I'll take the peace when the rest of you do, not before and not after." Then he looked at Maffitt, briefly but with a glinting speculation, and went out.

"I guess we better go home, Pedee," said Maffitt. Men were riding away from town. Charley Chavis had gone from the lobby. Majors watched Maffitt and Pedee leave, and made no motion. But he knew he had lighted a bonfire in each of those men's brains, and the fire wouldn't go out. He thought of it with a dismal amusement, feeling weariness weight him increasingly. Edith Sultan came out of her corner, across to him; she touched his arm and smiled and went on to the street.

Broderick stared through the window, his back to Majors. "Sundown," he said, "how long you figure to live?"

"Long enough," Majors grunted and crossed to the doorway, not fully appearing in it. Sultan and Ketchum and Hyde were grouped by the corner of the empty building, their men gathering slowly. Maffitt's partners had lashed the dead Ed Dale across his saddle. They were over by the half-shadows beyond the saloon. The Barrs stood with them. It was a matter of pride that made those two groups reluctant to be the first to pull out of Reservation—not a desire to go on with the fighting. There was always a peak moment in scenes like this. Men's emotions carried them up to that moment, and sudden madness cut the wires of reason and drugged their instinct of fear, and then the raw primal fighting lust pushed them on. Reaction came soon afterwards. The terrible fire of the moment burned them out, leaving them empty and tired and unable to feel very much. He could see that fatigue pull all those men. They stood with their feet apart, heads lumped down and dully silent, almost past the ability to break the deadlock. And so he stepped from the lobby and walked on as far as the edge of the square, the only moving figure on the street.

It was that motion which supplied the answer for them. Ben Maffitt suddenly called, "All right," and swung up to his saddle. In a moment all that crowd moved out of town by the south fork road; and presently Sultan and his friends turned back toward the east fork's valley.

The town lay empty and exhausted beneath the black hulk of the Silver Lode. Dust rolled pungently with the small cold wind, and the only sound to be heard was that of Matt Oldroyd's boot-heels dragging down the walk.

Jim Majors swung to find the yellow-headed youth idly halted near him—halted and smiling.

Majors said: "Thanks, Matt. You realize, maybe, you've put your neck out?"

"A man," considered young Matt in a gentle voice, "has to come to that sooner or later. If he figures to be a man."

"A hard lesson, Matt."

"You handled 'em like sheep," Matt said in a wondering way. "Like sheep. I sat back and watched. There's a time for silence and a time for talk. Time to drift and time to get tough. Where'd you learn all that? I'd give a leg to know what you know."

"No, Matt. When you know what I know you'll lose some-thin' worse than a leg. Don't aim for that kind of learning. Brings you no comfort and no peace."

"Peace?" Matt Oldroyd laughed, the sound of it soft and careless and gay. "What's a man for? Listen. I don't know where you're going or how you figure to get there. Hell or high water. The chances are plumb equal this minute. But if you ever want a thing done which you want another man to do—let me do it."

Majors only nodded. He noticed change in the young fel-low's face, a change from smiling to grave wonder; and turn-ing about, he saw Tony in the doorway of the hotel. The light was kind to the girl, showing the full, soft lines of her body; showing the womanliness in breast and shoulder. She was looking at him, at Majors, the expression of her eyes hidden to him. But Majors could see how it was with Matt Oldroyd, who remained humbly there and waited for her attention to come to him.

Weariness made Majors' legs heavy. He swung over the square and walked into the Old Dixie. The barkeep and Cal Soder were standing behind the bar, with Charley Chavis in front of them.

Soder said: "You can get your drinks somewhere else, my friend."

Majors moved against the bar, seeing these men without il-lusion and without patience. He had spent the active years of his life dealing with their kind, trading on their fears and weaknesses, matching their sly and hidden trickeries, avoiding their traps and settling his own, with always the stark knowledge in his head that someday the game, for him, would go fatally wrong. No luck lasted forever. There were times, as now, when the loneliness of this knowledge knocked down his guard; when he remembered the peace and personal happiness he once had wished for and now knew could never come to him. This was his present feeling and they could see it in his eyes like a sullen flame.

He said: "Soder, be careful."

Soder drew his arm back and reached for a bottle and for a glass. He brought them to Majors. He was at white heat, his poker expression failing to hold that stung resentment al-together below surface. He left his hands on the bar, so that Majors might see them.

"Captain," he murmured, "you drive men too hard. They are not dogs, though you think them to be."

"You have lost your backing, Soder. Ben Maffitt is about through."

"It may be," said Soder. "But the time comes to every man, if he's pushed far enough, when he'll try it alone. Don't forget that, captain. You cut a wide track and a deep one. Deep enough to make your own grave. I will tell you something, captain, from experience. Tonight you lost. It may not be clear to you, but tonight you lost. And whatever the politics of this country may be, you'll never live to see the other side of the Silver Lode. You have got a weak spot."

Majors took up the bottle and glass and moved across to the swinging doors. He turned there, a half-smile pulling his lips into a long, tough line. "This will be on the house, Soder."

"A weak spot," repeated Soder, his talk growing hot and half-furious. "I saw it. It is what will kill you."

Majors crossed the square with the bottle tucked under his arm. There wasn't a soul in sight, and nobody in the lobby when he passed through. The stairs groaned under his weight; fatigue weakened his knees. He went into his room and lighted the lamp and dragged up the little table beside the bed and put the bottle on it. He poured himself a drink, but for a moment he let it stand, laying his big arms across the table while his mind began to flash up one image and another—which was always the after-effect of a fight. He thought, "Maffitt will leave the Barrs," and then remembered Katherine Barr as she had stood before him on the heights above Reservation, a proud girl whose emotions laid a sharp beauty across her face. He had felt then and could feel now the shock of her personality and that wildness which had swayed both of them for one long, dangerous moment.

Somebody tapped gently on his door. He lifted his head and sat with a heavier thought breaking his weary expression. Then he called: "No, Tony. No."

As soon as Majors left the saloon, Charley Chavis let out a tremendously heavy breath and stirred from his long-maintained attitude.

He said irritably: "I never saw no weak spot. That dam' man ain't human."

Soder's eyes were red and small and showed the strain he

had been through. His short words were burdened with outrage.

"No man alive ever talked to me like that before, Charley."

"I saw no weakness," repeated Chavis.

"Maffitt was a dead man—and Maffitt knew it. Oldroyd and Sultan and Dobe Hyde and Majors all had him hipped. There was the break—right in Majors' hands. But he dodged it. See that, Charley? He ain't as tough as he makes out. Well, he's fightin' boys that won't make the same mistake when they got the drop on him."

"Maybe," said Chavis, doubtfully, "he's got another idea."

Soder, who seldom drank, lifted a bottle and two glasses from the back bar.

"No," he said; "this was his break and he backed down. Ben Maffitt will never give him another."

The two of them stood taciturnly up to the bar and drank.

Chavis said: "I wish to God I was out of it."

"You'll live to see him squirmin' in the dust," prophesied Soder, that hope surging wickedly through his talk.

Buff Sultan galloped down the road with his sister, Ketchum and Dobe Hyde, and Dobe's four hands. Nothing was said until they reached Ketchum's turn-off. Here they stopped.

"Boys," said Dobe Hyde in his piping voice, "Ben Maffitt's walkin' on his socks. This Majors took the play from him. I reckon the time's right for us."

Ketchum grumbled: "Majors took the play from us."

"We can handle *him*."

There was a thoughtful silence, the horses blowing into the night's sharp air. Then Dobe's scheming words came out again.

"Might be somethin' in what he said. Maybe we could line up Ben Maffitt. Never does no harm to try."

Ketchum said flatly: "I don't work with outlaws. Not ever. How about it, Buff?"

Buff's answer dragged a little. "No," he murmured. "No. I guess not."

"Buff," challenged Ketchum, "you better stiffen up on that. Whatever we do, we'll do by ourselves."

"Sure," said Buff Sultan. "I'll see you in the morning."

The party went on, leaving Ketchum shaped blackly under

the night. Later, at the entrance to the Sultan place, they
halted again. Buff went ahead with Dobe Hyde and parleyed
with him a long while.

Edith Sultan trotted into the yard, but she didn't get down
from the saddle. She waited there a good ten minutes until
her brother came up.

"Wait a minute, Buff. You're not going to have anything to
do with Dobe?"

"What's the matter with Dobe?"

"That's no answer. He never played square with Dad in
the old days, and he never played square with anybody else
in his life."

"I can use him, can't I?"

"He'll use you."

He came closer, leaning out of the saddle to catch a vague
view of her face. "What's the matter with you, Sis?"

"Nothing. I guess I'm just tired of fighting."

"I thought so. But you better get over it. There's going to
be a fight."

"When?"

He delayed his answer, which, when it came, was evasive.
"Pretty soon."

"Are you telling Majors about it?"

"Majors," said Buff impatiently, "can look out for himself."

"So you're getting shifty, like Dobe Hyde."

"Look here, kid. You used to be different. Who've you
been meeting up in the hills lately?"

At once she lost her temper. "None of your dam' business,
Buff! I'm not the only one that's changed. You're getting sly.
I can see you sit and scheme. You'd throw in with Maffitt if
you thought it would help get rid of the Barrs."

He said directly: "Why not? That's what we all want, isn't
it? Who started this thing in the first place? Who's put the
fear of God in everybody since you and me was old enough
to talk? Who broke up the country and made it impossible
for a man to ride the hills without eyes in the back of his
head?"

She said, wearily: "I know. But it never gets any better.
We keep going deeper."

"Sure. You want to soften up. Maybe I don't blame you.
But I'll keep on till I see the Barrs dead. That's the only
way." His voice dropped to a gentler pitch. "It's a dirty

business. It's wrecked the country. But someday maybe I'll be married and you'll be married. When that time comes, I want our kids to be safe. . . . Where are you going?"

She had turned away. She called back, "For a ride"—and drummed back down the Reservation road, leaving her brother thoughtfully behind. He had his suspicions then, but he let her go, knowing no other way.

Three quarters of an hour later she reached the deserted house in the pines, left her horse, and walked inside, not certain Dan Barr would come this way tonight but desperately hoping he would. She needed the comfort of his arms; she needed to hear him say again, "There's a way out of this for us, somehow."

Meanwhile the Barr party reached home. Maffitt sent the rest of his crowd on to the Pocket, himself walking heavily over the porch and following the Barrs into the living room. Standing in a corner of the room, Katherine saw how short a temper possessed them all. She did not know, until they began to talk, what had taken place in Reservation, but clearly the events there had tremendously disturbed her father and brothers and had reached into Maffitt as well. Usually he maintained a rather wooden expression. His temper broke that solidness now.

Her father said: "You permitted Majors to force your hand, Ben. It has weakened you in this country. Why didn't you broach him when he first walked across the square? You let him slip into the stable. After that everything was out of your hands."

"Not satisfied?" challenged Maffitt.

"No," said Pedee Barr. "Majors has brought you to a stand twice. They have lost their fear of us."

The shadow of trouble was over him. He stood gaunt and tall in the middle of the room, not able to conceal his disfavor and not wanting to conceal it. His pride was unbending. It tempered his will to the same metallic hardness, and when his pride was touched he was a match for any man on earth. She had a fatally clear picture of him then. He could not change, and he could not recognize any power greater than his power. He was wholly single-minded, believing his own position to be thoroughly right. He could not question his judgment and would permit no other soul to question it; and rather than bend he would break. He had found a weakness in Maffitt and, despising weakness in any form, he showed Maffitt his open contempt. All this Katherine saw in her father.

Maffitt's huge shoulders were swung forward; a bold, gray insolence controlled his face.

"Pedee," he said, "if I pull out you're a gone goose. But say the word and I'll pull out."

"No," answered the old man with a grinding calm. "You'll stand with me. You'll stand if we all die for it."

Maffitt's eyes widened. "I reckon," he drawled, "you don't know me very well."

"I know you very well, sir. You are a crook and a thief and it is in your mind to betray me. But you will not do it. I stood behind you in Reservation tonight. I shall continue to do that. But the moment you stray off you'll find me in front of you."

There was a quarrel storming up between her father and this burly outlaw who looked on with so much sly amusement. Fay and Ring stood behind their father, exact replicas of him. Katherine turned suddenly from the room and went to the porch. There was another brief word passed and after that Maffitt's heavy step came behind her. She turned with some surprise to see him outlined by the window light; he removed his hat and the force of his eyes was very real. Somewhere in her a small fear stirred up again.

He said: "Your dad is a fool, Katherine. But you should be smart enough to see that the Barr family lives or dies accordin' to what I do. I have watched you a long time, as maybe you've noticed, though I never meant unpoliteness by it. I know my limits."

She said, "I'll answer that question now, Ben."

He said, almost gently, "I have asked none."

"It is in the back of your head. I've never had anything to do with you—and never will."

She saw no change in his expression. He remained a huge block against the light, his words easy and almost windless.

"Man's life is a funny thing. I can look back and see where mine might have been different. I can trace every step of the way. But I don't cry now. Maybe you'd like to know this: Mighty few people in the world I ever have admired. Most of 'em have got a price or a weakness. But I admire you. And I admire one other in this valley, which is Jim Majors, who stands like a man. When this business blows over one of us won't be here, which is a pity—for there's a fellow I could ride with. Him and me—we could lick the world." He clapped on his hat, letting out a great sweep of a breath. He went by, descending the steps. But he halted momentarily to add, "Your family, Katherine, is lost," and went to his horse.

She stood by the porch post, listening to his horse pound across the bridge. Those long echoes flattened down the valley and soon faded into the great silence of the hills. Even the shallow rustling of the river seemed to diminish. There had been a ring in Ben Maffitt's words, like a bell tolling out dismal tidings; and in her own heart she felt its truth. The day of the Barrs was over, its ruin brought on by a big and solemn man who had once looked at her with hunger in his eyes.

Her brothers came rapidly from the house, swung to their horses, and rushed on out the back trail, apparently bound for the lower range.

12

Attack

DOBE HYDE and his four men got home around ten o'clock
that night. A light came out of the middle room of a house
that ran its low shape against the darkness like a wheelless
boxcar. A Negro, who was Dobe's cook, appeared; Dobe
dressed him down with a few high-pitched words.

"Baker, what you burnin' good coal-oil fer? When I want
you to use a lamp I'll tell you—and that'll be a dam' dark
night. Jett here yet?"

"Nooh," said Baker, softly and grudgingly.

"Slower'n sleepin' Judas," grumbled Dobe, and stamped
into the middle room, slamming the door.

It was a room belonging to a man who had all the acquisi-
tive instincts of a magpie. Here was a round stove, a chair
and a table, and a bed; a rifle rack, an extra saddle—and the
accumulated plunder of fifteen years. The walls were covered
with old newspapers, their edges loosely pulled away through
the disintegration of flour paste. A bunch of cured hides took
up one corner of the room. There were fragments of broken
rope lying in a pile, cases of canned goods,—which Dobe
personally doled out to the cook,—a mound of burlap sacking, a stack of *Harper's Weeklys* reaching from floor to window, each issue having been read to the last line and
scrupulously added to the stack, and a miscellaneous assort-
ment of junk which somehow satisfied Dobe's need of pos-
session. Here was a man who saved because of a craving like
that which led other men to drink.

He brought a bottle of whisky out of a cupboard, which
was a soapbox nailed to the wall, and held it against the lamp-

light, measuring its contents against a thumbnail scratch on
the label. He poured a small drink into a glass on the table,
and ran his small red tongue around the bottle's neck to
catch the final drip; then sat down in the chair, his legs
loosely extended before him.

He bawled through the closed door: "When Jett comes, tell
him to hurry here." Nobody in the yard answered him, but
he knew Baker heard. Baker heard everything, and never answered anything. So sitting there, a small bundle of a man
with a dry unwashed face and a single lock of gray hair spi-
raling up on an otherwise bald head, he took his whisky in
small sips, getting the last bit of savor from it.

Dobe Hyde was a Connecticut man who had sold his
wooden nutmegs and shoddy goods from door to door as a
youth; while still a boy he had gone to the Civil War—but
not as a fighter. Behind his uncertainly colored eyes lay thoroughly sharp and altogether unsentimental calculations, and
since there was no profit in personal glory, Dobe followed the
Union armies as a sutler, retreating and advancing as rapidly
as any, but to infinitely more personal advantage. The end of
the war found him on the Texas gulf. In this land of grass
and countless herds of almost valueless cattle, Dobe had had
the methods of quick ownership demonstrated to him by
other men with careless branding irons and fast-traveling
horses. Here was a man who never needed a lesson repeated
in order to learn it; so presently, with a few foot-loose riders,
he was making his first drives out of Texas, up through the
Nations, to Abilene and Hays and Dodge, with beef that cost
him nothing and sold very well.

In those days that land lay wild and dangerous, crossed
and recrossed by Indians, desperadoes, and ranch outfits in
search of beef that Dobe Hyde and other men like Dobe had
stolen. Yet though Dobe was aware of the danger, and never
met a fight if he could avoid one, there was behind that dry
face and seemingly colorless personality a driving force that
carried him on. Thoroughly cold, wholly without the emotions of pity or the scruples of honesty, he kept his pale eyes
on the main chance; and when the southern trails grew too
hot he rode into the still largely untouched northern range
and found his valley.

The war between the Barrs and the cattlemen along the
east fork was then in full swing and both sides courted him
for his support. He stayed aloof, nursing his herds and

watching men die and hearing rifle shots sound by night though the timber, and seeing the Barrs push up to the ridge where Tony's father had been. In those years—and until now—he was an enigma, no man knowing his politics; for Dobe had learned to keep his own counsel, he had learned how to bend with the wind and how to run with the wind. Steadily his secret glance lay over the land and he watched those forces play back and forth and reach uneasy deadlock: and now he saw his way to profit, as always, by other men's mistakes. What Dobe wanted to see was his own brand running a range that extended from his home ranch up to the Barrs' valley and back down the fertile east fork. There were times to drift and there were times to push. The time to push had at last come, after patient and inscrutable waiting.

This was what he considered now, waiting for Jett to come. Jett rode up half an hour later and dragged his spurs into Dobe's room. Jett was little more than a kid, with a face pale and prematurely wicked.

He said: "I sat out in the timber a long time. The two Barr boys—Fay and Ring—rode up to the line cabin after dark. That second cousin and another feller, the uncle, is there too. That makes four."

"You go tell Sultan to come. Tell him to send a man down to Ketchum. Then you go over to the Oldroyds'. They'll know."

"I ain't et," said Jett.

"Sultans will give you bait," said Dobe.

"You God-condemned old skinflint," said Jett.

"Stay with me, boy," shrilled Dobe, "and I'll teach you how to wear diamonds."

"Diamonds melt in hell," said Jett, and whirled out. Dobe listened to the boy drum off down the road. He got up and found his glasses and reached for the most recent issue of *Harper's Weekly*; he settled himself down in the chair and read that paper's editorial comment on President Hayes. This was Dobe Hyde—a man with a mind as cold and clear as glass. In his native state he would have been a rich man living in a white house on the fashionable hill, driving his own carriage of a morning down to his factory; thin-lipped and frugal and hard-driving and respectable. The truth about Dobe was that he took the world as he found it, asking no favors, and made his way.

Jett reached Sultan's and said, "Glass Eye, the old son of a

biscuit, wants to see you. You should send a man to tell
Ketchum—and by God I'm hungry."

Buff jerked his thumb at the kitchen, whereupon Jett went
that way. Afterwards Sultan walked to the porch and yelled
for Sam Veen, giving him orders to ride to Ketchum's. In a
little while Jett pounded away, leaving Sultan alone in the
house. Edith hadn't yet returned from her ride, and he felt
uneasy about leaving.

The truth was, he wanted to hear her speak against Dobe
Hyde, and so crystallize his growing doubt. He knew Dobe
meant to ride towards the Barrs', and that in itself met with
his approval. But it was Dobe Hyde's growing aggressiveness
that worried him, for this was a quarrel Dobe had never before taken part in. The man had always kept his skirts clear.
His entry into the fight now meant that he had some ends of
his own to serve.

Buff walked the living room floor a good five minutes,
threshing it out and finding no argument to stay him. He had
a good deal of pride, and a keen memory of the damage
done to his father by the Barrs in times past. There wasn't
anything complex about Buff Sultan. His angers were quick
and his judgments swayed by the need of the approval of his
neighbors along the east fork; and it was this fact which in
the end turned him out of the house. The rest of the valley
would go with Dobe, and he had to string with the valley. Before leaving he wrote a note for Edith saying he'd be gone
for a while.

Sam Veen reached Ketchum's and delivered the message;
and presently Ketchum and Ketchum's six-foot boy, Hallem,
were on the road with Veen.

Meanwhile Jett fogged on through the perfect darkness, diagonally across the valley to the Oldroyds'.

He hailed Oldroyd from the yard and waited there while
the light in the house went off. Oldroyd was one of the old
fighters who remembered the sudden ambushes of other days.
When he opened the door he made no shape for Jett to see,
but Jett knew the man was there, holding a gun on him. Jett
said:

"Dobe Hyde wants to see you. Sultan and Ketchum are on
the way up there now."

Oldroyd's wife lighted the lamp as soon as Jett had gone.
Matt came back from a corner window and the elder
Oldroyd turned slowly around. He was a six-footer with a

full beard and a pair of small, straight eyes. He had a habit of running the back of his hand along the edges of the beard; he did it now.

"Dobe?" said Mrs. Oldroyd. "He never helped us before. You stay home, Oldroyd."

"Don't understand why Buff and Ketchum string with him," pondered Oldroyd.

"You stay home," repeated his wife. "Dobe Hyde wants nothing good."

"Why," said Oldroyd, "I know what he wants. It will be to ride over to the Barrs'."

Mrs. Oldroyd shook her head. She was a quiet woman, a motherly woman who had seen a good deal of violence in her time and had her own secret opinions of the cruel mistakes made by men. But she had said little to Oldroyd, for he was a headstrong man. "Don't ride with Dobe."

"It ain't Dobe," said Oldroyd. "It's Buff and Ketchum. I reckon I'll have to go. Matt—"

Both of them observed, then, that Matt had quietly gone from the room; and while they stood there they heard him ride suddenly around the house. Oldroyd's eyes showed a sparkling, unpleasant surprise. He started for the door, and changed his mind; he listened to the horse pound away.

"Toward Reservation," said Oldroyd—and at once swore. "By God, he's running away!"

"Maybe not," said Mrs. Oldroyd.

"Stick up for him," said Oldroyd irritably. "He lives on the east fork and he's got to stay with his crowd. If he don't then he's nobody I want to know, Allie."

Something else occurred to him. "I hear he's been talkin' with Tony."

"Yes," said Mrs. Oldroyd in the same quiet way.

"I turned her out and she stays turned out. She's no good."

Mrs. Oldroyd looked down, not meeting her husband's clear-black glance. "Maybe not, Oldroyd," she said very gently. "Maybe not, according to your lights."

"There's right and there's wrong," said the old man with a ringing definiteness, and he moved toward his gun hanging beside the fireplace.

Mrs. Oldroyd sat down and folded her hands across her lap, soberly resigned, and watched him get himself together. She didn't say anything, since, long ago, she had learned there was nothing for her to say. Oldroyd came over and bent and kissed her, and paused awkwardly that way.

"I'll be back rather late."

"It has been a long time since you have said that. I thought those terrible days were gone."

"Save up some coffee for me."

"It will be on the back of the stove."

He went out with a slow and definite stride; a big man who had always believed in the simplicity of black and white and could not change. Mrs. Oldroyd began to swing the rocker back and forth—and would do that until he came home.

Paused under the river willows, Matt heard his father run down the dark road toward Dobe Hyde's valley, and long after that reverberation had died out he remained there, finding discomfort in his thoughts. In the morning he would have to face his father. That would be a tough scene, for the old man still regarded him as a kid to be ordered around, and would pound at him with an even, severe voice about his duty. All the older ones had been indescribably hardened by the long war with the Barrs; it had taken their reasonableness out of them and it had taken sympathy out of them. And none of that older crowd could understand that the young people growing up around Reservation had their own thoughts about this endless fight.

What he really wanted to do was to ride into Reservation and warn Majors of the fight to come. But much as he admired the big deputy marshal, much as his imagination was stirred by Majors' lone-handed courage, he could not square that with his conscience. Secrecy had been drummed into him since childhood; the sin of a loose mouth was, to the people of this country, the greatest sin. Thus he stood, hating the blind rage that made his father ride to renew the old war and yet unable to carry information to Majors. The only thing he could do was drift over toward the Barr house and see what happened.

So he crossed the bridge and headed for the broken country; and as he rode he kept thinking of Tony, his conscience not clear and his emotions vaguely stirred by the remembered sound of her slow and wistful voice.

Edith Sultan rode directly to the deserted house in the broken country after her half-quarrel with Buff, stopping once along the way to see if she were being followed. When she reached the little clearing she had no hope of finding Dan there; and he was not there. She waited in the thorough darkness of the house for a considerable time and occasionally broke the monotony of the wait by walking around the rooms until the echoes of her steps became unbearably loud in the empty place and brought her to a stand. She had about decided to return home when she heard somebody ride rapidly over the meadow and jump down. As soon as the newcomer crossed the porch she identified his stride.

"Dan."

He came into the room, a vague shape against the lesser black. He said: "I dropped by this afternoon and didn't see you. Just figured you might be here tonight." His hand reached out and caught her hand; and they stood in this attitude, not speaking for a while. A rat's faint scratching came through the floor and the slow wind was quite cold.

She said: "It is getting no better, Dan."

"Worse." Afterwards he broke out with a quick, resenting energy. "This man Majors! If he'd only left things alone!"

"I've seen him, Dan. I like him. He looks so big, and so lonely. I was in the hotel tonight when everybody came in. I could look at his eyes. He knows how little chance he has here. It made me feel sorry for him."

"I heard what happened. You'd better feel sorry for us, Edie. He's raised hell. We had some sort of peace around here, but now he's set all the dogs to barkin'."

"It would have happened anyhow, sooner or later."

"Maybe it would have just died down."

She said: "When? After you and I were old and gray-headed? We can't go on forever like this."

He said, "I know, I know," somberly. "But maybe you don't see what's coming now."

"There will be a fight."

He asked his question with a sudden intensity. "What do you know?"

She delayed her answer a long while, finally saying with a soft directness: "I can't tell you anything, Dan. I can't betray my people."

He withdrew his hand and she heard him walk violently around the room, and come back. He was only a shadow before her. His voice was harder than it had been, the grind of desperation in it.

"Oh, my God, Edie, don't you see?"

"I know. The fence between us gets higher. But, Dan—how would you want me to be? Would you tell me what your people were doing right now?"

He said: "I've often told you I can't excuse the things my folks have done. But I can't run away from what's coming. Majors has let hell loose, and your crowd plans to wipe us out. Is that what you want—the Barrs wiped out?"

"Dan—don't."

"It's come to that," he said with the same bitter, strained conviction. "Well, we both knew it would. So here we are. We made a mistake in the first place—ever knowing each other. There ain't any way out, and I guess there never will be. This damned fight goes back too far. It's like a poison that gets into everybody. Some of it is in us, and we can't do anything about it."

Edith Sultan stood still and silent in her place, near tears. Dan Barr's bitterness whirled around her, leaving her helpless, leaving her without answer. All this she had long ago seen. Even while Dan remained hopeful she had known it would come to this end. So, because she was a woman, with a woman's realism, she had taken the sweetness of their meetings with that really tragic knowledge always lurking behind her lips and behind her eyes, asking for nothing except the little moments of his laughter and the hardness of his arms. He was a man with the wildest of imaginations and at times it had swept her up and made her temporarily forget. Afterwards the return of memory was harder to bear.

He came on and took her by the shoulders, his talk calmer. "It doesn't mean much, Edie, but I do love you."

She was in his arms, definitely crying then—she who hated tears. He kissed her; and they stood this way, locked together in the thorough darkness, like two children desperately afraid of that darkness.

There was a drumming in the night and a rider slashed across the clearing, his winded horse sawing heavy echoes through the otherwise quiet place. Neither of them stirred.

He said: "I guess this is the end of it, Edie."

"Someday," she heard herself saying, "people will be kinder."

It was around midnight when Dobe Hyde got the valley assembled at his house. They were all crowded in his living room: his own men, Sultan, Ketchum, Ketchum's son Hallem, and Oldroyd. There was, also, one more man from the country east of Dobe Hyde's—a taciturn fellow whom Dobe called Godry. None of the east fork people knew him; and his appearance here didn't quite square with their feelings. Ketchum distinctly showed that, impelling Dobe Hyde to say:—

"Used to know Godry down the Chisum trail. One more man won't hurt."

Ketchum retorted: "Not accustomed to ridin' with strangers."

The taciturn Godry said nothing. He sat idly on the bale of burlap sacking, a short-stemmed pipe bitten between his teeth; he had a thin mustache running down into the corners of his lips, and a pale-green cast to his glance. Ketchum flashed a quick look at Sultan. Sultan briefly shrugged his shoulders. Dobe Hyde spoke in his high, reedy voice:—

"I'm no hand to shoot when it ain't necessary. Jett went over and had a look. Old man Barr's got his two oldest boys and a couple of relations down at the south corner of his range. In a line cabin. Most of the Barr cows are yander. We'll just ride over and about daylight scare hell out of that crew and scatter the beef. I reckon the Barrs will take the hint."

Sultan said gloomily: "Bad judgment on your part, Dobe. The Barrs don't scare."

"Maybe," Dobe piped mildly, "we can make the thing clear to 'em."

"You're still wrong."

Dobe Hyde's light eyes touched Sultan briefly. There wasn't any heat in the glance, nor any particular force. But Sultan saw something that pulled his face together. He reached over and seized Dobe's bottle and poured a good half-glass of liquor—and drank it. Dobe almost winced.

"It's five hours till daylight," pointed out Ketchum.

"Two to get there and three to wait."

Oldroyd had been meanwhile studying the stranger, Godry. Oldroyd was a hard character himself, and knew another hard character when he saw one. The length and force of his deliberate stare lifted the stranger's attention and he met Oldroyd's eyes with a strict reserve, and finally looked aside. Oldroyd rubbed the back of a hand along the edge of his beard.

"Dobe," he said, "politics is a hard thing. I never trusted you, and I don't now. You held out when this quarrel was toughest, years back. Now we go along with you, but it ain't for any of your profit. Ketchum runs this party tonight and you will take orders from him. That clear?"

"Gentlemen," said Dobe, "anything is agreeable to me."

"You see you stay that way," warned Oldroyd. "And I will remind you of another thing. We are dealing with dogs, whom we will destroy, God willing. But when the Barrs are gone from the south fork, that valley will not be open to you. It will be split up among the families who have borne this trouble since '65. Is that clear?"

Dobe sat loosely in the chair, his bald head somewhat bowed and a faint flush creeping across his face. The dryness grew more apparent, the thinness of his lips increased. Godry looked over at him, something in those green eyes suddenly. Everybody was listening and watching. Dobe's four men stood in the background; Jett's lips stretched into a surreptitious grin and he winked at the rest of the crew.

Oldroyd repeated, "Do you hear?" in a grating intolerant voice.

Dobe's eyes flickered a little when he looked back to that bearded old warrior who bent to no man. Dobe said, smooth and agreeable: "I got no intentions on that valley. All I want is a piece of the broken country, which they're usin' now. No conflict, gentlemen. I wish to be agreeable."

"Part of that belonged to Tony's dad," observed Sultan.

"Who is dead," said Oldroyd. "We got no debts to dead men. And we owe nothin' to his daughter, who is no good. We will settle this. We will make a bargain, here and now. The scope of range you want is yours—and nothing else."

"Fine—fine," said Dobe Hyde, his voice rustling like rubbed paper.

Oldroyd and Ketchum and Sultan were all weighing him, without friendliness or trust.

Oldroyd said: "It had dam' well better be. And get no ideas about that, later. You are a sly man, Dobe, which we all know. You don't fool nobody. There's ways of handling men who go balky. . . . Now let's be about this job. It's been a long time delayed."

They turned out of the room. Dobe and the stranger were the last to go. At the doorway Dobe looked back to the stranger close behind him and winked, slyness like a film of oil in his eyes.

They swung up. Ketchum said: "Some of you boys are green at this business. So I will mention certain things. Make no noise, keep behind me, and do as I tell you. Nobody fires and nobody shows himself—until I say so. In case we get bushwhacked, every man find his own hole."

After that they swung off, saying nothing more. They crossed Dobe Hyde's small valley, followed the stage road a short distance and afterwards entered the broken land. This was a roundabout way, avoiding the trail that passed the deserted house; it was a good twelve miles through a darkness solid enough almost to have body, and Ketchum set a slow pace, choosing to waste time this way rather than to stand a long wait for daylight after reaching the Barr line cabin. And so, three hours or better from Dobe Hyde's valley, they came out of the broken land and filed gently downward along a bare slope that presently ended at a kind of low rim.

Fog rolled off the heights of the Silver Lode in steady waves. Below the rim was a shallow canyon, which all of them knew to be there but none could see; and somewhere in the canyon lay the Barr line cabin. A creek made a faint racket in the night and the idle run of the wind dragged low, washing echoes out of the solid pine mass that covered the shoulders of the range.

Ketchum said, "A hundred yards, dead in front. Hallem, catch up all the horses and take 'em back a piece. We wait here."

The horses raised a muted scuffing as Hallem led them back. Ketchum spoke again, laying his talk smoothly against the black. "We'll spread out here—and we'll wait."

They were shapes dissolved against the earth while time passed. The wind made a down-draught from the mountain, piling the raw, cold fog against them. But the patience of these men was colder still—and they waited here without sound and without motion while the last of night turned on and light began to dilute faintly the solid dark. The mountain mass heaved up gigantically through these first perceptible shadows, and then the streak of low-lying fog showed the course of the canyon, hiding the line cabin completely.

Dobe Hyde permitted himself a faint whimper of discomfort and scrubbed his round belly against the earth. Light suddenly sparkled through the fog, at last placing the cabin;

and later, when the world was a wool-gray color, the fog rose and showed the cabin's shape beside the creek. Sparks sprayed from the chimney and the door opened, letting out a quick rectangle of yellow glow. One of the Barr men walked through it and went to the creek, dipping up a bucket of water. This was a hundred yards away, yet the voices of the others in the cabin came plainly across the heavy air. The man with the bucket—it was the oldest of the Barr boys, Ring—straightened and ran the canyon's rim with his glance. The squeal of the bucket bail was a clear sound when he turned back to the cabin. The stranger, Godry, rolled half on his side and brought his rifle forward—and was stopped by Ketchum's taut rumble: "Quit that." All these men were flattened at the edge of the rim, grayly blended with the earth. Day's light stepped up a full tone and the fog rolled back into the pines along the slope of the range. Woodsmoke drifted up and cut across the nostrils of these men; and farther along the creek the shapes of cattle began to stir.

"Not yet," murmured Ketchum. "We'll wait till they all come out."

13

---•◦•---

The War Comes

AT FIVE O'CLOCK day had come, gray and still sunless. Hallem was three hundred yards behind, holding the horses in a half-hollow. And farther back still, the land rose up to the thick pines of the broken country. Buff Sultan, who had said no word all during this vigil, thought now to look behind him and consider the exposure of this spot should anybody come out of those rear pines. But he said nothing, for Ketchum had grunted and all the men lying along the rim stirred a little, dragging their rifles forward.

Ring Barr had stepped out of the house again.

Ketchum murmured, "Wait," and Sultan looked toward the man, seeing how stone-set his face was, how bright the shine of his eyes. It shocked Sultan a little, this thing they were so coolly prepared to do; it was a sensation that crawled along his nerves and made his stomach muscles tight. Ketchum and the bearded Oldroyd were alike. They had been through the old fight and they remembered it too well; and all these years the memory had burned in them, tempering their hatred to a hardness nothing could break. To them the Barrs were savages, to be treated as such. It was, he realized, an honest attitude, untouched by any matter of conscience. All that they had been through made them this way. He could recall that his father, too, had been this way. But for him the moments got worse and he lay there and went down suddenly into a private hell. These Barr boys were his own generation, they were people, they were human. Only, it was too late to tell this to Ketchum. His pride wouldn't let him draw back.

He rested there while the moments piled up, and he

113

watched Ring Barr stroll around the cabin toward the corral.
He turned his head, the strain of waiting growing too great,
and saw Oldroyd's face in profile—calm and unstirred, his
bony hands relaxed on the rifle stock. Dobe Hyde was at the
far end of the row. And at once, for some fathomless reason,
Dobe Hyde brought up his rifle and took aim.

Ketchum began to speak. Ring Barr was almost around the
corner of the cabin—and one of the Barr relations had come
to the door. At that moment Dobe let go.

The bullet caught Ring Barr in the back, literally breaking
it. The force of the blow bent him in the middle and pushed
him on a foot or so; and this was the way he fell, wheeling
forward and sidewise, and never moving after he struck. His
hat rolled along the earth.

Ketchum hauled himself on his knees, passionately cursing
Dobe, and dropped flat again. The man in the cabin's door
ducked back and at once one of them began firing out of the
window, dusting up the soil along the edge of this rim.

Ketchum, still bitterly cursing, said: "Well, let 'em have
it."

Afterwards all of them here began to pump shots at the
cabin's exposed window. All but Buff Sultan. He lay flat, rifle
extended in front of him but not lifted.

There were seven guns pouring bullets at the cabin and no
shots coming back. All the glass of the window was carried
away and dust boiled around the doorway. Ketchum said,
"Some of you boys start workin' on those cows."

Dobe Hyde instantly complained: "Don't shoot beef. We
can get that later."

Shots unexpectedly began to reach up here. Ketchum said:
"They climbed out the back window," and Sultan could see a
rifle's barrel project around the cabin corner.

Oldroyd crawled back and took another position on the
rim, targeting the cattle in the lower end of the canyon. He
sighted and fired quite coolly, like an old buffalo hunter;
bringing down the beef farthest away so as not to stampede
the herd. Meanwhile the Barrs had quit answering. There
was, Sultan could see, a blind spot running back from the
cabin toward the nearest timber, a distance of perhaps thirty
feet that could be run in safety. Beyond that lay another few
yards of exposed ground that the Barrs would have to cross
before they reached the timber. Dobe Hyde had already calculated that, for he called out:—

"Take a sight beyond the cabin. They'll make a run."

"Crawl down the rim farther," said Ketchum, "so you can get a better shot."

Dobe grunted, "Whope," and fired. One of the Barrs was rushing over that exposed strip, low and fast. The bullet from Dobe's gun broke dust behind him; and suddenly all the line had let go at him; but he faded into the timber and from this shelter began to rake the rim with a steadier fire.

Ketchum said at once: "All right. We crawl out of this."

Sultan backed up on his belly a good hundred feet before rising. The rest of them followed suit and walked on to the horses. Sunlight began to show in the east and the fog had faded from the broken country. They climbed into their saddles and sat there momentarily, waiting for Ketchum to make up his mind.

"They got the idea," he said at last. "We might of done better—but they won't venture down here again. Anyhow this racket will be pullin' the rest of the family over here. So we fade. God damn you, Dobe."

Sultan considered the timber above them, not liking this exposed location. He said so. "We better get out of this meadow."

Ketchum and Oldroyd regarded him with a close, sharp interest. "Didn't get your barrel very hot, Buff," suggested Ketchum. "Buck fever, maybe?"

"Let's go," said Sultan irritably.

They wheeled and started upgrade for the trees. Oldroyd lagged back. He said, "Wait," and got off his horse to tighten the cinch. The rest of them had gone on a little way; and afterwards he straightened beside the horse, looking back toward the cabin.

They were all waiting for him, their horses fiddling restlessly, when the morning quiet was again broken, this time by the flat explosion of a gun in the pines before them. It was a blast almost in their faces. Dobe yelled at the top of his lungs and wheeled and rushed for the timber at a headlong pace, towing the others behind him in whirling confusion. The ambusher let go again and Sultan ducked low in the saddle, feeling the bullet pass near. After that they were safely in the pines, rushing along a faint trail.

But Sultan, who was last, looked behind him as he reached the timber, and saw Oldroyd lying dead by his horse.

After leaving Edith at the deserted house, Dan Barr started homeward through the broken land, his mind confused and his thoughts reaching no end. Somewhere in the depths of the ridge he pitched a cold camp and rolled up in the saddle blanket, staring at the cold glitter of stars so remotely above the treetops. For him, at intervals like this when his personal affairs seemed hopeless, there was a comfort in this kind of aimless, lonely wandering. The wildness of the earth flowed around him, getting into his bones and into his mind, erasing the tension of his troubles. In the night was a timeless swing, a vast rhythm that caught him up and bore him away from the little things of man; in the night ran the undertone of a life that had no break and no end, while above him was a space that laid its everlasting mystery across his thoughts, humbling him and yet reaching into the farthest corners of his being and rousing there the faint immortal flame that lies in every man.

So he camped here, falling asleep with the half-howl and half-bark of the coyote in his ears; and he woke before the gray dawn fully came. Thereafter taking the trail homeward, by way of the line cabin canyon, he heard the firing of Dobe Hyde's party from afar, and reached the edge of the timber just as those men were rushing away. He knew the meaning of it when he looked down from this high place and saw a shape motionlessly sprawled in the dust by the cabin. All his hopes fell in ruin, and he knew where his part lay, regardless of his wishing. Pulling up his gun he killed Oldroyd with a single shot. His second bullet missed its mark.

Afterwards Dobe Hyde's party had rushed on through the timber—the sound of their departure dying a little too suddenly to convince him that they actually were gone. So he galloped across the clearing and found a trail down the rim's side into the canyon, calling out to protect himself from chance fire. His brother Fay and the two other men, his cousin Creed and his uncle Will, trotted out from among the trees. All of them gathered around the dead Ring.

Fay said: "They gone?"

"I guess so."

"I saw somebody fall up there."

"Oldroyd," said Dan and looked down at Ring. The bullet had killed his brother instantly. There had been no time, he thought, for Ring to show shock or pain or fear. One minute he had been alive; the next moment he was dead.

He lifted his head and saw no expression on the other men's faces, which was their way—the Barr taciturnity covering whatever they might really feel. Coldness explained part of it; and a kind of Indian stoicism explained part of it. It was that iron quality in his family he most hated, that taciturnity which placed Katherine and himself so much apart from the rest. There were no light and no laughter in his father nor in his brothers, and light and laughter were things he had needed.

But he could look now at Fay, whom he had never really understood, and see in his brother's eyes the flash of a spirit that was like his own. And between them, though nothing was said, was a sudden closeness. Neither wisdom nor desire had any part in it; it was, really, the old, old pattern that made a man answer to his blood. It compelled him to say now, as laconically as his brother would have said it: "Guess we better get out of here."

Fay said "Yeah," and went over to Dan's horse. He drew the Spencer from its boot and removed the round magazine from the gun's butt, his eyes examining the load. He replaced the gun and turned squarely on Dan: "You fired twice?"

"Second shot didn't hit anything."

"The first one counted most," said Fay gently. "I reckon you're all right, Dan."

After that they said very little more. They lashed Ring across the saddle of his horse, let out the extra stock, and turned up the canyon toward the ranch house five miles away.

"I guess," said Dan, "we won't be comin' back to this canyon very soon."

Fay's lips were small and close and his lids squeezed most of the light out of his eyes. "Soon as we get Ben Maffitt down from the Pocket we'll do some visitin' of our own."

Dan murmured, "I wouldn't be too sure."

An hour later they came into the yard. Pedee and Katherine were there, waiting. Dan saw his father's frame grow higher and thinner; he saw his father's face lose all expression. Katherine cried out, "Ring!" Her face whitened under the sudden sunlight pouring out of the low east. There had never been any sympathy in Dan Barr's heart for his father, but he could feel the old man's grinding hurt; in Pedee's eyes for a moment lay something hard to watch. But it was only for a moment. Afterwards Pedee's eyes were empty windows opening into an empty room.

He said: "Bring him into the house."

Dan and Fay lifted Ring's body from the saddle. It was Cousin Creed who stood by and explained the fight, his slow talk not accented at all. Dan and Fay carried Ring into the front room and put him on the couch, and it was Fay who bent down to wipe the dust from Ring's pale face. They came out just as Pedee walked along the hall. He passed them, closing the living room door as he went in. They heard his feet drag across the floor in there—and stop.

Fay muttered, "He liked Ring best," and went out of the house rapidly.

Dan cut into the kitchen and sat down at the table, laying both his arms across the cloth. He was like that, struggling with his hard thoughts, when Katherine came in. She walked around the table so that she could see his face.

"We're all in it now, Dan."

He said: "I guess so."

"Nothing," she said bitterly, "nothing good will ever come to any Barr. I feel most sorry for you. You didn't want this kind of a life but you're pulled into it. And I think you've lost something else."

"Maybe you know," he countered.

"I have guessed."

He looked down at the table, shaking his head at the strange feelings slicing so painfully through him. "I have always figured the Barrs were a little more than half-wrong on this thing. But right or wrong, a man can't run from his family. So I guess that's all."

She said: "Jim Majors started this."

"I guess he did. But it's funny: I can't hate the man or wish him poorly. It's a job he came here to do and he never made any bones about it. I can admire him for that."

She said with a desperate intensity: "I wish I could hate him!"

"We got enough hate in this family now. Don't add any more."

The Ketchums, father and son, branched off from the party, the older man continuing on to the Oldroyds' with the hard news. A few miles later, Buff Sultan left Hyde's group and cut over the ridge of his place. Edith was waiting anxiously for him; she saw the worst of the story in his face. She didn't have to ask him. He blurted it out.

"We caught part of the Barrs in the line cabin and Dobe killed Ring. Then we started back home. There was a man up in the timber—coming out of the ridge trail, I guess. We don't know who it was. He got Oldroyd." He looked at her with all that fresh and brutal fight in his eyes. It weighted him down. "What a hell of a thing, Edie," he groaned. "I didn't want it to be murder!"

She said; "And now Dobe has you all."

He groaned: "I shouldn't have gone with him. What am I to tell Mrs. Oldroyd?"

She was a fair girl, a full-hearted girl. Her lips and her eyes showed her feelings then. "What about Ring? Ring was a human being, too."

"Well, we're in it now. If that damned Majors had only stayed out of this country . . ."

She stopped him, quite sharp with her words. "Don't blame the wrong man."

"Well, we were getting along all right till he came."

She shook her head. "No, we weren't. But everybody will blame him—and hate him that much more." She was thinking of Majors then, remembering the sadness lying behind his smile; remembering how his eyes had mirrored so much that he knew about people. "He knew in the beginning how it would be," she murmured. "How terribly lonely it must make him. How he must hate people for their blindness. Buff—there is the only honest man in our valley. And probably he'll die for it."

He said: "'I wish to God I knew who that was, up in the timber," and went restlessly out of the room.

Edith Sultan said quietly, to herself, "I think I know—I think I know."

It was for her, as for so many others in this valley, the end of hope. The lines were drawn tight and the war was on, and her own personal happiness, little as it had been, went down into the ruins. She stood quite still in the room, her expressive face sad as she thought of all this. In the end she went out of the house, saddled up her horse, and left the yard.

Buff called after her: "You've got to quit riding the ridge, Edie."

She said, "I'll be back," and struck into the timber. When

she reached the deserted house she wrote a single word on a scrap of paper and hammered it above the fireplace with an old nail—and looked at it with eyes blurred by tears, and then went away.

The word was: Good-by.

14

Hidden Maneuvers

MATT OLDROYD came into Reservation with a team and light wagon at nine o'clock that morning and found Jim Majors lounging in the sunlight at the edge of the hotel.

Matt stopped there. He said: "I'm going over the ridge to pick up my father. He was killed three hours ago."

The big deputy's head lifted but he didn't stir from the wall and he didn't show surprise.

Matt said: "You already heard about it?"

"No," said Majors. "You're the first to tell me. I'm sorry, Matt."

It was this unbreakable calm, this capacity to resist surprise, that always stirred Matt Oldroyd's wonder. There seemed to be in the big man a strange foreknowledge of things to happen, a kind of intuition regarding the acts of men. He stood there now so quietly, as though he were looking into the future and seeing other things Matt could not see.

"Dobe Hyde sent his riders over last night," said Matt, "to pick up Dad and Sultan and Ketchum. Ketchum came back early this mornin' to tell us what happened. Was eight or nine of 'em, includin' Dobe's outfit. They camped on the rim above the Barr line cabin. Dobe shot Ring Barr. This was about daylight. The rest of the Barrs got into the trees. Ketchum led the outfit back for home. Somebody in the broken country happened to be watchin'. His shot caught Dad. Nobody knows who."

"Matt," repeated Majors, "I'm sorry."

Matt looked over to the dining room doorway and discovered Tony. She had been listening to him, her cheeks soft and

121

sad. He stared down at his boots, a gawky young man turned uncertain by all that had occurred.

"I knew somethin' was going to happen," he murmured. "But I couldn't come and tell you last night. You understand?"

"Sure," murmured Majors. "So what now, Matt?"

"I reckon I'll ride over and get Dad."

"And what next?" said Majors in his easy voice.

Matt shook his head. "I don't know. It's kind of beyond me."

"You'll string with Dobe, maybe?"

Matt drew a long breath. "Maybe that's what I'm supposed to do. Maybe I ought to lose my head and go shootin', like everybody else. God knows. He was my old man and I reckon I ought to take up the grudge. That's the way he drilled it into me. That's the way all the old ones drilled it into us young fellows. So I ought to go kill a Barr—and then a Barr should come and hunt me. And twenty years from now my kids would be shootin' the Barr kids, if any of us grow up to have kids."

He ran out of breath. Majors' lips made a long, faintly smiling line; but it was the wistfulness of that smile which now, as before, stirred Matt's wonder. The big man was tough and he had a streak of raw courage in him that could be brutal. Matt had seen it. Yet always, behind that smile and behind the heavy gray of the man's eyes, was something like profound knowledge and profound regret. It made him different, it set him apart. Maybe it was a loneliness that came of knowing too much and seeing too much. Matt thought about it, his admiration as strong as ever; and he said:—

"If I pack a gun it will be to bust this whole damned thing up—if anybody knows the way to bust it up."

"You've got a head," said Majors gently, "and you think like a man. I'll remember that."

Matt suddenly lifted his hat at Tony, his cheeks distinctly red. He grabbed the reins and clucked at the horses, sending them out of town by the ridge road. There was a fullness in his heart, rising from the big man's compliment. He cleared his throat two or three times and settled the team to a steady trotting until the road began to climb the ridge's quick grade. Around eleven o'clock, having threaded the rough country by one dim trail and another, he came upon the clearing where his father still lay.

He was in risky country and knew it, yet he stood over his father a moment and felt a quick rage at the crowd who had run on and left him here; a rage at their indifference and their lack of sympathy. Afterwards he lifted the elder Oldroyd into the wagon and tucked a blanket around him and turned from the clearing, taking another set of trails which would lead him past the deserted house.

He was thinking then, with the regret common to all men, of the understanding he had never achieved with his father. He could go back far into his memory and recall his first boyhood impressions of a tall man looking down at him with a pair of eyes, so cold . . . with a voice that was so impatiently blunt with him when he made his mistakes . . . He was a kid wanting affection from his father, but he knew now that his father, embroiled in the first war with the Barrs, had tried to drive some of the steel of his own belligerent, righteous nature into him, had tried to mature him early for other fights that were coming. His father had grown up in a dog-eat-dog world, and he had wanted his son to take a proper part in that world. Maybe it was his way of showing affection, this hardening of a kid to roughness and discipline and hurts. Maybe. All he knew now was that the distance between them grew always wider, and now there was no way of closing it. His mother had taken Tony in as an orphan; but it was his father who had sent Tony away as soon as she was old enough to work, fearing the girl would bring out a weakness in him, in Matt.

The weakness, Matt told himself, had been there. The wildness of youth had been in him and in Tony, and something strong and bright as fire had powerfully impelled them. That too was in the past, beyond repairing now. So he thought, and so he rode, his blond head bowed and his eyes fixed on images so vivid yet so everlastingly gone.

As soon as Matt Oldroyd left Reservation Tony went up to her room and put on a pair of old riding pants and a man's blue shirt, and crossed to the stable to borrow a horse. She rode directly to the deserted house which once had been her home.

Her mother had died; her father, one day ten years ago, had been killed. On that day old man Oldroyd and his wife, riding up in a buggy, had packed her few things and taken her home. She had not said anything to them, nor had they asked if she wished to go. It was something that had happened to her, beyond her control, as so many pieces of her life had been beyond control.

Since that time she had never returned to the house, not wanting to be hurt again as she had been in that day of departure. She could not precisely explain to herself now her reasons for turning up the ridge along the well-worn trails of her childhood, nor did she try; for there was in this girl a simplicity that seldom sought explanations and a sweetness that lived on emotion and not by thought. But it was, though she did not know it, a flight backward. Suddenly in her was a hunger for a peace and warmth and security she had so long been without. And so because she could remember those things in childhood, she turned up the ridge to that old hearthstone.

The sight of the house, shabby and windowless and sagged, was a shock that stopped her on the margin of the clearing. She had remembered it as a home, its doors closed against heat and rain, with a light shining out of its windows and a curl of smoke at the chimney top. It had been that way when she left it—and so it had remained in her memory. And this now was the cruelty of time, fading and killing and decaying all things; she knew at once there was no comfort here. And though her life had ground into her a patience and a kind of dull fortitude she felt loss go through her and leave an emptiness that was pain.

Afterwards she went inside and saw how hard the place had been used by weather and cattle. She saw the note nailed above the fireplace and read it incuriously, and went up the unsteady stairs. The large bedroom had been for her parents, through whose thin partitions she had once heard the drawling talk of her father late at night, a steady tone to comfort her in the darkness. She went into her own room. There had been a little crib in the far corner for her brother John who had died so young; and the other corner had held her bed, made of pine slats and rawhide thongs. Lying here at night, just before her mother took the lamp away, the cone of light had shone on a cluster of rosebuds in the ceiling wallpaper. She could remember her mother coming in and casting a shadow against the wall, and waiting there while she repeated: "Now I lay me down . . ." And with each word of that childhood prayer her eyes had counted off one of those rosebuds. Then her mother had bent to kiss her and take the lamp away. All the paper had long since fallen from the ceiling. There had been a fragrance to her mother's clothes and to her mother's hair.

· At the window, she sighted the base of the nearest pine tree, where her father had built the doghouse for Pete, the woolly shepherd. The tree itself, in that day, had reached only as high as the roof; now it was half again as tall. Beyond it lay the trail to the spring. She had thought, from all the times she had packed water up that little hill, that it would be beaten into the ground forever; but the trail was buried now beneath the forest mat.

These were the things she remembered, turning back down the stairs. They were fresh, vivid images that came to her, one after another, as though all this still was and would always be. She could close her eyes and bring everything back. And did. And opened her eyes again and saw the gray ruin.

She stood with her back to the wall, a full-breasted, soft-bodied girl with long lips turned gentle and eyes filled with the shadows of misery. There wasn't any anger in her and there wasn't any resentment, for these were qualities of a fighting spirit and Tony wasn't a fighter. She was a girl turned humble and half-afraid by hard ways of life, and taught to expect nothing; a girl who, hungering for warmth and affection, had known little of it since that long-gone day when she had stepped out of this house. The world was a brutal place, as Tony well knew; yet the knowledge only made her more wistful. In many ways she was still like a child, cherishing her dreams while the crying and the dusty brawls of the world passed over her head entirely.

This way she remained, her expression lightening and darkening to the play of her thoughts, when a rider galloped across the clearing and jumped down. Dan Barr came through the door and saw her and stopped immediately. Surprise widened the thorough darkness of his eyes and went away. He looked tired and nervous and at the end of his rope. He said, "Hello, Tony," and walked straight to the fireplace, attracted by the sheet of paper tacked over it. Tony watched his shoulders hunch forward and drop as he read that single word. She didn't know the handwriting, but he apparently did and it seemed to mean something to him, for when he turned back all the expressiveness of his face was gone. He was the best of the Barrs; but now, to Tony, he looked as black and as faithless as the rest of the tribe.

Her voice was a faint melody in the empty room. "What's the matter, Dan?"

He looked at her a long while, strangely and without hope. "You grew up in this house, didn't you, Tony?"

"Till I was ten."

He said: "Sure I remember. You must hate the Barrs. God knows you've got plenty of reason."

It was the way men spoke of hate that always disturbed her. It was their unrelenting memories of injuries done that she could never understand.

She said, "I don't hate anybody. What good would it do me? What good does it do anybody?"

He kept his eyes steadily raised on her, strain continuous in them. "Tony," he said, "it's a terrible world."

She shook her head, wiser now than he would ever be. "Not the world, Dan. Not the hills or the rain or the sky. The world is so beautiful. It's the people who are fools—who spoil everything."

"Sure. And still you don't hate 'em for what they've done?"

Her lips turned to a faint smile. "No," she murmured. "No."

A wagon's wheels set up a groaning in the morning's quiet, the sound of it whipping Dan Barr around. She had not noticed this muscular tension until now, but he went across the room in quick catlike steps and paused there, both hands lying flat along his thighs. He had his body swung forward. His head turned slowly, to show how carefully he kept his eyes on that approaching wagon. Out there Matt Oldroyd's brief, seldom-stirred voice rose:

"Well, Dan?"

In Tony was a thorough indifference to the quarrels of men, yet now she moved suddenly across the room and pressed Dan Barr aside and stepped to the porch. Dan Barr said, irritably, "Don't get in front of me," and moved down from the porch into the yard. He said, "Hello, Matt," with a distant civility, with a high faint ring in the words. She remained on the porch, so wise in the ways of men, and felt hostility flow along the yard. They were like two strange dogs, stiffened against each other and waiting.

Matt Oldroyd was a slack shape on the wagon seat. His big hands clung idly to the reins and his shoulders were dropped forward. Beneath the shadow of the hatbrim, his long face remained darkly composed. The edges of his yellow hair showed against his sun-darkened skin and his eyebrows made two short bleached lines. He was a larger man than Dan Barr and a quieter one, and once all three of them had been children roaming these hills. From her place on the porch she saw a shape in the wagon box, covered by a blanket. It was that which moved her quickly across the yard until she stood below Matt. Dan Barr called again, "Don't get in front of me, Tony."

Tony said, "Matt—I'm sorry."

Matt Oldroyd watched Dan Barr, the solemn composure not stirred by any expression.

He said: "What are you afraid of, Dan?"

She looked carefully at Matt, and was sure of him; and wheeled and saw Dan Barr turned altogether still, with the iron of the Barrs showing like a stain in his eyes, with the gaunt lines of the Barrs dug into his cheeks.

Dan said: "We're not friends, Matt."

"That may be. I do not know—and I'm not passin' judgment."

Dan Barr said swiftly: "I don't want to talk to you."

She saw them both, one man deliberately locking himself behind a barrier, and one man slowly growing before her eyes. It was Matt who grew. He sat loosely on the wagon's seat, thoughtfully refusing a quarrel. He made a big and patient shape against the sunlight, with a quietness that came out like water damping down flame. Somewhere in his riding silence he had risen above his careless youth.

"Then," he remarked, "you'd better catch up and go, Dan."

"You'll be fighting against me soon enough."

"Not sure," murmured Matt. "Not sure."

Dan Barr shook his head and his eyes traveled to the wagon box and jerked away with a recoil Tony could plainly see. He went about the head of the team to his own horse and swung to the saddle, thin-shaped in the day's long light. A moment later he rushed out of the clearing.

Matt said to the girl: "What brought you here?"

"I wish I hadn't come," she told him. She noticed the change of his face and instantly added: "Oh, no, Matt. I came alone. But there isn't anything left that I remembered. I wish I hadn't come."

He turned the reins around the brake handle and slid his long legs down. He took off his hat, as he always did before her, with a gesture half-awkward and half-humble. "For you," he said, "nothing has been right. You've had the worst of it all the way through—and none of it was your doing. I have thought of that a lot."

She said: "I'm sorry about your father."

"I believe you are—and that's a strange thing, for he never did you a kindness. He put you out of our house."

"Maybe he was right," she said, in a long low tone.

He said, "Tony, there's something in you, like—" but he couldn't put his tongue to it and stood there with his bronzed forehead marked by one deep line. "A sweetness you always had—and never lost."

She said, "Don't feel sorry for me." But his eyes watched her in a way that was quite personal, with something in them that sent warmth into the cold places of this girl who had been starved for warmth. Her lips changed and color ran along her cheeks pleasantly.

He said: "Certain things I have never ceased to regret."

She had a pride—and that pride was touched. "I don't want regret, Matt."

"I know," he said. "I know. I'm not tryin' to give out charity."

She looked at him. "Why, what made you that wise?"

His shoulders lifted a little and dropped. "I've had a long time to think."

But she was remembering the years between and all that had happened to her, and what she had been and what she couldn't be to a man like Matt. Fatalism covered her expression and deadened her voice. "Maybe once, Matt. For us. But it is too late now."

She went away from him to her horse and rode quickly from the meadow. Matt remained there by the wheel of the wagon, his glance going after her. When she had disappeared he got back to the wagon seat and drove on.

From the corner of the hotel, Jim Majors watched Matt drive the wagon toward the ridge and later saw Tony ride from town. The sun was up, but the scent of winter cut the windless morning rather sharply. The spires of the Silver Lode showed a deeper dusting of white. In a week or so the first winter storm would sweep the land.

These were idle thoughts dropped into the main stream of his thinking. He lighted a cigar and put the corner of a shoulder more comfortably against the hotel wall, reflecting that Matt had brought in the first news of a fight now almost four hours old. It was a little strange, this delay, in a country where news of violence spread on the wings of the wind. The stable hostler had been across the square, listening to Matt's talk; and now the hostler was telling the town. The little man limped into the Old Dixie, and limped out; and went on down to the print shop, and crossed the street with a pegging briskness. The saloonman came from the Old Dixie and strolled directly up to Charley Chavis' office. Broderick came as far as the doorway of the hotel, speaking across Majors' shoulder. "You have played hell," he said, and stamped back into his place.

It was ten-thirty when another rider trotted down the Barr ranch road and entered the Old Dixie. The saloonkeeper meanwhile had returned to his place. Presently Charley Chavis came down and beckoned to the feed store man. Both of them went into the Old Dixie. The printer walked out of his shop, destined also for the saloon. But he paused at the door and threw one glance across to Majors, his face rather oddly white in the morning sun, and went in.

The town, usually so asleep, was wide awake. Majors could feel that change and understand it. Reservation was the cockpit of these stormy hills, extremely sensitive to the forces that played against it from either direction. These shopkeepers lived for profit, not caring a great deal which side held the upper hand, but fearful always of any change that might draw the wrath of the factions down upon it. This, Majors knew, was the prime reason for the hatred the people of Reservation showed him.

At eleven his cigar, carefully nursed, was smoked out and his patience, always so difficult to control, was about gone. He crossed the street and went beyond the vacant building into the general store operated by a quiet man named Webber, and by Webber's wife. He bought two more cigars and went out, and was walking away when Webber's wife called his name: "Majors!"

Like that. Quick and peremptory. He turned, seeing her ample shape sway through the store. She was a solid, red-faced woman with high cheekbones. She faced him intolerantly. She said: "Why couldn't you leave this country alone?"

He lifted his hat and said, "My apologies," and saw Webber futilely waving his hands, inside the store. He turned from her but her voice went up to a strident pitch and she ran after him and caught his arm and pulled him around.

She was angry in the way a man grows angry, with the desire to inflict physical punishment. Her voice lost its restraint. "Answer me! Why don't you leave us alone? My God, here's two more men dead, and now we'll have a war! Nobody wanted you here! We can run our own business. If I was a man I'd do what no other man around here has the nerve to do. I'd shoot you!"

He had no answer. He stood there while people came into the square and stood listening. Mrs. Webber's voice lifted upward and upward. Blood rushed to her cheeks until they were raw red. She yelled: "Before God, I would!" and slapped him twice with a swinging force. Her nails dragged welts upon his skin and she waited uncontrollably before him while the silence got past enduring. The rounds of his eyes were pale gray, and he said with a wicked quiet: "Are you through?" And then she struck him again and cried out something he didn't understand, and walked away.

Majors wiped his face. The cigars were still in his hand. He put them in a pocket and crossed the street, going into the hotel. Broderick waited there, grayly grinning. Broderick's voice was as dry as dust. "Gives you the idea."

Majors cruised the lobby at reaching, restless strides. Fury shook his muscles. He said, "Waiting's hardest, Broderick."

Broderick grunted: "What's to wait for?"

Majors stopped. He kicked a chair before a round poker table in the corner of the lobby and sat down. His fingers reached out and closed around a pack of cards lying there. He didn't answer Broderick.

Broderick repeated the question: "Waitin' for what, Sundown?"

Majors swung hard enough to carry the chair half around, its legs squalling on the boards. He looked at Broderick, the paleness of his eyes brighter and brighter. Broderick closed his mouth and went out of the lobby.

It was a wildness working its way through Majors. It was a weakness that unsteadied the balance of his mind and turned him rash and pushed him toward thoughtless action. Better than any other man, he knew that he balanced now on the edge of something that would destroy him if he gave ground.

That was why he sat in the chair, his shoulders crowded forward and his hand squeezing the deck of cards out of shape.

He waited for that terrific gust of recklessness to pass by. He waited for the stinging feel of Mrs. Webber's slap, which was the symbol of Reservation's hatred, to wear away. He had been a peace officer long enough to know the loneliness of that job. Whatever he did and whatever he said would be misunderstood, nor could he speak in a way that would make them understand. He dealt in the worst part of the man-animal's nature, in passion and prejudice and evil. People watched him for weakness and they watched him for partiality and sooner or later, somewhere along the line of his work, he would lose even the confidence of the honest ones. There was a cruelty in the death of Oldroyd and in the murder of Ring Barr that was a direct result of seeds sown long before his time. Yet Reservation blamed him for those deaths because he had upset an uneasy peace. His actions had a far purpose few people could see—which was a real peace and an open country. People had to die before that came, and somebody had to lose before that came. Of all the actors in this gray scene only Matt Oldroyd seemed to know that.

So he remained thoroughly alone, as he had known he would be. Yet there were times when his isolation was hard to bear, when the hostile silence of people stung his temper and, as now, turned him rash. He sat still, squeezing the deck of cards more and more tightly, and waited for that tempest to pass by.

Broderick came back. "Sundown, Dobe Hyde's in this fight now. Up to the hilt. He organized that raid."

"I was waiting for that."

"Why?"

"I had to see him tip his hand. You can't fight a man unless you know which side he's on."

"Well, you know now. So, then—"

"Not yet. One more man has got to show his hand."

"So you wait," said Broderick, the rumble of discontent in his voice, "while somebody else prob'ly dies."

"Just so," said Majors. He laid his long fingers on the table, narrowly watching them. The bones of his face showed flat and heavy through the skin.

Broderick cruised the length of the lobby and back again. He stopped at the table, the point of his steel arm resting on it.

"Sundown," he said, "I kinda been likin' you. But you're dodgin' somethin'. You brought on this war. It would of come anyhow—but you brought it on quick. Oldroyd's dead, and the east fork folks have gone to Dobe Hyde for help. So the east fork folks are out of it, because Dobe will make it his own fight and take the rewards. All right. It is Dobe Hyde against the Barrs. One is no better than the other, but you brought that on—and it's your responsibility. You'll take one side or the other. You got to. Which side?"

"I'll wait," said Majors, gently, "for one more thing to happen."

"Wait?" yelled Broderick and struck the table with his steel hook. "No! By God, you can't dodge! One thing or the other."

Majors said in the same dead tone, "Just so. One side or the other. When the time comes I won't duck."

Broderick growled: "You got a hell of a choice. Both sides are wrong—and you carry a star, which makes you responsible for your conduct. I think you played it poorly."

Majors looked up at Broderick. "Why are you worried?"

Broderick stared at the big deputy for quite a while, and finally shrugged his shoulders. There was a dry reluctance in his voice. "Hate to see you make a mistake, Sundown. You're a man I admire."

He evidently meant to say more, and didn't. For at that moment a pony rushed across the square and halted by the hotel. The next moment Katherine Barr half-walked and half-ran through the lobby door. Riding color flushed her cheeks, and her eyes were brightly bitter when she turned them on Majors.

She said, "I want to talk to you."

Majors pulled his long legs from beneath the table. He took off his hat and laid it on the table; and stood up, a heavy and tough and taciturn shape in the room.

He said to Broderick, "Close the door on the way out,"—and waited until Broderick had gone.

15

Majors Makes His Mistake

HE SAID: "You are going to tell me I have brought all this on your family, that I'm responsible for your brother's death. You're going to say I am a killer, like Maffitt."

She flung one word at him in a throaty whisper: "Yes!"—and squared her shoulders. She wore her habitual riding suit, trousers tucked into short boots, and a man's cotton shirt whose opened collar lay back from the whiteness of her throat. She held a quirt in one hand, the knuckles pale from the pressure she put on it. Her cheeks were quite colored from her riding and her temper, and that brilliant anger kept brightening her eyes. There was a fire in this girl that made her lovely, that brought out the rich and headlong qualities of a spirit otherwise hidden behind the cool reserve of her lips. He could stand here now and admire the stirring picture of a full woman and feel the strange things a man feels when he looks upon beauty, and knows that it will never be for him.

He said very slowly, very quietly: "For whatever I have done to your family, Katherine, I'll pay out in regret."

She cried: "Why do you make it so hard for me? I came here to hurt you as much as I could!"

"A man's conscience will do that to him."

"Then you know you've been wrong?"

He looked at her with a smile shadowed by wistfulness. He shook his head. "No, Katherine, I don't think I have been. I said I'd regret all that's happened. But it had to happen."

She flung her question at him: "Do you think Dobe Hyde is better than the Barrs?"

"No," he said. "No."

"Remember that, Jim. For it was Dobe who killed Ring. And it will be Dobe who tries to run us out of the valley. Maybe my family has been wrong. As wrong as the Sultans and Ketchums, who always have hated us. I don't know. Maybe we've been wrong to be friendly with Maffitt. It's hard to know what's right and what isn't when you're fighting to live. That's what my family has been doing for ten years. It's hard to be fair when your people are killed. I had an older brother who was shot in the first fight, years ago. That was Clay. And all this time the man who killed him has ridden this valley as though he had done something to be proud of. Matt Oldroyd's father killed my brother. Now Matt's father is dead, and you're blaming the Barrs."

His question prompted her gently: "How did Tony's father die, Katherine?"

She looked at him, her anger showing its first break. She said, in a quieter way: "I know."

"So," he said, "we have blood on both sides, and the quarrel would never die out."

"It might have died," she said, "if you had left us alone."

He lifted an arm, pointing through the door. "Before I had been in Reservation two hours a man was shot down. That's your country, Katherine. But I tried for a compromise. I got everybody together in this room. When I got them together I knew nothing would work."

"This is what I came to tell you," she said. "My brother Dan and I have always been less bitter than the rest of our family. We have wanted to be peaceful. But the east fork people are using Dobe Hyde, who will have his own way, who will stop at nothing. The Sultans are fools to trust him and the Ketchums are fools—and we will fight because we have to."

"I expect that," he said.

She said in a quick, protesting tone, "You can be so cruel at times."

"I have no hope of a kinder judgment," he told her. "Maybe I deserve none."

She stood still, watching the way his heavy face settled. Anger left her eyes completely and her lips softened from her thinking.

"There might have been a time," she murmured, "when I

could have judged you differently. I think you knew that yesterday on the ridge."

He nodded, not speaking, and watched the expressive turning of her features while a deep hunger woke and threshed through him and left him heavy-tempered again. There was a whiteness on her temples, at the edge of her shining black hair. He remembered that afternoon too clearly. One powerful flash, like heat, had touched them both—disturbing them in a manner they had both recognized. He thought of that and knew his chance had come to him then and had gone away; it wouldn't come again. The memory of violence and death would never let them reach that moment again.

She said, "Good-by, Jim," and left the lobby.

Broderick came immediately in from the street, breath running strongly through the man's deep lungs.

He said: "Charley Chavis dropped somethin' to Soder, which I caught on the bounce. Somebody saw Ben Maffitt ridin' the ridge a while back. Ridin' toward Dobe Hyde's valley."

Majors had started toward the dining room. He stopped and turned.

He said: "You think Chavis wanted you to hear that?"

Broderick looked steadily at Majors. "I didn't hear it. A certain friend of mine brought the news to me. I got a few telegraph lines of my own in this town, Sundown."

Majors wheeled into the dining room and ate dinner, and afterwards walked directly to the stable, saddling up. He had mounted and was lighting one of the store cigars when Doc Showers came in, on the half-run as usual.

Showers said, "Henry, get my rig," and watched Majors drag in the cigar's smoke with a thoroughly disapproving eye. "Hate to see you do that, son. Tobacco's like a common woman—a comfort you'll later regret."

Majors grinned and left the stable. He trotted across the square, turning into the east fork road. He let the horse have its run, afterwards settling to a casual pace along the willow-fringed Ute. Ketchum's house showed its white wall from afar and the afternoon breeze bit through his shirt. The land lay brown under the sunlight, with cattle here and there grazing the low pastures.

By Sultan's place he saw the girl Edith gaiting a horse in the yard. She waved at him and he drew in and waited until she came up.

She said: "You've heard about the shooting?"

"Yes."

"Well," she said with a directness he liked, "Buff was in on that. But he never lifted his gun. The thing has left him pretty sick. I want you to know that. Not apologizing, but you won't find any Sultans riding with Dobe again."

He said, "I'm glad to hear it."

She looked at him carefully. "Your horse is headed toward bad country. I think I'd better tell you so."

He lifted his hat and went on, soon turning into the canyon. Beyond it, he worked eastward through a high piney country, and around the middle of the afternoon came out on a ledge above Dobe Hyde's car-shaped house. Squatted down on his heels, he waited there.

The Pocket was two thousand feet higher than Reservation, and the bite of approaching winter had driven Maffitt's crowd into the kitchen. They sat around the table, playing an idle game of poker. Brick Brand now and then left the game to stoke up the stove. Maffitt, not playing, sat watching the other four, and was like that when Little Peters rode back from the valley.

"Well," he said, "the ball sure has opened. Dobe Hyde and some of the east fork crowd caught the Barr boys flat-footed this mornin' down at the line cabin. They killed Ring, knocked all the glass out of the cabin and trotted back home. Dan Barr walked into it and got Oldroyd."

The card game died. Maffitt said, "How'd you find out?"

"Stopped in at the Barr house." Little Peters' nose was red from riding and he went over to the stove, slapping his hands together. "Pedee said for you to come down. He wants to see you."

Maffitt was a thoroughly indolent shape in the chair, his huge bulk spilling over its edges. One arm lay on the table; his blunt fingers set up a slow, steady tapping and his lips crawled back from his teeth, as though he squinted at strong sunlight. All of them were quiet and thoughtful, considering their own fortunes in this. Brand reached out and collected the cards and laid the deck on the table, shuffling it and re-shuffling it.

Little Peters said: "The Barr family can't cut in, Ben."

Maffitt shook his head. "Through. I saw it comin'. This Majors is a smart man. He played for a break and he got it."

Brick Brand's eyes laid a narrowing attention on the cards. The cuts on his mouth—from the fight with Majors—were beginning to heal into long, irregular scars; and the fight had put something in his head that showed through his eyes like a permanent shadow. But he remained silent.

Little Peters spoke again. "Maybe. Still, he didn't figure on Dobe, who's been sleepin' in the background. Dobe's a wolf waitin' for the smell of meat."

Maffitt nodded. "Dobe will beat the Barrs—and he'll use Sultan and Ketchum for a while. Then he'll beat those boys too."

Brand broke his silence. "What about us?"

"You want to fight Dobe Hyde?" said Maffitt.

"Well, Pedee has stuck by us."

Little Peters came back from the stove, standing across from Maffitt. "If you figure to help Pedee, Ben, you talk for yourself. Not for me."

"Why, hell," said Brand, "he's helped us. We owe the man somethin'."

The rest of the crowd looked at him. Maffitt's lips were pulled back in that grimace which looked like a smile. He said, "You're a crook, Brick, and so am I, and we can't afford friends. We play with the winnin' side. Which is the winnin' side?"

"Dobe," said Peters. "No question."

"So . . ." said Maffitt, and got up and left the house.

Brick Brand's fingers kept mixing the cards. His face showed stronger color. He looked around the group with a distinct irritability. "Man can play straight with his friends, can't he?"

Little Peters said: "Don't be a damned fool, Brick."

Ben Maffitt saddled his horse and took the down trail. Near the river bridge he ducked into the timber, climbing steadily until he arrived at a point from which he could see the valley and the open country rolling off toward the broken land eastward.

The Barr house lay perhaps a thousand feet below him, its sheds and corrals making an irregular pattern in the brown earth. Some of the Barr men were grouped in the back yard. One of the crew, obviously keeping guard, stood on the canyon rim above the house.

Here Maffitt stopped and laid his great hands across the saddle horn while he watched.

There was in this huge hulk of a man the stirring of an emotion as near regret as he had ever known. Not for Pedee and not for the Barr fortunes—but for Katherine. There had been other times when Maffitt, traveling these wild hills by night, had paused here on the rock outcrop to watch the lights of that ranch shine out, and to think of the girl and to think of his own life with a hard wonder.

He laid no blame on anybody else for the turnings of that life. Bad as he was and merciless as he could be, he remained a thorough realist and permitted himself no excuses. He had been born to be what he was, and he knew it; and though the tricky and altogether brutal lessons of his life had been largely taught him by others, he knew that he had wanted to learn them and that he had been an apt pupil. He was not the kind to look back with self-pity. He had made his fun and he had kept his freedom. He had made his kills. He had matched his wits against the best of them. He had a name and he had the power to make men show fear in his presence. Life was a matter of survival. That was the greatest game of all and, for him, the only game worth playing—to stay alive when other men wanted him dead.

All this he felt without reasoning it out, for he was in no sense a philosopher. If he looked back now and saw those forks in the trail where he had stopped to make his choices, it was only because of a kind of impersonal curiosity, and not from regret, knowing well enough that those were the choices he would take again. Nevertheless he thought of them because of Katherine Barr, who was the first woman ever to break through the gray materialism of his mind and bring to him a hint of what he had missed. There had been a time when he had considered his chances with her, but as he came to know her better his innate realism had showed him the deep gulf he could not cross. Some things a man could have and some things a man could not have; and with this thought he put Katherine Barr behind him, and turned and rode on. He crossed the valley near the line cabin, reached the broken country and struck out for Dobe Hyde's.

Riding this roundabout way in no haste, his thinking came around to Jim Majors, whose first appearance in Reservation had been like a warning of something to come. Maffitt had ridden the trail too long not to have developed perceptions which were spooky and intuitive. He had felt the big man's power definitely. Certain qualities Majors possessed—a smartness to be seen in the corner angles of his eyes, a coolness, a nerveless kind of courage that could whip him to a point of deliberate killing.

Maffitt had made his cautious tries at the big man and had failed; and now, single-handed and deliberately, Majors had thrown the valleys into war, while standing back and watching. Yet even as he stood back he collected power into his hands. And because Ben Maffitt had a pride in the matter he saw the time soon coming when, if Majors still survived, the two of them must meet. The greatest game of all was to stay alive. But there were rules a man couldn't duck, if he wished to keep his self-respect and maintain his name. It was part of the game.

This was what he thought when he dipped into Dobe Hyde's little valley and rode up to the house. Dobe and two of his crew sat out in the sunlight, Dobe shabbier than the others. None of them made any motions when he came forward, nor did he give the place much inspection. He had a good deal of contempt for the outfit, knowing it to be wholly crooked; and so he had the assurance of one crook speaking to another.

He didn't get down. He stared at Dobe, who rested so indolent on the ground. He said: "So you made a play."

Dobe looked at him with his pale, smart eyes. "Thought you'd come along."

"Pretty sure of that, was you?"

Dobe grinned. "A man always bets accordin' to his hole card. Never saw that fail. What's your hole card, Ben?"

"You tell me."

"Well," drawled Dobe in his high voice, "you backed the wrong horse and now you're lookin' for a better bet. So you're here."

"I'll listen," said Maffitt.

"You're payin' the call," countered Dobe. "I'll listen."

Ben Maffitt's glance fell on one of the two other men lying on the ground—on Godry. He said: "Never saw you around this country before."

Dobe gave out a short bleat. "You'll see a few more strange faces pretty soon, friend."

"I'll make you a proposition," said Maffitt finally.

Dobe Hyde suddenly rose to his feet and abandoned his indifference. He had a sharpness in his voice. He was telling Maffitt what to do.

"No, I'll make the proposition, friend Maffitt. You stay up in that Pocket for a week and don't interfere. If the Barrs have trouble, don't come down."

"And what for me?"

"Same thing you had before," Dobe told him coolly. "Protection."

"You can promise that," pointed out Maffitt. "But can you fill the bill? How about Sultan or Ketchum? How about Majors?"

"Always like to handle one thing at a time," said Dobe, and let it go at that.

"All right," said Maffitt.

Dobe said: "This is Wednesday. Friday night you stay in the Pocket. Don't go near the Barrs."

Maffitt continued to look down on this dirty little man whose eyes were so cold and intelligent and sly. He considered Dobe through that long silence and saw him clearly, knowing there was nothing in the man he could trust. But if Dobe had far purposes he wasn't revealing, so had Ben Maffitt. They could make this bargain now with mutual profit; and fall out later.

So Maffitt said, "All right, Dobe," and turned and rode away. Godry made a faint gesture with his arm, at which Dobe shook his head. And these two and the kid Jett watched Maffitt fade into the timber.

"What'd you tell him Friday night for?" complained Godry. "He'll tell the Barrs."

"Because it won't be Friday night. It'll be tonight. I want you should run to your shack, Sam, and bring up those extra boys."

"That fellow," prophesied Godry, "will rustle you blind if you move into the south fork."

"One thing at a time," said Dobe, and let go his shrill, tittering laugh.

From his position on the ridge above Dobe's, Majors saw Maffitt arrive and later depart, and at last he knew a bargain had been reached by that pair. This was the final move for which he had been waiting, as he had told Broderick. He had not expected to see the transaction take place under his eyes; but he had believed that it would soon come about, knowing Maffitt's type of mind as he did. Here it had happened, and the politics of the country had reached balance again, temporarily and uneasily, so that one purpose might be achieved, which was the wiping out of the Barrs.

In Reservation he had seen that it was time for him to make his move. All things pointed to an attack on the Barrs by Dobe Hyde. He, himself, had brought that on. Now, since Dobe Hyde finally had come into the open, the matter was simplified. He could break the backbone of the fight by seizing Hyde on a charge of killing Ring Barr and by hustling him over the Pass into Jeff White's hands. The fundamental antagonism of the factions would still remain, even after Dobe's removal. But in getting rid of this one source of trouble, he would at once weaken the east fork's power to cause trouble; and in his mind was a half-formed plan to move against Maffitt once he had captured Dobe, thus reducing the Barr power. This was the way he saw it: to quench the fire bit by bit.

Meanwhile he saw one of Dobe's men trot from the ranch yard, heading eastward. It left only one man with Dobe, which was fair odds. Majors crawled back to his horse and stepped into the saddle; but looking again toward the house he found two more riders coming in from the broken country. He climbed off the horse and squatted down, waiting for a break.

It was four o'clock then. At six-thirty, the four were still moving around the house and he had no hope that he could better his chances. So, with dusk running heavily off the heights, he went to his horse and rode quietly down the slope. A light sprang suddenly from one of the house windows and he heard a voice, strongly Southern, murmur a few words. The smell of coffee lay in the wind.

He was within twenty yards of the house when one of the men came around from behind it and saw him. The shadows were fast thickening, and at this distance nothing was very clear. It was plain to Majors that the man wasn't sure.

The later slowed his step, and got as far as the open door of the house. Then he said: "Who's that?"

A chair scraped inside the house. Dobe Hyde's shrill voice called out: "Who's what?"

Another door opened and Majors saw a Negro pause there. This made three of them, with two more somewhere about.

The one who had challenged him called again in a quicker voice. "Sing out—what the hell?"

Majors said, "Dobe."

Dobe Hyde was in the other doorway, small and thin against the light. His head swung over and he said, "Well . . .?"

And at that moment the other two men showed up in the shadows, walking away from the nearest corral.

The man who had done all the talking yelled back at them: "Wait a minute! Something wrong here!"

Dobe said: "Sing out, friend."

Majors stepped from the saddle. In one quick motion he pushed the horse half around, making a shelter for himself against the fire of those five men.

Dobe Hyde took a backward step.

Majors said:—

"Walk out here, Dobe. I'm taking you in to town."

Dobe Hyde's voice was thin and squeaky in the semidark, and yet very cool, very sure. "Oh, no, friend Majors. Oh, no."

The two men near the corral began to run forward.

16

***

The Fight

MAJORS' SPENCER lay in the saddle boot, its butt touching his chest as he came against the horse. He hauled the gun out with a jerk of his arms, laid it across the saddle and drove one shot at the two men running up the yard. Dust broke in front of them. He said, "Wait a minute," and held his fire.

These two halted, their bodies slanting backward from the sudden effort. The Negro cook raised his arms high above his head, murmuring, "Nooh, Nooh." Dobe swayed from side to side in the central doorway, his thin shoulders seeming to shrink. Majors threw the gun's muzzle around on him. Dobe yelled, "Careful, friend!"

"Walk out here."

Dobe came a few feet forward and stopped. Majors called to the two farthest away: "Come up—come up."

Meanwhile the man nearest Majors hitched himself half-around. The light from the house came out and touched him, showing the sharp, scheming speculation in his eyes. He was a kid—pale-lipped and full of wickedness. He was calculating his chances, dangerously cool about it. Something got into this yard definitely then, and all that crowd caught it. It was a break they had waited for.

Dobe said, to the kid, "Well, Jett?"

Jett said, "Who's callin' the turns for this dance?"

The Negro, still holding his hands toward the sky, repeated, "Nooh, not me."

Dobe Hyde said, "Shut up, Baker." But a dry, gray grin broke over his face. "Friend Majors, you don't want me."

Majors felt the drift of their thoughts. They were deliber-

143

ately standing fast, putting the weight on him. They were watching him through these shadows and they were listening, and pretty soon recklessness would have its way and the break would come. He thought of that, and worked the Spencer's lever. It was a sharp, metallic sound in the silence—and like cold water on a fire, as he well knew it would be. He saw Dobe Hyde's shoulders twist at the report.

Majors murmured: "Tell the boys to mind, Dobe, or I'll blow a leg off your skinny carcass."

Dobe let out a reluctant, angered bleat. "All right, boys."

The two farthest away marched forward. Majors stopped them with a curt, "Wait."

Jett had started a slow turn, but the command froze him still and he laid a bright, wild glance on Majors. Wind lifted and dropped his chest rapidly.

Majors drawled, "Careful, kid. All right. Dobe, stay right where you are. The rest move over and back up against the shanty wall."

Jett retreated to the house wall and joined the other two, who moved up. The Negro sidestepped along the wall until he was with that group.

"Dobe," commanded Majors, "go get their guns. Be a little careful about it. Belts and all."

Dobe moved over. They were all bunched together, as he wanted them to be. But they were a tough lot, seasoned by trouble like this, and coolly waiting for the moment. He had trouble coming up; they knew it, and knew that he knew it. Dobe unbuckled the three belts—the Negro not being armed —and hooked them over his arm.

Majors said, "Back up to me."

Dobe obeyed, stepping around the gelding. Majors reached out and seized the belts with his free arm, throwing them over his saddle. He lifted Dobe's gun from its holster and hurled it behind him, far into the darkness. Two horses, all this while, stood near the corner of the house, and now Majors said: "Get on one of those horses."

Dobe spoke over his shoulder: "You're makin' a mistake, friend Majors."

"Go on."

Dobe shuffled to the nearest horse and climbed up. He waited there, putting all the work on Majors. Majors said, "Move into the yard and stop." He pushed the Spencer back into its boot, and drew his pocket knife and stepped over to

the other horse and slashed the webbing of the cinch. Dobe
had drifted down the yard a short distance and had stopped
again; he turned in the saddle, sending some silent signal
across to his still-placed crew. Majors walked back to the
gelding and slid into the saddle, pinching the captured gun
belts with his thighs to keep them in place. He shook out his
rope and dropped a loop over Dobe Hyde. "Pull your arms
through," he said, and afterwards took up the slack. He had
the little man held by the flanks, letting him use his arms.

Jett said: "Nice, mister. But what comes next?"

The kid was throwing a challenge at him. The kid was
waiting, and would never rest till he tried his luck. Majors sat
in the saddle a moment, realizing the dynamite lying behind
the dark and motionless patience they showed him. Dobe had
picked his men well.

Majors said to them: "Trot out there fifty yards."

They didn't trot. They walked slowly away from the house,
sinking into the darkness, becoming blurred shapes out there.

Majors' voice turned tight and flat. "When we move, Dobe,
we move on the run. Lag behind and I'll drag you to Reservation at the end of this rope." He had a fair view of the
lamp sitting on the table, inside the center room. He drew his
revolver and took a fair shot and saw the light explode into a
bright-blue ball of flame. The spilled kerosene suddenly rolled
up a quick fire on the table and another fire began burning
on the floor. Jett's voice pitched out of the darkness with an
accumulating rage. "By God, Majors . . . !" But Majors
waited until he saw the fire creep along the floor toward the
piled junk. When he saw the junk catch hold he spoke to
Dobe.

"We move," he said, and laid his horse into a dead run.

Dobe was slow in following. The rope jerked him around
the saddle and the bite of it dragged a yell out of him. "Wait,
damn you!" He caught up, reeling back into his seat. They
were both side by side, shooting across the small valley
toward the road. Dobe's men had made a sudden break for
the house. Looking back across the increasing distance, Majors saw them rush through the door, and he heard Jett's
voice sing out: "Never mind! Baker, you watch the fire!
Come—come on!"

A moment later a rifle began to break the night with its
beating shots. One of them, by pure chance, came close to
Dobe, and Dobe howled out his warning. "Hey—hey!" Ma-

jors reached the road and followed it. There was a turn here that took them into a low pass. A shoulder of the hills blocked out all further firing. They rode steadily on.

Dobe said in his child-high voice: "Friend, you'll never get to Reservation."

"Better plan on it, Dobe."

"No," said Dobe, "you never will."

The road was definitely upgrade for a mile or more, winding with the contours of the country. The gelding began to pull wind; Dobe's pony lagged back. Majors said, "Bring him up."

"I worked him all day. He ain't fresh."

"Bring him up."

Dobe brought him up. All the hills rolled formlessly under this night and a wind came out of the east, very cold. They passed the mouth of another road.

Majors asked: "Where does that go?"

Dobe's voice was dry and smart. "Short cut to my ranch, friend. And the boys will be comin' along it. You ain't ever goin' to get to Reservation."

The road reached a summit and fell away, its yellow dust showing the curving grade in a kind of phosphorescent glow. They passed from the hills into the narrow canyon of the Ute's east fork. Darkness dripped along those walls and the run of the ponies' feet rebounded in hollow waves. Beyond the canyon the lights of Sultan's ranch began to wink over the far flats.

Dobe's pony had again fallen behind and Dobe was howling about the sudden jerks of the rope. Majors pulled in. Dobe overran him, the rope again almost unseating him.

He said, in a passionate rage: "No man ever rawhides me, friend Majors! By God, I'll see you kickin' in the dust for it."

Both horses were hard put, the wind sawing in and out of them; and the following run of Dobe's men began to disturb the night. Majors listened a moment, placing them somewhere along the canyon. It would be the canyon walls that threw those echoes forward. He had his hard moment of thought then and knew he could not tow Dobe Hyde into town this way. The alternative was to duck into the river willows, or strike for the ridge behind Sultan's and thus throw Dobe's crowd off-scent. If they missed him they'd go on to town, making his entrance tougher when he finally brought

Dobe in. But this was the only way now. The horses had lost their snap.

The sound of pursuit rolled more strongly forward—a mass rush of hoofs on the road's cushioning dust. He said, "All right, Dobe," and put his horse into a run. There was, suddenly, trouble beside him. Dobe's horse went up on his hindquarters—which was strange for an animal half-spent— and the rope snapped Dobe out of the saddle cleanly. He fell beneath Majors' gelding and kicked around in the dust and got to his feet, fighting the rope with both hands. He cried out in a broken, gusty way: "I'll kill you for this!" The other horse wheeled off to the road's ditch and stopped. These minutes were running by, and Dobe's men kept closing the distance and Dobe, suddenly turned mad, never stopped fighting the rope. Majors said; "Get on, Dobe."

"You can go to hell!"

Majors pulled his gun. He spurred his horse against Dobe and brought the gun barrel down on the little man's head and knocked all the sense out of him at once. Dobe wilted, and it was only Majors' sudden pull on the rope that held him against the horse. Majors jumped from the saddle and boosted Dobe into it. The gun belts slid to the ground but he let them lie; the steady pound of the other men drummed harder and harder against his ears. He got up behind Dobe and looked back and saw the shadowed substance of that crew against the night, and looked ahead at the glitter of the Sultan ranch lights—and thought of Edith Sultan's words. He put the gelding into a run again. Dobe's riders were no more than five hundred yards behind him, coming on without a break.

He wheeled into the Sultan road and rushed toward the house. He was at the house porch and wrestling with a Dobe Hyde suddenly half-alive when the door opened and Buff Sultan's big shape partially blocked the light. Another man ran around from the back, challenging: "Who's that?"

He got out of the saddle, dragging Dobe with him. Dobe swung at his face and missed. He gentled Dobe with one flat-knuckled smash on the temple and carried him up the porch. A gunshot banged behind him and Jett's voice sailed on.

"Dobe—drop down!" Majors rushed through the door and Buff Sultan slammed it, moving backward on his heels. Majors let Dobe fall. The little man crawled half-across the room on hands and knees and turned, and sank down. Blood dripped from his nose, but he watched Majors with a maddened brightness and his lips stretched back when he shouted: "Far to town as you ever git, friend!"

Certain things Majors saw with a quick eye. Edith Sultan was in a corner of the room. Sultan stood by the table, his hand ready to whip out the light, his cheeks very ruddy; and one of Sultan's men rushed in from a back room, lugging a rifle. This he saw; then the yard was full of sound and a bullet smashed through the door, aimlessly flung. It missed Majors by the spread of a hand, near enough for him to feel the wind of its passage. Sultan flung up his head and his arm dropped from the lamp and he gave a quick groan. Edith cried, "Buff!" Afterwards, the door was kicked open and Jett and the other two men rushed in and halted there.

Majors had wheeled to face them, his gun lifted on the doorway; and so they remained, Jett with his weapon swinging in his fist and the others posted beside him, caught at that fine balance between violence and caution. They were breathing deeply and their shifting boots scraped up little echoes from the boards. Sultan had groaned again. Dobe Hyde crawled along the floor and stood up. He held his hand to his lips; his words mushed through his fingers.

"Get him, Jett."

It was this kid Majors watched—this thin stripling who was seasoned by so wild and wicked a knowledge. He had a greater daring than the rest of them, a courage that was savage in its way. He paused here now with a white grin on his sallow face, with a luminous shining in his eyes that had neither heat nor depth—like the reflection of light in the eyes of a cat.

Dobe Hyde mumbled, "All right, Jett."

It had turned still in the room. All of them, Majors thought quickly, had taken hold of something and none of them could let go. He could see that Jett was ready to shoot and willing to make the try: and Dobe Hyde's thin voice kept urging him, "Jett—go on!" Majors thought of Edith Sultan in the room's corner, and knew he was whipped.

But he said, to Jett: "Want a try?"

The glow of Jett's eyes got brighter and brighter. He seemed like a man enjoying himself.

"Any time, mister."

"Wait a minute," said Dobe, and began stepping to the far

side of the room. He was near the wall when a voice came across it and stopped him. "Hold on, Dobe."

Majors was turned away, but at once he remembered that this was Sultan's man who had charged in from the kitchen with a rifle. From the corner of his vision he noticed Dobe suddenly freeze. Dobe spoke to Sultan with a shrill intemperance. "What are you doin' in this? You're ridin' with me, ain't you? A hell of a thing! Tell that man of yours to drop the rifle."

Majors could not turn, though the grind of something in Sultan's voice urged him to look that way.

"I'm through with you, Dobe. Your man shot me."

"An accident," said Dobe Hyde. "Drop that rifle, friend."

Sultan's counter-order cut in. "Keep it lifted, Sam. Maybe an accident, Dobe. But you shot through my front door. That was no accident. I'm through with you."

Dobe snapped out: "You was through with me before now. Else why did friend Majors run for shelter here? A tricky thing. Put the rifle down."

The Sultan rider said calmly, "It ain't heavy."

Jett's grin seemed a permanent crease. "I'll risk it, Dobe, if you can risk it."

"No—no," said Dobe Hyde. "Dammit, put your gun down, Jett. I ain't armed nohow."

"So what do we do?" said Jett. "Jest stand here?"

Majors said; "Go on, Dobe. You can ride back."

Dobe shuffled across the floor. He stood between Jett and Majors, blanking Jett's gun, but also sheltering himself from the rifle held by Sultan's man. He twisted his neck uncomfortably and wiped the drying blood from his lips. "Said you'd never get to town with me. If I had a gun . . ."

"Go on," grunted Majors.

"You bet I'll go," burst out Dobe. "But I'll have your skin before I'm through! All right, boys."

He went out first, crowding in front of his riders. Jett pulled slowly away, a step at a time, gun half-lifted. Dobe walked out to the road, where his horse stood; and, excepting Jett, the rest of them were rising to their saddles. Jett stepped from the porch, and backed against his horse. He went quickly into the leather. Majors called: "Go on. No shooting." And there was a voice deep in the yard's darkness calling up: "Careful, you fellers." It was another Sultan hand crouched out there. Jett suddenly wheeled. All of them rushed away.

Majors turned and found Buff Sultan dropped into a chair, his left arm hanging straight. A red stain slowly spread away from the fleshy part of his upper arm, showing where the bullet had torn through. Edith Sultan came over from the corner. She called, "Sam, put the teakettle on the stove." She was quite calm and her fingers moved lightly along her brother's shoulder. Buff looked up at her, the ruddiness draining out of his cheeks. The pain was beginning to punish him, but for a moment Majors saw the strong affection between those two.

Edith said, "Buff—I'm sorry."

"No," said Sultan. "I got what's coming to me and I'm lucky it ain't worse. When a man plays around with skunks he gets to smell like a skunk. I made a mistake ridin' with Dobe. I know that now. The man is after his own schemes and he'll kill all of us to have his own way. The old man told us that before he died. I should have remembered." The broken nerves of his arm jerked him badly and he fell silent a moment, dumbly waiting for the spasm to pass, and spoke again in a defeated tone. "What a hell of a mess." Afterwards he looked at Majors.

"What made you figure you could get help here?"

Majors said: "It was a mistake."

"No, you guessed right. Only I wasn't much help. Caught me too sudden. But I don't get it. Sam had the drop on Dobe and you were doin' pretty well with those other fellows. Why'd you let him go?"

Majors looked at Edith Sultan. "I put you in considerable danger. I apologize."

"Afraid of that?" said Sultan. "Afraid she might get hit in the scrap? Well, you're a white man. I wasn't so sure of that when I first saw you in town. You looked kind of tough. What did you figure to do with Dobe?"

Edith Sultan had gone from the room. She came back with a pair of scissors and cut away the sleeve of Buff's shirt. There was a dull-blue hole showing in his bicep muscles. When Edith touched the surrounding tissue Buff flinched and put his teeth together.

"Get him out of the way," answered Majors.

Edith made another round-trip to the kitchen and back. She stood over Buff, washing out the bullet's gash. Buff's legs squirmed around the floor. He said, to Majors, in a groaning way: "What?"

"Run him out," repeated Majors. "He's top man here now. When I came here it was Pedee Barr who controlled the country. So I worked on him, through Maffitt. Maffitt has just switched to Dobe Hyde and that puts Barr out. Now it's Dobe."

Sultan groaned, "Wait a minute, Edie! By God, that's painful!" Sweat glistened on his pale skin. Edith stood back, watching Majors with a long, odd glance. Sultan shook his head at Majors. "You're damn' cool. It's all calculation with you. You make your moves count. You sure Maffitt went with Hyde?"

Majors nodded, whereupon Buff Sultan took on a little color. "I got to thinkin' of that. It was you that put the idea in Maffitt's noodle and made all the rest of us suspicious. Kind of clever. And now everything's in a hell of a mess. Where do I stand? God knows."

Majors said: "You boys in this valley are about through. Dobe carries the ship."

"What would you have done with Dobe?"

"Took him over the hill to Jeff White—on a murder charge."

"And bust up his crowd. Sure. But you lost him."

"Yes," said Majors, "I lost him." It was a soft tone; too gentle and too mild. His eyes gave him away. They were pale with temper. He made a poor play and knew it, and the knowledge fanned up his temper. He could not admit defeat equally. Something violent and thoroughly relentless showed on his face for the Sultans to see. It was a quality that made him hang on and try again. For him, in a fight, there were only two ways—to break or to be broken. He stood above them now, big-shaped in the lamplight, ungentle and unforgiving.

"I got no use for Dobe," said Sultan. "I'll help him no more, and if he pushes me I'll stand against him."

"You'll make a poor show of it, alone."

"Maybe," said Sultan, not liking the direct statement. He had pride. "Maybe. But neither have I got any use for the Barrs. Be a better country when they're all gone. Let Dobe go fight 'em. Drive 'em out. Then maybe we'll have some peace."

"No," said Majors, "you won't. Then you'll have a man up

that valley who'll be lyin' awake thinkin' of ways to drive you out."

Sultan quit talking. He hunched over in the chair while Edith wrapped a piece of cloth around his arm. When she tied it down Buff lifted his weight from the chair, and settled again, freely sweating.

He said, "He ain't that crazy."

But Edith Sultan broke her long silence. "Yes," she said. "Yes, he is."

Sultan showed an irritable weariness. "I guess this has got beyond me and Ketchum. But I'll never lift a hand to help a Barr. Not ever."

"Buff," said Edith, "Maybe we've been a little bit wrong."

"Not about the Barrs," contradicted Buff and let his big head roll downward. He stared at the floor, disillusioned and altogether helpless at this moment. Majors turned his glance to the girl. She stood behind her brother, and she met the big marshal's long inspection with a straightness that was like defense. Color came to her face.

Majors turned to the door. He said, "I'm sorry I brought this risk on you. It was my fault."

"Where you goin'?" asked Sultan.

"I have just made a sucker play," Majors grumbled. "So I'll have another try."

Sultan's voice followed him through the door. "I don't figure you," he said, almost in complaint. "And I'll be damned if I see what keeps you alive."

Majors went out to the gelding and stepped into the saddle. The girl came quickly from the house; she stopped beside the horse. He was thinking about Dobe Hyde, the sense of his defeat burning his nerves like salt and alkali. But he could admire Edith Sultan for the way she spoke, so free and self-willed and so definite of voice.

"Do you know anything about me?" she asked him. "You looked at me. What was it?"

"Maybe I know."

"Maybe you do. Nothing can ever come of that. Too much has happened. But"—and her voice had a long descending swing to it—"I can't hate the Barrs quite as much as Buff does. I could live in peace with them, if they let me."

"Time's past for that."

She said, quite gently: "Have you ever thought that you have some responsibility for their ruin?"

"Yes," he said. "Yes."

"I'm not reproaching you. I was only curious. There's so much in you that doesn't show. It has been very hard for you. You are so deeply hated here. I just want you to know that I admire you."

He said: "I'm sorry for your personal fortunes."

"Thank you," she whispered. "What are yours? There seems nothing at all for you. Nothing but trouble."

"I guess," he said in a dry way, "that's all a man can expect, if he looks for it. Good night." He removed his hat with a little sweep of his arm. It was a gesture unconscious and gallant, and this was what she remembered after he had ridden away and the sound of his pony's hoofs had died in the night.

When Dobe and his men returned to the ranch, Godry was already there with four extra riders from the Cache country. They were standing around the yard, nerved up by the wait and a little bit uneasy from what the Negro, Baker, had told them. Godry said: "I didn't know whut the play was. So I figured I'd better stick here." He stared at Jett and the other riders with Dobe. "Little trouble, hunh?"

Jett started to explain.

Dobe, in a thoroughly bad temper, shrilled: "Never mind! We got no time for foolin'. You get your cinch fixed up." He stamped into his room. Baker lighted another lamp, whereby Dobe could see how the fire had eaten into his burlap sacks He stood there, his narrow shoulders bowed and his magpie's thriftiness terribly shocked. "No," he grumbled, "he can't do that to me. I will take it out of his hide."

Godry came in. "We ridin' pretty soon?"

"When Jett gits his saddle fixed."

"Well, it's cold. Tell that dinge to boil up some coffee and warm the beans.".

"You should of et before you left your own shack."

Godry was no man to back up. He stared at Dobe. "It's maybe not a bad idea. I'll just take my crowd home. See you next week."

"Hold on," argued Dobe. His small rosebud lips made a petulant frame. He gave ground grudgingly. "Just coffee. Baker—boil up some coffee! Just coffee." Baker didn't reply, but Dobe knew the Negro heard him.

"If I was you," said Godry with a show of anger, "I'd make that dark boy give me an answer."

"Was you me," stated Dobe, "you'd be better off than you are."

Jett was swearing around the outer darkness. It was half an hour before they came into Dobe's room and took their coffee out of the big pot the Negro brought from the kitchen. Dobe sat in a chair, the very picture of a pale little bookkeeper. The single tuft of gray hair stood up on the fore part of his head and he looked at this crew in a way that bitterly begrudged them the drink. But behind that expression was a sly satisfaction with these men. He had picked them and he knew them: they would do what he wanted done. He said, presently, "We ride," and went into the darkness. Baker stayed behind, a gloomy shape in the shadows. The rest swung up.

Dobe said, to the Negro: "Don't burn that lamp."

The Negro said nothing at all, whereupon Godry growled: "You speak up, nigger."

"Nooh," murmured Baker. "Nooh."

Afterwards Dobe Hyde led his crew across the small valley into the broken country, pointing toward the Barrs. Darkness ran the land completely, thick in the way smoke is thick. Overhead the stars showed a diamond scatter in the sky, but none of that light illumined the earth.

17

---◆◎◆---

The Hard Choice

THERE WAS no change in Pedee Barr that his daughter could detect. He made a stiff shape in the center of the living room, as iron-sure of himself now as in all the years past. Ring lay in a fresh grave at the top of the rim, beside that older brother, Clay, killed so long ago, and beside her mother. Closely watching her father, Katherine understood him no better and was puzzled no less. He would remember Ring as he had remembered that other son, in hard silence. Somewhere in him, she thought, some affection must lie, though he had seldom, by any act, indicated it. But if there were affection in him, this added loss would be fuel to feed his undying anger toward the rest of the world. He was a man who would never bend; when he surrendered it would be at once, in a clean break. She often had wondered if he felt the end of sympathy, and wondered now, seeing the somber flare of his eyes. She could not penetrate his mind, could not believe that he liked her, or that he even gave her any consideration at all. That was the barrier between them, and all that she could think of now was that he remained as consistent in tragedy as otherwise. She feared him and yet in a way she admired him for the changeless quality that made him what he was.

He said: "I want to remind you all now of something you should not forget. I came into this country and took what I wanted, as other men did in those days. It may be that some of you feel something wrong on our part as regards Tony Black's father. I will only say that he once spoke against me and I could not trust him. If I cannot trust a man, that man

155

is my enemy. A man must stand the consequences of his words. I have—and expect others to."

All the Barr men listened in heavy silence. She looked particularly at Dan, and thought that something had at last gone out of him—that lightness of spirit which had set him apart from the rest of the menfolk; and with its departure he had become one of them. Katherine felt at once lonely and without hope.

Her father continued. "This valley hates us. The people in it have waited a long time to get back at us. Nothing's held them still but fear and I have seen to it that they have had plenty of reason to fear. The way to handle people is to crack the whip over them, which I have done, knowin' that all of them want somethin' and would take it if they could. I took it. They lacked the nerve."

Katherine thought: "So that is all that he feels about people—a contempt for their weakness."

"I have never asked a favor in my life," said Pedee, "I have never apologized. This is what I want to tell you. We will no doubt soon have to fight. Do not—any of you—ask for anything from them now. Those people are dogs, which I knew in the beginning. They are still dogs. You will go up to the rim, Dan, and keep a watch there until I relieve you. I'm riding to the Pocket."

They remained in the room's stone-cold silence, listening to old Pedee drum across the bridge. Wind ran through the open door and the rustle of the Ute water over the gravel had a frigid sound.

Dan put both hands in his pockets, staring across the room in lightless discouragement. "Always thought this was a pleasant place for a house. Occurs to me now it is a trap. They'll stand on the rim or in the timber and shoot hell out of us. Dad must have been pretty confident in the old days."

It was one of the older men who answered. "In those days nobody got near enough this house to do any shootin'. Pedee was king for a long while. If he'd shut out those new families in the beginnin' he'd still be king. It was Dobe Hyde he let alone. And it's Dobe who will come for us."

Fay took command naturally. "You better get up on the rim, Dan. Cousin Creed, you go yonder of the corrals. We got nothin' to fear from the timber."

Dan went toward the front porch. Katherine followed because she felt altogether lost. They stopped out there. The river showed a dull silver streak as far down as the first bend, but the shadows of the rim lay in velvet pools along the road. Long, undulant waves of sound washed down from the wind-stirred pines. A coyote, far up the slope, broke into its halfbark, adding the last indescribable note of wildness to this night.

Dan said: "Guess I might as well tell you it was Edie Sultan I been ridin' to see. We used to meet at Tony's old house. No harm now in admittin' it, for it's all over now."

"How," said Katherine, "could a Barr ever come to speak to a Sultan?"

"A long time ago, I met her on a narrow trail and one of us had to step aside. I stepped aside and it kind of surprised her. Ordinary politeness from a Barr was somethin' she never expected. So she smiled at me." He stopped to consider that distant scene and his face softened from thinking of it, and Katherine saw how terribly deep his emotions were at the moment and how hard the break was for him. "So that's the way it started. That's the pleasant part of my life, and it won't come any more."

She said: "I'm sorry, Dan."

His words were at once intense and gusty. "She's so damned beautiful, Katherine. Almost as beautiful as you are. I won't ever forget her voice. It always had somethin' in it like . . ." He went silent, groping for a word that would express the completeness, the richness he felt in Edith. He remained that way a long while, watching the river's shining streak. "Like music that makes a man feel strong enough to whip the world." Afterwards he added very softly: "But it was always a little bit sad, as if she knew it wouldn't ever come out for us."

"Won't it? Won't it ever, Dan?"

The question turned him around. There had been so forlorn a note in it; and he was not so self-occupied that he could not observe misery in her eyes.

He said: "No. This damned fight has ruined a lot of things and it's ruined our chances for good. She knows by now I shot Oldroyd. In a way he was one of her people. I've got that blood on my hands. It's between us and nothin' under God's sky can wipe it out."

"But if she really loves . . ."

He said with a rapid vehemence: "She's got pride. She'll stick with her own side. I'm glad she has, and I'm glad she will. No, there's nothing left for me, no matter how this comes out."

The misery in her eyes was greater and greater. It rode her shoulders down like weights, those shoulders which had always been so proud, so buoyantly presented to the world. She said in a way that was begging, pleading: "How about me, Dan? How about me?"

It took him a little while to clear his mind of his own troubles. Then he said: "That big deputy? Why, Katherine, there's the man that's caused all our troubles."

"I know."

"Why, my God," he burst out, "how can you think of him? He made Ring die. Just as sure as if he'd shot him. He's turned Dobe loose on us. He's put us here in this shape. He's wrecked everything. You got pride, Katherine."

She said, so brokenly soft: "I suppose."

"Now he's watchin' us bust up. That's what he's played for all the time. To hell with him!"

At that moment he was hard in his anger, almost as hard as his father. She didn't answer and she turned her face from him; and long afterwards he touched her with his hand.

"Tough," he said, and wheeled away at a long-legged stride.

She was thoroughly lost in her own strange and humble thoughts. She was saying to herself: "I suppose I have pride. A month ago I hated him. I suppose I still should." But all this while there was before her eyes the distinct image of his big shape, so loosely powerful, so deceptively hiding the tremendous vitality that made him great. She saw the scar on his temple and the breadth and the solid irregularity of his face, and remembered all the tumult of his feelings as his eyes had revealed them to her that afternoon on the ridge above Reservation. Like storm, like fire. She had seen little of him, yet knew him so well. Behind his faint smile was a hunger and a loneliness and a temper that could sweep tremendously through all the ranges of emotion, disturbing her even now at a distance. And this was the man she must hate.

Pedee Barr traveled up the trail to the Pocket, through the drip of solid blackness. The certainty of Dobe Hyde's attack on the ranch was in his mind, yet he didn't hurry; for his life had been keyed to a certain pace and nothing could break the iron assurance of his mind and make him change that pace now. Though, in a way, it was not so much assurance as a

feeling for the inevitable. A man's life had its destined
course, the end of which was written in a sealed book, and
no earthly power could amend or scratch out that writing.
What happened would happen. Governed by this gray mood,
he rode the night with no fear and with no hope, thinking as
the trail took him upward into the sharper chill of the Range,
of the two boys he had so secretly cherished and had lost.
The older one, long buried, was as clear-featured in his
memory as on the day of his death; and so it would be with
Ring, ever-remembered in the long silences of his mind. He
could not show pleasure, he could not show affection—and
now his pride would not let him show sorrow; but he traveled
the night with a regret that would never leave him and would
never diminish—which was the regret of a man who, loving
his sons, had failed to let them see it. A light had dimmed at
the older one's passage; the light grew dimmer with Ring's
death. He had three children left, but of these only Fay
showed him the image of himself; and it was Fay he considered as he climbed the last stages of the trail and caught
sight of Maffitt's house light glinting through the timber. In
his mind was a fear of failing again with that son as he had
failed with the others.

Before he went down the last slope to the house's yard he
unbuckled his gun belt and strapped it outside his coat. It was
a significant action. He had a thorough knowledge of the sins
of men and a perfect understanding of the things that
prompted them to loyalty and to betrayal; and he knew that
Ben Maffitt, having smelled a taint in the wind, would be
wavering now. Men of Maffitt's kind, like animals, always
obeyed the instincts of fear and hunger and hate. Halted at
the edge of the timber, he called across the yard.

"Maffitt."

He had heard the easy run of voices inside. That suddenly
quit. A chair scraped the floor and the lights went out.
Presently the rear door opened and Maffitt's voice called
through. "Who's that?"

"I want to talk to you, Ben."

"Pedee? Light that lamp, Brick. Come in, Pedee."

"Privately," said Pedee, and pushed his horse a little beyond the trees. He said, "Come up here, Ben," and got down.

Light flashed in the kitchen windows and ran a square
shaft through the doorway. Maffitt's body rolled back and
forth across that shaft as he came confidently up. Pedee ob-

served that sureness with instant thought: The man hadn't
changed his mind. Or else he had changed it and was very
certain.

Maffitt halted, his head rolling a little as he searched the
timber behind Pedee. "Come alone?"

"Yes."

Maffitt scratched a match across his trouser leg and
touched it to the dead cigarette between his lips. This light
laid its shining across the swart face, deepening the bold
angles, accenting the gray-green glitter of Maffitt's eyes; and
went out.

"What's the trouble?" asked Maffitt.

But the tone had changed, tightening and pressed flatter.
Pedee knew Maffit had seen the gun belt buckled outside his
coat.

Pedee said: "Bring the boys down to the house. Dobe will
be along. Tonight or tomorrow night. Or maybe the next. But
he'll be along."

"You sure?"

"Ben," said Pedee, "don't dance around with your talk.
Get the boys."

"We had an agreement," said Maffitt. "We made it a long
time ago. I'm tryin' to think how we had it."

"No," said Pedee. "You ain't tryin' to remember. You're
dodgin'."

"Just so," agreed Maffitt coolly. "Well, Pedee, I won't
dodge. Protection for protection. That was it. But you got no
more protection to offer me. So I can't give you any. I think
you're all through."

"I admire honesty, Ben. Otherwise you are a scoundrel and
your word is worth nothin'."

"Dog eat dog," murmured Maffitt. "You know that. It's
what you'd do to me, if the time came."

"So you've seen Dobe?"

"That's right," agreed Maffitt and threw the cigarette away
and stood short and broad in the vague limits of the light
beam. His arms hung idle. "It's a hell of a world, Pedee."

"Then," said Pedee, "you are better out of it"—and drew
his gun.

He never got it lifted. The slap of Maffitt's palms against
the butts of his guns was a sharp echo. His elbows bent and
his double fire laid two violent-orange fingers of light across
the shadows. That pair of bullets drove Pedee's breath out of

him in a hard gasp and knocked him backwards to the earth. He never moved. Up in the trees his horse pitched mildly and stood still again. One man came from the house. He said, "Pedee?" and turned into the house again when Maffitt said, "Yeah."

Maffitt went back to the living room. All of them were standing around—all but Brick Brand, who sat at the table and piled poker chips one upon another. A cigarette hung between his teeth and the smoke rolled against his red cheeks and he had his eyes half-closed against the light. Faint sweat beaded his upper lip.

Nobody spoke until Maffitt said:—

"The old man was a hard one. He came up here to make this play—and he made it. I give him credit."

Brick Brand piled the chips into a high column, his glance narrowed on the motion of his fingers. The beads of sweat grew larger. Suddenly he pushed the stack over and stood up going toward the back door.

Maffitt said: "Where you goin'?"

"To get Pedee's cartridges. I'm shy."

Maffitt and the other four remained in the room, listening to Brand hit the doorsill with his boot toe and step out. Maffitt turned his head, his chin rising, speculation in his eyes. Suddenly he said, "Hell," and rushed at the door. Brand had just stepped into the saddle of Pedee's horse. He was beyond the yard, in the timber.

"Hey!"

Brand called back with a sudden outraged passion: "To hell with you fellows! A bargain is a bargain and by God I'll stick to mine! You fellows think you're pretty smart in pickin' Hyde for the right man. I'll pick a righter one, which you'll soon see." And, having said it, he rushed up the hillside. Maffitt threw a few scattered shots that way on pure chance, and then stopped to hear the horse fade on the trail.

Long afterwards Maffitt spoke to Little Peters, behind him. "Tie the old gentleman on Brand's horse and take him down to the bridge."

Jim Majors came into Reservation and left his horse by the hotel. It was past the dining room's closing time, but he went on to the kitchen and found Tony cleaning up the last of her chores. He didn't say anything. He sat down by the serving table and put his arms on it and let his legs sprawl out, watching her move silently around to find him a meal. Broderick came in.

"You went," said the hotel man with a driving directness, "to get Dobe Hyde. Where is he?"

"Didn't get him."

Tony put a plate before Majors and drew silently into the background, watching him with round, soft eyes. Her lips changed, drawing faintly apart; and breathing stirred her breasts a little. Majors went about his eating, but Broderick stood over him, his vast belly steadied against the opposite side of the serving table. He had been an enigmatic man and was not now. Discontent showed and restlessness showed and a latent temper, so long concealed from Reservation, began to find its way out.

"You tried?"

The question freshened Majors' sense of defeat. He wasn't a humble man and he wasn't patient; and the knowledge that he had failed to bring in Dobe jabbed at his pride and pumped blood into his tanned skin.

He said, "Be quiet, Broderick."

"You're roughin' up the wrong man," Broderick instantly warned him. "I have got to—"

Majors laid down his fork. He put both hands flat on the table, the fingers spreading and whitening from pressure. His legs crept backward along the floor and he looked at Broderick with his muscles set for a dive across the table; his face was white and stone-still. Wildness was in the shine of his eyes, pulsing life the flow of his blood.

Broderick didn't give ground. He shoved the steel arm hook half across the table and rapped it sharply on the wood, and let it lie, point upward, like a weapon. They faced each other in this manner, implacably and deadly willful.

Majors abruptly settled back. He said: "You're right, Broderick. My apologies."

Relief loosened Broderick completely, from head to feet, and a great breath swept in and out of him. "You're a great man, Sundown. I will say it again, I admire you. If I talk out of turn it is because I hate to see you go wrong. All right?"

"All right," said Majors and slouched quietly back in the chair.

"Well, you came here to break up the valley. You have done it, which is somethin' no other man could do. I have watched you make your plays, some seemin' very foolish.

Which was my mistake and the town's mistake. None of 'em have been foolish and I have learned somethin' I never expected to learn, that bein' how one man with nerve and smartness could bust a country wide open. I take my hat off to you, Sundown."

He looked away from Majors, remotely embarrassed at making the compliment, and drove his even words on again. "Everybody hates you, which is natural, and that has been a prod in your ribs, day and night. I don't want to see you give way now. For you have brought the game this far and you have got to carry it to a finish. The Barrs are through and the east fork people don't count any more. Dobe Hyde is the power now and Dobe is no better than what we had. That's your responsibility. It won't do. It just won't do."

"I know," said Majors.

Broderick shook his head. "I can't see how you'll work it. I just can't see. You know how?"

"Yes."

Broderick picked up his chin and stared. The silence went on considerably and in the end Broderick grinned. "Maybe I've underestimated you, like the rest of the town. A fool always talks too much and I'm a fool."

He went heavily out of the kitchen and Majors resumed his meal. The echo of an incoming horse drifted through the building and somewhere back of the hotel two men talked in stray, muted phrases. Tony watched the big man finish his meal. She brought up the coffeepot, refilling his cup, and took her station in the corner again, her breathing still disturbed. When he rose and turned toward the dining room she shifted over to that door and came in front of him. He was deep in his own thoughts, but her presence there drew his attention and stopped him.

She said nothing. Her hand came uncertainly up and she touched the lapel of his coat. Rose color stained her features strongly and her lips were caught in an uncertain, crooked smiling. For a moment he was deeply stirred by an expression in her eyes that was strange and glowing and hopeful in a way he could not interpret. Whatever she had been and whatever mistakes she might have made—and he had his own intimations—there was a sweetness to her and a fragrance. It was, he thought, a love of life, a hunger for some richness which she had never had and yet could see in the world. That childlike simplicity survived the tragic poverty of her life, like a small light bravely shining out through the surrounding stormy dark. He had one moment to think of all this; and afterwards he smiled at her.

"Tony," he said, as gently as he could speak, "someday you'll find a man, and that man will be getting solid gold. I hope he knows it."

He went through the dining room and up the stairs. The kitchen doors swung slowly, grinding on the hinges. Tony settled her shoulders against the wall. Her head went down and after a while she began to cry, silently, hopelessly, terribly.

In his room, Majors walked to the corner window and watched the square below, one hand working two silver dollars around his trouser pocket; and to him during the following five minutes came the hardest thoughts of his life.

He had known, as soon as Dobe Hyde slipped away from him, what he must next do. His mind was made up to it now. Yet it was a decision hard to face, breaking the long record of which he was so deeply proud. He remained there, reviewing that record in his mind, seeing its high lights with clarity, while occasional riders drifted into town and lights went on here and there and the smell of winter entered the open window with keener insistence. Doc Showers rounded a corner and went toward his office at a characteristic bustle. Chavis strolled from the jail, tracking toward the saloon at a loose-kneed pace; and a man idled in the shadows of the vacant building directly across from the hotel watching his— Majors'—horse. His attention stuck to that man a long while and presently he recognized the redhead outlaw, Brick Brand.

He swung to the little table in a way that was abrupt and forced, and sat down and drew out a pencil. He wrote Jeff White a careful letter, making a few explanations. Afterwards, on another sheet of paper, he printed an announcement in rather bold letters. When he had finished this he unpinned his deputy's badge from his vest and laid it on the announcement, which read:—

To Those Interested:—
    I have this night resigned as U. S. Deputy Marshal.
                             JAMES J. MAJORS

18

A Man Changes

MAJORS took the letter and the announcement and the badge and went downstairs. Broderick sat as usual in the rocker, facing the window.

Majors said: "Got an envelope?"

Broderick hoisted himself up and went behind his desk and produced the envelope from a pigeonhole in the key rack. Majors put the announcement and badge to one side on the desk while he addressed the letter. When he got through with that chore, he saw Broderick staring at the printed sign, astonishment breaking purely across his dish-round face. The man had huge black eyebrows; they went up like awnings withdrawn from a window.

Majors said: "See that the letter gets on tomorrow's stage."

Broderick didn't have an answer. He watched Majors take the announcement and badge and walk to the door. He found his voice just as Majors was about to step into the street.

"Brand's across the way."

Majors stepped to the edge of the walk, seeing Brand across the top of the big gelding near by. He moved around the gelding, into the dust and away from the hotel lights, and stopped with the shape of Brand shadowed against the wall of the opposite building. He had meant to call out to Brand. The redhead beat him to it.

"Majors—no. I want to talk to you. That's all."

Night's cold ran against Majors, bringing in the smell of dust and the resin scent of the pines and the wildness of all this land so darkly crouched around the little core of light that was Reservation. An Indian left Webber's store, his moc-

165

casins taking him soundlessly away. Soder and Charley Chavis were suddenly standing on the saloon corner, watching him. A man coming down from the stable behind Brand at once saw this scene and wheeled out of range at a jerky stride. It was the old pattern rising again, without change, without mystery.

But Brick Brand's voice lifted once more, quickly concerned. "No, Majors. No."

Majors went across the dust, even-footed, and came before Brand. The shadows of the building dropped like a cape over both of them. He could see the vague, pale track of the scars on Brand's lips, which he had put there. Brand kept his shoulders very still; he kept his arms folded. He spoke down in his throat, for only Majors to hear.

"I took a lickin' from you once. I know when I'm second best, friend."

"Go on," said Majors. "Finish your speech."

"No. I left the Pocket. Pedee Barr came up there tonight. We always had an agreement to help him. He wanted help. Maffitt shot him dead. I don't go back on my promises like that."

There were two more men on the saloon corner, making four. Their faces were four pale spots in the corner of Majors' vision. Somewhere about this town another citizen kept gutterally whispering. Majors held his place, weighing Brand with a long judgment, listening to the run of the man's words, waiting for the tone or the gesture that would give Brand's intentions away.

"Maffitt's made his dicker with Hyde," said Brand. "He figures Hyde is top dog now. Maybe. I'll pick my own top dog."

"Who's that?"

"I'll string with you, friend. That's what I came to say."

Majors did a strange thing then. He let his right hand drop toward the butt of his revolver. It was a quick, startling gesture, intended to set off a man who was cocked for trouble, or expecting it, or looking for it. Brand's shoulders ducked and he pulled his stomach in, but he kept his arms locked across his chest.

He sighed out his protest. "No, not any. I've made up my mind."

"Stay where you are," said Majors, and went by him. He crossed the street and traveled on to the jail office. He laid the announcement against the outside bulletin board and tacked it with the loose pin of the badge. Announcement and badge remained there on the board for Reservation to see. Afterwards he walked down to the saloon; that corner was suddenly empty.

Chavis and Cal Soder were inside, with a few idlers at the bar and the pale gambler sitting thoroughly alone at his table, head bent down with the weight of some moody thought. Cal Soder was behind the bar and Chavis in front of it. Majors crossed the increasing silence of the room, whereupon Chavis cut away from the bar and went over to take a chair at the gambler's table. Majors put his elbows on the bar, waiting there. Soder stood fast, making a gesture at the barkeep, who produced bottle and glass. The man next to Majors stirred and stepped back. It was the printer. The printer caught Majors' glance and swung on his heel and left the saloon. Majors took the bottle and glass and trudged over the room with his heavy shoulders slung forward. His lips were pushed together; lines ran fan-shaped away from his eye corners and the room's light built up a glass-gray sparkle in his eyes. The silence here was as though the breathing of all these men had drawn in and stopped. He went by Chavis and sat down at a table in the far corner, and poured himself a quick drink and took it.

He had the room before him but he didn't, at the minute, give it any interest. One man walked out, his steps making a lonely racket on the floor. Somebody's horse arrived in town at a fast gallop and somebody else ran along the walk just beyond the saloon wall. These were distant tones to Majors. He sat in the chair at odds with himself. The drink of whisky hit him in the stomach and ran some ease through his nerves, but it wasn't enough. He had reached a fork in the trail he didn't like, and a good many memories were feeding the old restlessness again, pitch-dry kindling for an eager blaze. Mrs. Webber's tongue-lashing . . . Dobe Hyde walking out of Sultan's door, a free man . . . Katherine Barr's voice carrying its slow richness across the hotel lobby . . .

He had pride, and that pride was his weakness, and this was a fact he knew as well as anybody. It was a flaw old Jeff White had recognized, which was why old Jeff had said, "You can be tough. Maybe you'll come out of that valley and maybe you won't." Pride had caused him to turn in his star.

The gambler rose and walked to the door, leaving Chavis alone at the next table. Chavis sat there in a kind of dreaming silence, watching his hands as they rested motionlessly on the green cloth. Majors observed this altogether indifferently, for he was searching his mind for some logic that would halt the tremendous dissatisfaction flowing through him. He had a responsibility for the things he had done in this country, and that responsibility included the Barr family. To this point he had acted within the limits of the star. But if he proceeded now as his conscience indicated, the star couldn't cover him. There were limits to what a deputy marshal might do, and though old Jeff had hinted that the sky was the limit, it wasn't in reason that a peace officer could openly take sides in a fight. Even old Jeff wouldn't agree to that.

A cooler man would stand back and let this ancient quarrel play out its course. Yet he knew that impartiality was no longer possible for him. To this point he had played his hand as he saw it. The power of the Barrs was broken and he had shaken the outlaws from their old allegiance. The east fork people were no longer disposed to take up the battle against the Barrs. So much he had done, deliberately.

Having carried it this far, he couldn't step aside now and watch Dobe Hyde smash the Barrs and usurp their power and place. He had an obligation here, star or no star. He had no recourse.

Altogether idle and withdrawn from the affairs of the saloon, he tried to visualize old Jeff's reactions and could not. In other hard situations during the past he had always found an answer within the limits of his duty. This time there seemed no answer that old Jeff would approve. Thus impelled to break with his past record, left thoroughly alone and uncertain by that decision, a greater discontent got hold of him and dredged up his old impulse to be on the move, to act, to work a way out with the power of his hands regardless of consequences.

This was his state of mind when the light of the saloon faded to a dismal glow and drew him out of himself. Looking across the saloon he saw Chavis standing by the next table. Soder was just then stepping away from a lamp whose light he had whipped out. All the other men were gone.

"Captain," said Soder, "I've seen tough ones come and I have seen tough ones go. You have made your mistakes. Comin' into my place tonight was one mistake too many."

Soder stopped in the middle of the room. He wasn't a big man, and the saloonman's trade had trained him to hide his feelings. They were hidden now, not even his voice giving him away. But he had settled his shoulders and he set himself on his legs, and by these signals Majors judged him. Chavis moved away from the table, backing up and turning somewhat in order to watch Soder. Chavis showed excitement. He lifted a hand to push the brim of his hat away, and let the hand fall with a touch of caution. His face betrayed strain, its fresh color marbled by patches of growing pallor, its cheek hollows more pronounced. He was second fiddle in the scene waiting for Soder to set the tune.

Majors remained as he was, his shoulders pushed over the table and weighing down his idle arms. The whisky bottle stood directly in front of him, the liquid in it throwing out a bronze shine. Soder had extinguished the two lamps behind the bar, leaving that corner in semishadow; the smoldering wicks of those lamps ran a faintly acrid smell through the room. There was a lamp bracketed in the wall near Majors, playing its yellow glow against him; and one more lamp near the door.

Certain things he saw now with an exact attention. The swinging doors jiggled from outside pressure. A man stared through the crack thus made—and stepped back. There was one window on the far wall and two on the wall beside which Majors sat, all painted green to shut the street away. Pressure began to pile up here. Soder never moved. He had closed his mind, Majors saw, and would stubbornly stick it out. But Chavis moved farther back from his table, one pace at a time.

"You're proud," observed Majors, and noticed no belt on the saloonman. If he carried a gun it would be tucked behind the band of his trousers or in a harness under his arm. It would be a slow draw, Majors decided, and made his calculations on that. Chavis' gun was on his hip.

"You have made some fool plays in this town, captain," murmured Soder. "The worst of them was to use your talk on me like you was handlin' a club. I take that from no man alive."

Chavis kept drifting rearward until he stood within arm's reach of the far wall lamp. His glance kept swinging to the lamp, and away, and back again.

"A little late in your decision," suggested Majors. He didn't move. The weight of his shoulders rode against his arms on the poker table.

Soder said: "You're a private citizen now."

"Any difference?"

He put the question at Soder but it was Chavis he watched. The town marshal's nerves had begun to creep. They were pulling at him. He couldn't stand fast. He kept shifting his feet. Suddenly he burst out:—

"Nobody asked you to come here! You have played hell with everything!"

Soder said: "Shut up, Charley. You talk too much."

"I want him to know," growled Chavis. The swinging doors teetered inward again, minutely squealing. There was a difference between the two men that Majors saw then. Soder stood cooly composed. Chavis went half way around at the noise and bawled at that door, "Get the hell away from there!"—and wheeled back, suddenly shocked by his carelessness.

Majors ran out his words as slow and as soft as possible.

"You're an orphan around here now, Chavis. Maffitt's runnin' with another crowd." He thought of something and used it. "He's in with Dobe Hyde, and I hear Dobe is after your scalp. Where'll you get help?"

"A lie!" yelled Chavis. He twisted his neck, as though to relieve a cramped muscle, and looked at Soder in plain appeal. Soder didn't speak and he didn't stir. Bulldog tenacity controlled that small figure and caution held him steady through the strain. Majors knew then they were still not quite sure of their luck. All the details of this room were deep-cut in his head. He saw the distance to the door, the shape and length of the bar, the three green-painted windows, and the light burning beside Charley Chavis. He still held the weight of his shoulders against his arms. He said: "Charley, you'll have trouble in makin' a good draw. Skirt of your coat's in the way."

Chavis looked down; and then his head snapped up and a pale fright showed whitely in his eyes. He pulled his arms away from his hips; their fingers spreading apart. Majors' lips made two long rolls above and below his teeth; he was smiling at Chavis and he was thinking of how it had to be done. When he got up from the table it had to be on the left side of the table, near the wall, so as to avoid the converging tracks of their fire.

Soder said: "You owe me one dollar for the last bottle you took out of here. Reach down and get it."

Majors pulled his shoulders back. He looked beyond them, to the door. He said in a full tone: "Watch out," and came out of his chair.

Certain things he expected to happen. In his mind he had built these things up into an orderly pattern by which he meant to operate. But he had miscalculated the nerve-strung Chavis. He had figured Chavis would turn his head toward the door, as the man had done once before. It was a break that Majors counted on. Chavis, meanwhile, had been thinking of another thing, and so now his mind was equally divided by two urges. He turned to look behind him, but as he turned his hand swept out and knocked the neary-by lamp from its bracket.

All this motion flowed together, half-seen and half-felt. Soder's arm ran upward across his chest, beneath the coat, and he took a full step backward. The rattled Chavis made a delayed grab for his gun; and Majors' thoughts rushed down another channel. He knocked the poker table away from him, not drawing, turned in toward the wall and batted out the remaining light. Then he plunged forward through the sudden black of the room and his right hand, all the while holding to a rung of the chair he had been sitting in, swung that chair overhand at Chavis.

He had little chance of missing Chavis, sightless as it was in the room. He heard it hit. Afterwards Soder's shot exploded like a stick of dynamite in those close quarters. Majors' feet struck the chair and he went over it in a long fall, driving into Chavis and carrying him backward. He got his arms around Chavis, and when he struck the floor his head smashed into Chavis' nose.

They rolled violently along the boards, Chavis trying to get his arms free. Majors' legs were tangled in the rungs of the chair. He kicked it away and rammed both knees into Chavis' stomach, driving a hot breath out of the man. Soder fired again, rattling every stick of furniture in the saloon. It was a wild, wide shot and afterwards Soder called: "Charley—get clear!"

Chavis was beneath Majors, still trying to bring out his gun. Majors punched his knee into the town marshal again, lifted him a foot from the floor and slammed him down. He felt Chavis go soft and took a chance, releasing his grip and sliding it down Chavis' arm. He got the gun and threw it away. All this was near the swinging doors, for he could hear

men out there talking and he could feel the cold wind pour
in; and then Chavis' arm, swinging around, caught him in the
mouth and sent him backwaard.

Soder yelled: "Where are you, Charley?"

Chavis was on his knees, wind sawing out of his throat.
Majors rolled clear and sprang up and closed in again,
catching Chavis as the latter also rose.

He had Chavis against a wall and he threw a blow at the
marshal's face and missed—and drove his knuckles into the
wall. Chavis hit him freely in the belly while Majors stood
there, shocked by the pain of his fist. Chavis suddenly yelled:
"Come here, Cal! Come over here!"

Majors bore against Chavis. They wrestled savagely along
the wall, striking and being struck, fighting closely and um-
mercifully with their knees and arms. Chavis kept butting at
Majors' chin, cracking Majors' teeth together. Blood ran
warmly in Majors' mouth. He heard Soder stumbling forward. He wrenched Chavis around, putting himself against
the wall; and when Soder came in, it was Chavis he first
struck with the whole force of his body. He kept yelling:
"Charley—pull out—pull out!" Majors, reaching out with a
free arm, caught Soder by the neck.

Soder was trying to use his gun. Majors felt it brush along
his flank, but the saloonman was afraid of hitting Chavis
who, caught between, put up a weaker and weaker struggle.
Majors slid his arm around the back of Soder's neck until he
had it locked in his elbow crook; he got his other arm away
from Chavis and completed the lock, grinding the face of the
saloonman against Chavis' head.

All three of them were milling the floor with their feet. It
carried them away from the wall. They went wheeling around
and around; they struck the bar, with Majors' back against it.
Soder gasped, "God damn you!" and fired and missed. Breath
came painfully out of his throat and he pushed against
Chavis, grinding Majors' spine into the bar. The pressure
tipped the bar. It swayed and went over with a solid crash,
all three falling with it. The collision broke off part of the
back bar, and bottles dropped and rolled around them and
drinking glasses splintered and began to cut into Majors' back
as he threshed from side to side.

Chavis was plainly out, squeezed unconscious, his body a
dead weight locked between the other two. Majors tightened
in on Soder's neck, feeling the man's legs kick stiffly, desper-

ately. Soder's gun came down on the bar, clipping the point of Majors' ear. After that Soder's fingers lost the gun, and he choked up a faint, "All right—all right!" Majors knew the man was going out then; holding that steady pressure, he lay there until he felt the saloonman's body lose all resistance.

He shook them off and stood up, and spewed the accumulated blood from his mouth. Silence came back to the saloon.

Men beyond the doors were sibilantly talking. A voice—it was Matt Oldroyd's voice—said: "Who's standing up?"

Majors grunted, "Come in," and spread his legs wide apart. Men came gingerly through the doors, careful in the way they placed their feet. He had to bend his shoulders a little to give his lungs a better bite on the wind that rushed in. Blood flowed from his head, making a steady drip on his shoulder. He moved the fingers of his left hand and felt no break, but the pain there was pretty bad. Light flared up from one of the wall lamps. Oldroyd came over, his young face actually shocked. He said, "Why, my God—!" Brick Brand pushed through the forming crowd in the doorway. Majors saw the printer look in at the scene with an odd, disturbed expression.

Oldroyd went on to the bar. He said, "You busted Charley's arm." Other townsmen came into the saloon then and it occurred to Majors to look around. Soder lay on the floor, the side of his face showing a round spot like a permanent burn, which was where Majors' arms had ground it against Chavis' head. Chavis had fallen against the capsized bar; one arm was unnaturally placed behind his back. Both of them were out and both of them showed punishment, Chavis particularly so. All the tables and chairs in the room were down. Glass littered the floor. Brick Brand prowled the place, finally returning to Majors. He said: "They had a dose of what I had, friend."

Majors wheeled away, pushing the crowd ungently aside. His shoulders brushed the printer and he saw the strange rigor of the printer's cheeks. As he went on across the square it was something that unaccountably stuck to his mind because of its peculiarity.

He went through the lobby and up to his room and stripped off his coat and filled up the washbowl and scrubbed the sweat and dirt and dried blood from his face and hands. Soap and water crept into bruises he didn't know about; his lips began to burn and the throb of his knuckles got worse. A small fragment of whisky glass had plowed a track across the back of his hand and remained half imbedded.

He put on his coat again and stood in the room's center and considered what he had done; and, as always, clearness came to his mind, and he looked back at himself as he had been during the fight with a faint astonishment. He could not remember the details of the fight, or the blows he had struck or the blows he had received. In a way it was as though he had stepped out of his skin for that space of time, becoming somebody else. All the restlessness and all the anger piled up in him had at last broken through, spilling free in one rush of action. He stood here now, very calm, purged of uncertainty. He was himself again, his nerves unnoticed and his muscles loose. And at once he had a feeling that what he was about to do was the right thing to do. He could literally feel old Jeff White's approval. So, restored to his self-confidence and his self-control, he returned to the lobby.

Broderick was there and Matt Oldroyd and Brick Brand were waiting for him.

Oldroyd threw Brand a friendless glance; and looked at Majors. "What's this brush jumper doin' here?"

But Majors was smiling at Broderick, and saying: "A favor for a favor, like I told you in the beginning. I'll take my favor now, Broderick. You got a gun?"

When Majors left the saloon the printer had gone to the swinging doors and watched him cross over the square; and not until Majors had disappeared in the hotel did the printer go back to have his look at Chavis and Soder. Doc Showers had arrived and was now kneeling over Soder. The rest of the crowd were reconstructing the fight; and the barkeeper, who had been temporarily out of the room, went around righting the chairs and tables with a great gloom on his face. The gambler and two others were pulling the bar back into place.

Doc Showers said: "Must have the muscles of a horse in his arms. Ain't a solid front tooth left in Charley's head."

Talk became general.

"Well, Soder will kill him."

"The hell he will. The big fellow buffaloed the both of these boys final. They'll be gone from this town tomorrow night. You see."

"Nope. Not Soder."

"That's twice this Majors has stepped out of a hole. He was at that far table. Soder must of put a shot . . ."

The printer drank it in, meanwhile watching Doc Showers work over the two on the floor. In him was a strange feeling, like growth; his chest deepened, his thin arms had the weight of heavy muscle, and in his heart was a pride as great as if he himself had smashed the lights out of that pair. He found his voice and said gruffly: "They'll run." When the gambler looked curiously across the room the printer returned the stare, the back muscles of his legs tightening.

This was the change in the printer, as complete as the change from adolescence to manhood: On the floor, thoroughly smashed, were two men he hated with a depth and a passion very near to the border of madness. He could look at them now and feel the wine of freedom run through him, making him brave, making him hopeful.

It all went back to his entrance into this town five years before, when he had been a man with self-respect and some conviction. He had started his print shop and his small weekly paper, and his first lessons had been bitter ones. He had meant to speak his mind as a brave man might—and for his pains he had been horsewhipped in public. A weaker man would have left Reservation overnight, but there was in the printer a pride even greater than his physical fear and pride made him stay and weather the contempt and the indifference of this hard town. Silent and bitter, he endured the evils and brutality he saw, and wrote polite stories of men he hated, and begged printing business from merchants who used that business as a club to keep him humble. He was a shadow in this town, scarcely a grade better than the riding bum who swamped out the Old Dixie, and he knew it and slowly shriveled, and came to despise himself and to fear the sound of footsteps dragging near his office door. And the little flame of pride sank down, and he saw life with a hopelessness that got blacker and blacker, and nothing but drink would cut the nagging misery of his mind, dulling it but never completely killing it.

Here he stood, seeing the symbol of all that he hated lying as so much pulp on the floor—put there by one man who didn't know fear. For the printer it was like the passage of a long and terrible night whose nightmares he would never forget. So strong was the rush of his feelings that, though he didn't know it, he was crying.

He heard Doc Showers say: "Majors? Who told you he resigned his star?"

"On the jail office wall," grumbled the gambler.

The printer opened his mouth, and shut it. He said in a dropping voice: "No, no! My God, he wouldn't give up!" He turned out of the saloon and ran headlong up the street to the jail office. The feed store man, Lute Janes, stood in front of the bulletin board, working his jaws steadily around a cut of plug as he read. The printer pushed against him and saw the notice.

Lute Janes said: "Get your damned elbows out of my ribs."

"He wouldn't do that," groaned the printer. "Why should he? It ain't right!"

"Ain't it?" said Lute Janes. "Well, he's smart enough to know he can't beat the country."

The printer yelled, "You're a liar!"

Janes stepped back. His eyes were round and yellow above a thin nose and a crescent mustache. "You been feedin' on meat?"

The printer went at him wildly with his fists. He had never known how to fight and a cooler man would have slaughtered him, but all the burning intensity of five years was behind his erratic blows. He hit Janes a dozen times, in the chest, in the stomach and once in the face. Janes never got his rawboned arms unwound; he never managed to brush the printer away. As far as he was concerned, the printer might have been two men, those small fists hooking in from all angles, and his skinny body bumping up against Janes, crowding him, his boots stamping on Janes' feet. In the end Janes simply got tired of backing up, tripped himself and sat down on the walk with a huge grunt, more shocked than hurt.

"Now wait," he said reasonably. "What've I done, Billy?"

The printer had exhausted himself. His heart sledged against his ribs and the lining of his mouth was dryer than cotton, so dry he couldn't immediately swallow. But he looked at Lute Janes, another of those men he had so long feared, and saw no more arrogance, no more threat in the man. Janes had called him by name; was looking up to him with a degree of respect. The printer had the bitterest of moments then in reflecting how different his life would have been had he made that show of force five years ago.

He turned from Janes, walking spraddle-legged down the middle of the dusty street. He crossed the square and went into the lobby. He was in a state of mind to recognize only Jim

Majors, the rest of the men in the room being formless blurs on the edge of his vision. He stopped and stared at Majors, his breathing quite uneven.

"Why—why did you go and do that? What can a man believe? Listen. I was a white man once, when I came here. But what did they do to me? I have crawled on my belly to these people. They're the scum of the earth but I crawled on my belly to them so I could live. I have written nice lies about them when I knew they were rotten all the way through. I see men killed but I say nothing. No. I talk about Webber painting his store. I see Soder and his gambler trim all the fools, but I mind my manners or else I get my face kicked in. I call Maffitt 'Mr. Maffitt' when he comes to town because I have been horsewhipped in public and I know when to cringe to my betters. So here I am, a coward and a barroom tramp. Then I see you do what I never expected any man in the world could do, and I stand in the saloon and know there's some justice in this world and that there is such a thing as courage. It takes fifty years off my shoulders. I'm a white man again. But what do you do? You turn in your star and everything is lost and the crooks are right after all! Oh, my God—Why? Why?"

He bent back until his thin shoulders touched the door's casing; and remained there, spent and hard-breathing and terribly shaken by the outpour of all that he felt. It left him empty and it left him futile; and gray hopelesssness began to settle again.

Only, it was odd to see the way the big man listened to him . . . Saying nothing. Smiling with his long lips in a rather sad, crooked way . . . With a deep kindness in his eyes, as if he knew the despair behind those words . . . It was something the printer could feel, like warmth. The silence ran on. He looked around, recognizing Matt Oldroyd and Brand and Broderick. They didn't say anything. The exposure of his emotions had embarrassed them. They didn't understand. But Majors did.

Majors' voice was gentle. "You're all right. Don't worry, son. A man can only go through hell once, and you're through it now. You got a gun and a horse?"

"Yeah," said the printer, winded and indifferent.

"You ride with me. We're going up to the Barrs'. Dobe Hyde will be comin' that way. May be a fight. I'm telling you."

The others were walking toward the door. The printer said, "Sure—why not?" He had been through terrific swings of emotion and he was slow to comprehend. He repeated, "Sure, I'll go," and went toward the stable with his head down and his arms swinging. He didn't have the thing clear until he had saddled and swung up. Then he said aloud to himself: "Why, it doesn't mean a thing. It's all the same—star or no star." He galloped across the square and turned into his own shop. He caught up a .44 and tucked it beneath his trouser band. When he got back to the street the rest of them were coming by—Majors and Brand and Broderick and Oldroyd. He fell in with them, silently, his mind reviving and full of wonder at this odd outfit. But nobody spoke and he was content to ride, the cold air flowing against his thin shirt and something far down inside stirring. Like growth. And he could feel the weight of his arms, as though they were heavy with muscle. Majors' shape was high and broad before him, and he watched the sway of those shoulders, and was afraid of nothing.

Later, at the second bend of the Ute's south fork, they heard a burst of far off firing, which was a sound that raced the printer's blood. Majors dropped a single word, "Ride," and they jumped into a sweeping run that took them down the wholly dark road. The firing ran on steadily, now single shots, now quick volleys. The occasional rapids of the Ute sent up frigid, slashing echoes and the shoulder of the Silver Lode was a huge black shadow all up to the diamond-dusted sky. At the last bend of the Ute, long later, the lights of the Barr house threw their round beams across the dark. But the firing had quit.

Majors drew in, bringing them all around him. He said, "I think they have gotten into the house." The printer, closely listening to the big man's voice, heard no excitement in it and no anger. It was cool, like the even-sharp strokes of a bell; and without flaw. The printer pulled up his shoulders and swept the night wind into his chest; and heard the mourning wildness of a coyote's call high up on the ridge—and felt that wildness in himself.

"We'll get up on the rim," said Majors. Single file they hit a trail and began rising from the canyon.

19

━━━◆◎◆━━━

By the Ute Water

THEY CAME to the top of the rim, Majors and Matt Oldroyd riding together. Brand had paired off with the printer; Broderick followed behind. They drifted on at a casual walk, making little sound in this blanketing night. The air was very clear and the countless stars showed a cloudy brilliance, filling the sky all down to its lowest horizon, to create in the printer's bounding imagination the sense of riding beneath a dome whose edges he might reach if he ran far enough. The impressions of the night were all sharp to him and wine was in his blood and a kind of silent laughter stirred him at the thought of pacing beside Brick Brand, who was an outlaw. Laughter and pride in his new condition. They were drifting on the rim's edge, the shape of Majors, very solid before the printer. The light beams from the ranch house grew brighter, and now and then were cut off as somebody in the house passed in front of them. A dog in the yard barked steadily, those echoes breaking the stillness with an almost mechanical regularity. Majors murmured, "Wait," and disappeared.

Brand's face was a luminous, diffused disc before the printer. He said: "Friend, this ain't your style. It will maybe turn out tough. Better draw back."

"No," said the printer. "No."

Majors drifted up. "We leave the horses here."

They got down and went on afoot, holding close to the rim. The river's surface was a ragged silver streak in the canyon below. Wind dragged its steady waterfall echoes out of the pines along the Silver Lode. When they stopped again, long later, they were abreast the ranch house; they were on

179

their bellies, watching it. Woodsmoke smell drifted across the printer's nostrils.

The back door of the house stood open and from their position on the rim they looked directly down upon the horses waiting in the rear yard, half illumined by the light pouring out of the door.

Majors whispered, "I count eight. Where'd Dobe get the extra four riders?"

"Maybe Maffitt," suggested Oldroyd.

Brand said, "No, he was supposed to stay out of this."

"Makes it tougher," said Morse.

Somebody opened the front door and stepped to the porch, shaped definitely against the light. "Hyde," grunted Brand, and reached for his gun. Majors' single "No" stopped him.

All of them watched Dobe Hyde move as far as the porch steps, where he paused and seemed to scan the bottomless shadows of the canyon. When he turned into the house he left the door open. The dog kept on barking; somebody walked through the back door and crossed the yard. Night's chill began to shake the printer's body. He gritted his teeth and tried to stop it, feeling shame; and could not.

Majors murmured, "We'll take this trail."

The printer got behind Majors. They crawled down the trail single file, reaching a corner of the front yard. The house now was sixty feet away.

"That dam' dog," murmured Brand.

Majors said: "I'm going around the other side and see how it looks. Wait."

He rose from his haunches and walked rapidly over the yard to the corner of the porch. Here he ducked down, skirting the porch edge until he reached the steps. The beam of light flowing through the front door made a yellow hurdle before which he paused; and from this position he caught a partial view of the house hallway. He saw nothing. A few voices lifted from the depths of the house, but by the tone he judged Dobe's men to be in the back part. And so he took his risk, stood upright, and crossed the beam of light without haste. A moment later he reached the far corner of the porch. A window on this side of the house showed light. He put himself against the wall and crawled to the window's edge, and pulled off his hat and tried a quick look, ducking immediately back.

All the Barrs were in the room, and a man he hadn't seen before stood by the hall door, holding a gun on them.

He cut under the window, traveling faster. At the rear of the house he stopped and made himself a flat shape in the shadows. There was a good deal of commotion back here. Dobe's men had pulled up a flat-bed wagon and were hitching a team to it.

Dobe stood on the porch, calling: "The girl wants to take a trunk. She can take it. Go up to her room and lug it down, Jett."

Majors teetered on the edge of a break, and changed his mind when he thought of the man standing guard over the Barrs. But it gave him an idea. He cut back along the house and ran beside the porch. At the lane of yellow doorlight he paused long enough to take a look into the hallway again and, seeing it clear, walked through the light. A moment later he reached the spot where he had left his men.

They were gone.

He faced the black rock wall of the canyon. He said in a gentle murmur, "Matt," and got no answer. To right and left the shadows were black enough to cut. He could see nothing. Dobe's shrill voice traveled clearly from the back yard: "Bring down the trunk"—and the sense of a narrowing opportunity began to push at Majors. He walked along the canyon wall a few feet, following it toward the rear yard, expecting at any moment to bump into his party. He was almost abreast the back side of the house when he stopped and realized he was wasting too much time. He turned, growing a little careless, and reached the foot of the trail again, once more calling: "Matt."

Somebody in the rear yard sang out: "Who's in the barn now?"

Dobe's shrill voice said: "What?"

"In the barn."

Dobe's voice lifted a full tone in pitch. "Godry, you over there?"

Sweat began to sting Majors' face like nettles. Time ran short and trouble was about to break loose while the rest of his men were threshing around the darkness on a fool's errand. His temper lifted, turning him careless as he trotted along the porch and came to the beam of light again.

Without pausing, he walked up the steps toward the doorway. Dobe Hyde's little shape was at the moment disappearing at the far end, into the yard. Dobe was repeating a name rapidly: "Godry—Godry!"

Rooms opened into this long hall and a light came out of the doorway of that room where the Barrs stood and where Hyde's man would be. Hyde's man, he thought, would be facing the Barrs, his back to the doorway. This was the chance he gambled on as he lifted his gun and stepped into the hall. He went toward the doorway in long strides, and saw the back of Dobe's man just inside the room.

At that same moment the Barrs saw him appear and something on their faces warned Dobe's guard, who started to turn. Majors said, "Hold it," and hit the man soundly over the head with the barrel of his piece. Suddenly, outside, Dobe Hyde let go with a wild, high howl: "Oldroyd!" The guard buckled at the knees and fell forward on his face, whereupon Dan Barr made a long jump from the corner of the room to catch up the man's gun. The back yard was all at once full of firing, and a man's steps beat across the upper floor of the house. Majors came out of the room and and saw Jett's face hook over the second floor landing; he ducked back as Jett threw a bullet at him. Dan Barr seized the guard's gun and threw himself around. He wrenched up the side window and dove through; the other Barr men were breaking toward Majors.

Jett had fired again, smashing the hall light. As he raced toward the stairs and took them three at a time Majors heard Jett running through the upper part of the house. When he reached the upper landing he heard Jett somewhere in the back end. There were no lights here and he had no knowledge of the house at all. He ran dead into a wall, crawled along it until he felt a door frame. Jett said, "Majors!" and let go another bullet. Majors hooked a shot into the room, and heard a window give way with a full smash of glass and wood, and a man's great yell of pain rising from the yard below. Jett had taken his chances on a jump.

Majors charged over to the window. There wasn't any hall light to illumine the yard now, but the kitchen lamps laid a little glow on part of it, partially pressing back the dense shadows; and so he had his view of the fight.

Hyde's men were at the moment rushing toward their horses and little flashes from the back side of the yard showed where Oldroyd and those others had stationed themselves. Their lead laced the yard wickedly. Jett was on the ground, rolling from side to side and still crying. One of Hyde's men ducked behind the flat-bed wagon and then the bullets from the barn veered that way and the box of the wagon began to rattle like a drum. A horse went down, hindquarters first; all the yard was rolling with dust. Some of Dobe's men had reached their saddles. They were plunging away into the darkness beyond the barn.

Dobe Hyde came into the kitchen glow, running toward his horse. He had lost his hat and his bald head was a shining target from above, and he carried something in both hands. A bullet plowed in front of him, ripping up the earth like fire smoke, causing him to stumble and drop whatever he carried. This was the moment when Majors saw how fixed were the patterns of a man's life, for Dobe came to a full halt and bent down to retrieve that object; and so he stood when a bullet from the barn caught him, turned him like a flimsy straw dummy in high wind, and sent him wheeling to the ground.

The last man rushed by the barn, leaving Dobe dead in the dust, leaving Jett in his twisting agony. The printer raced from the barn and took a vague position in the yard, futilely firing at Dobe's vanished crew. Oldroyd trotted out of the murk toward Jett. Somewhere in the house Katherine Barr was calling: "Jim—Jim!"

He saw her when he came to the head of the stairs. She had brought a lamp from another room, and stood below him with her face tilted upward and a strangeness in her eyes. Afterwards her shoulders dropped and he didn't see her face until he went down. Oldroyd walked into the hall, carrying Jett in his arms. The printer still fired his shots at the dark, but the others were returning, crowding by Katherine and Majors. He removed his hat, not realizing he did so. She was so composed before him, so impenetrably serene. . . .

She said quietly, "I wasn't sure," and followed the other men into the big living room. Majors tramped after her. Oldroyd had dumped Jett on a sofa; he stood over Jett.

"Out entirely," he murmured. "He busted somethin' in that jump."

The Barrs were all here.

Brand faced Majors with a small expression of unease. He knew what was in the big man's mind and forestalled it. "My fault," he admitted. "But they were all in the back yard, and I thought the barn was a good spot to be. We crawled around the house and cut in from the back."

Majors only said, "All right."

The Barrs were watching him, neither friendly nor otherwise. But the situation was odd and hard to explain, and they didn't know what brought him here, or what was in his head. Jett's groan dragged across the silence. Katherine Barr's expressive face instantly showed a reflection of the kid's pain. She couldn't help it, however else she might feel toward Jett. Majors made a solid shape in the room, taciturnly trying to find a proper explanation. He found none, and gave it up; he went over to Jett. The kid's eyes were bad.

"Jett," he said, "Hyde's dead."

Jett's lips shrank back from his teeth. His knees worked slowly up and down. He sighed. "It's in my side."

"We'll get Doc Showers up here. But I'm asking you. Will the rest of your crowd come back?"

"Why should they? No. It was Dobe. They won't come back. I won't come back either. It's my side. Jesus!"

Katherine Barr came over the room. She crouched down and laid her hand on Jett's forehead. He was, Majors could see, going out again. He moaned faintly, "Thanks—thanks," and went still.

Majors said to the printer: "You go get Doc Showers. Make it a quick ride."

He stood there afterwards, thinking of the consequences of this fight. Dobe was dead and the pressure was off the Barrs. He was trying to see the end of his job—and couldn't quite see it. Maffitt was left, and the old hatred still lingered between the Barrs and the few east fork people, like Sultan and Ketchum. There still remained something to be done; and he was trying to see the way to do it.

Dan Barr spoke up bitterly. "Your switch came too late, Majors. Ring's dead. Our father's dead."

"I have made no switch," Majors told him.

"Then why come here?"

"Dobe," said Majors and let it go like that.

"They drove us into the house in a hurry," Dan Barr explained, as though compelled. "A bullet almost got Katherine. So we made a bargain. Agreed to leave the country. Too many people have died around here. I don't want any more."

Fay Barr said, "One of these days I'll look up Buff Sultan,"—and his dark face showed the old hatred fully—"and maybe Ketchum. Then, by God, we'll be satisfied."

Dan swung around. "Shut up, Fay. Shut up!" He looked at

Majors again, impatient with his questions. "Well, what do you want of us?"

"Why?"

"It's your show. You started it and I guess you end it. You've wrecked a lot of things for us, and for others, to get your point. But I will not fight again. What do you want?"

"We'll ride up to the Pocket," said Majors.

"It is one thing I can do with real pleasure," Dan retorted. "Creed, you stay on the ranch with Katherine."

They all went out, leaving Majors alone with the girl. She was on her knees, her hand supporting the kid's loose head. Her face was smooth and pale, and beyond his power to read. For a moment he remembered the scene on the ridge and a little of that tumult came back to him. She had power to stir him, to deepen his hungers and his sense of loneliness. But it soon went away and he looked at her as a man, lost in the desert, might look at some far light. Ring was dead and old Pedee was dead, and these were the things which she would remember and forever put against him.

She murmured: "It is so strange, and so sad—I remember now that I have never seen you laugh."

"No, I guess not."

Her voice was even, and gently curious. "You've gone through things like this before? Is that the reason?"

"That's the reason."

She regarded him with the same dark, remote serenity. "And other women, as well."

He had a blunt answer for that. "I have known other women."

The serenity faded. Her chin lifted and her lips were long and pressed even. Faint color came to her face. Her voice was curt with an anger he couldn't comprehend. "Go back to them!"

"No," he said. "Not to them, or to any woman."

She said: "My father is across the hall. He is dead."

He didn't answer. He turned from the room and found the rest of the men waiting in the yard. Brand had been talking to Dan Barr.

Dan Barr said: "I'm glad to know how you stand, Brick. I guess there's a few white men left in the world. But damned few. Majors, you ready?"

Brand spoke to Majors with an evident difficulty. "You're goin' to the Pocket, and I know what you intend to do. I'd just as soon not be in on that. I've changed my politics, but I can't raise a gun against those boys. Maybe you see."

"Wait here."

"Be a little careful. Ben's a wolf with long ears."

Majors led his outfit across the bridge into the quick-climbing trail. Presently the ranch lights died behind and they were absorbed by the pure darkness of the Silver Lode. Winter's smell flowed downslope with the wind and five hundred feet higher the big gelding's feet began to scuff up half-frozen dirt clods on the trail.

Fifteen minutes from the ranch Majors stopped. "Two men's not enough down there."

Dan Barr's voice came calmly from the rear of the column. "Uncle Will, you ride back."

They went on, with a sibilance of leather in the column and the soft heave of the climbing ponies. Now and then the trail came hard by the liquid turbulence of the fast-falling Ute, where mist from the river's wild churning spread like fog before them. Majors stopped occasionally, keening the night for its secrets. In darkness and uncertainty such as this, he had intuitions that worked for him, that had a sensitiveness to the intangible pressure of trouble; but nothing warned him now, and so he kept on.

As he traveled he had Katherine Barr in his thoughts. He had her features clearly before him, and could remember all her mannerisms—the even gentleness of her lips in repose, The color of her eyes in anger, the pride that strengthened her voice. He had known women before, and some need for honesty had made him tell her this. What he had afterwards added, silently to himself, was that no other woman had so stirred him as she had done. It was an outward beauty and outward grace. More than that, it was the stormy tide of inner emotions which set her apart. She was rich in the way a woman should be rich, at times gay and reckless, at times showing him the deep, mysterious glow of a softer mood. These were the things he remembered, with the old rankling hunger in him that he knew would never grow less, and never be satisfied. He had certain things yet to do. When they were done—if they were done—he would ride out of this country as he had ridden in, altogether alone. Only, somewhere along these last hard days, he had lost something he doubted he'd ever have again—a careless ease and an eagerness to know what life was like over the hill. He would be looking back, wherever he rode, to what he had left behind.

The trail leveled away from its climbing and began to dip. Through the timber he caught the first flash of light from the house in the Pocket. He stopped again, the rest of the party drifting forward, and said: "We'll stay clear of the trail," —and led them on into the timber. They made their way down the slope by cautious degrees, turning from tree to tree until they came upon the margin of the meadow. Light showed through the kitchen windows and through the side windows of the front room. Dan Barr bent near Majors, murmuring: "Corral's empty."

The corral was a blurred streak in front of them. Dan Barr whispered, "Wait," and left his horse, merging with the earth. Something splashed the Ute's water, out in the middle of the meadow. Majors kept watching the window lights and could find nothing there. Dan Barr returned, heavily breathing. "Horses gone. Far as I can see nobody's downstairs."

"Sparks comin' from the chimney," said Majors, and left the saddle. "I'll be back." He cut into the meadow. He came up against the corral bars and had his own look through the house windows, forty feet away. Kitchen and front room were apparently empty; the upper story of the house showed no light. He lay against the corral and debated this in his mind until the run of time turned him impatient. Dropping to the ground, he worked his way across to the house and behind it until he had reached the back door, which was closed.

Rising up, he laid his ear to the house wall and kept it there, listening for the vibration of voices or of footsteps. Wind played more fully against his face, but he heard no rumors of life in the house. The chimney sparks indicated they had been here recently, and might still be here, but there wasn't any sense of warning in his head, and the impatience he had carried up the hill got greater and at once he lifted his gun, took a good grip on the doorknob, and flung the door open.

He was inside instantly, closing the door behind. This was a small hall half-lighted by the lamps still in kitchen and front room. His glance raced up the stairway, and then, seeing no shape in that darkness above, he knew the house was empty. He knew what he wanted to do, and did it quickly. Ducking into the kitchen, he seized the lamp on the table and brought it back to the hall. He took off the globe

and unscrewed the wick, careful to keep the flame alive while
he dumped the bowl of kerosene on the floor at the base of a
wall. He dropped the burning wick into this pool of oil and
watched it catch brightly and make one vivid leap toward the
wall's loose paper. He remained there until he knew the wall
would catch fire. Afterwards he opened the back door to
create a greater draft for the fire.

Dan Barr's voice came straight over from the mouth of the
trail. "Here."

Majors crossed the clearing and found the group. He
stepped into the saddle. All of them waited silently, watching
the fire make a swift upward rush along the inner wall. Wind
had blown the back door completely open and at the end of
five minutes the hall was a mass of flame and the bone-dry
wood began to crack like gunshots.

Majors said: "That's all."

But Dan Barr murmured: "Wait. I want to be sure. It was
an evil dam' place. It always was. In Maffitt's time and before. That's where my brother Clay was killed. The east fork
people caught him there—when I was just a kid."

Majors saw Matt Oldroyd's shoulders swing. But nothing
was said, and they sat like statues in the saddle. All the back
windows were blood-crimson squares. Little by little the light
crept across the back yard toward the trees, touching them
faintly. A low humming ran out of the place, deepening
presently into a solid roar. And when the upper windows began to turn red they knew the fire had at last reached the second floor.

Majors repeated, "That's all," and led them up the trail.

They were back at the house in a half-hour. The printer
waited for them on the porch and Doc Showers' buggy stood
in the yard. "Guess the kid will make it," said the printer.

Nobody got down. Everybody waited for Majors to speak.
They were all looking at him. Dan Barr said, in the same
tone of irritable defeat: "Well, what do you want us to do?"

Katherine Barr came to the door. Majors saw her there,
slim against the light, her head lifted and her face vaguely
showing.

He said: "I'd like to see all of you in town tomorrow
morning." He turned suddenly out of the yard and fell into
the canyon road, towing his crowd behind.

Little Peters had been on the shelf above the Barr ranch

when Dobe Hyde struck, and later had witnessed Majors' surprise attack. This information he carried back to the Pocket. "I dunno who it was that put up that second fight and I dunno how it came out. Too far away. There was a hell of a bust of shots. Then everything quieted down."

Maffitt said: "Majors, certainly. Nobody else would buck Dobe."

"I dunno how it came out."

But Maffitt looked at Peters and at the others and his solid face was smart and hard and sly. "I know. It would be Majors who came out. His luck runs strong. I knew that about the big fellow the first time I laid eyes on him." His flat lips stirred and the gray surfaces of his eyes threw out a stronger and stronger brilliance. It wasn't anger and it wasn't fear. In Ben Maffitt was a coolness and a patience that rose above these things and now he was seeing the picture complete as it had to be. "But men like Majors and men like me always make a last mistake. Luck goes out—and the man goes out. We'll drift."

"Why?" asked Little Peters.

"Because they'll be up here. I can call the cards before they fall. I know just how the big fellow does his thinkin', for he's like me. Ain't much difference between us except a fence, which is the law. It's a flimsy fence and God only knows why it is he's on one side and I'm on the other. But that's the way it is."

So Maffitt pulled his companions out of the Pocket and halted them on the high bench overlooking the meadow. This was the old apple orchard from which Majors had first viewed the Pocket. And from this spot, a little later, Ben Maffitt saw the house burst into flames. He shrugged his shoulders in the darkness, too much of a gambler to express emotion. He turned to the others.

"Well, here's where we ran out our string. It was good while it lasted, but the big fellow changed it. Makes no difference now what happens to him, the valley ain't the same any more. I'll meet you in Jackson Hole, three weeks from today."

"Where you goin'?" asked Little Peters.

"One more card to drop," said Maffitt enigmatically, and left them.

At three o'clock in the morning he rode to the edge of Reservation and left his horse in Charley Chavis' barn. He went around to the bedroom window and knocked on the glass, but after a while, receiving no answer, he walked away—not knowing that Chavis had piled all his belongings in a buggy and departed from the valley not more than an hour before. The town was entirely dark at this hour, with a sharper and sharper wind pouring down the flanks of the Silver Lode. Ben Maffitt paced through the back alleys, crossed the main street near the bridge, and circled to the rear of the livery stable, sliding into the stable's dense dark. He made himself a bed deep in the hay and, thus hidden, waited for daylight and for his chance.

20

By Gray Morning

AT DAYLIGHT winter suddenly dropped out of the sky in a faint shifting of snow. By nine o'clock a rising wind drove in from the peak of the Silver Lode and the air was white and thick as meal, with the street ends lost to sight and the lights of the town vaguely sparkling through clouded windows. All Reservation's roofs were whitely quilted. Wind began to pluck a long, low whine from the building eaves, and drifts piled up against the street corners and against the weather walls, accumulating and being whipped away in violent eddies, and reforming elsewhere. Now and then a rougher gust of wind seized a drift and carried it the whole length of the street in sheets of glittering spray.

Majors had early sent Matt Oldroyd down the east fork to bring in Ketchum and the Sultans. The Barrs came in around nine-thirty: Katherine and her two brothers and the older pair, Creed and Will. It was about ten when the east fork crowd, bucking a continuously strengthening wind, reached town and stamped into the hotel lobby, their cheeks whipped red. Matt's blond eyebrows were beaded with little ice particles. The Sultans, Buff and Edith, had come in a buggy because of Buff's bad arm. Ketchum complained of this to Majors.

"A wild errand for Buff. This could have waited. It's been goin' on fifteen years and another week wouldn't hurt."

This early morning Broderick had set up a stove in the lobby; its belly showed dull crimson and heat ran the room gratefully. Brand came out of the street, but when he saw the

191

gathered group he withdrew. Tony occasionally passed the dining room arch on her travels to and from the kitchen.

Majors stood, back against the lobby desk, reading this crowd with a careful eye, feeling the remnant heat of the old antagonism between the two factors. The Barr men held themselves near the door, the clannishness of their tempers showing in that bunched posture. The two older men would never change and Fay, whose eyes showed an actual hate as he stared at Buff Sultan, would never change. But in Dan, whose hollowed cheeks revealed the strain he had been under, Majors placed some hope. He knew Buff Sultan's attitude, which, without friendliness, was nevertheless ready for reasonable compromise. Of Ketchum's disposition he knew nothing, nor did he much care.

The two women, Edith and Katherine, had come up to the stove, standing on opposite sides. It was the first time Majors had seen them together and for a moment he was free to make his comparisons. Edith Sultan was the smaller, with a fairness of skin and an expression that seemed to seek light, that seemed ready for laughter. She would forgive, Majors thought, because of a gentleness in her; and because of Dan Barr. He could not see that gentleness in Katherine Barr. She stood tall and slim in the room, her chin lifted and her eyes very dark from all that she was remembering. It was a pride, like steel, that held her this way; it was the force of emotions so deep and so strong behind the sustaining gravity of her features which held her this way. He saw it and felt a slow thrust of disappointment, as though she had failed him.

Dan Barr said: "Why wait? What is it you want?"

They were at once all watching him, and he knew that for some of them nothing but force would do. It was the old, old pattern and a reflection of that weary and irritable wisdom which showed in the slanting corners of his eyes and in the sudden roll of his lips. He made a taciturn, heavy shape against the desk; and physical threat lay in his muscles. He knew he had made himself master of these people, and knew that they knew it. For better or worse it was his strength he had to use.

"The job is not quite done, but it will be when we leave this room. Some of you hate me, and I can't help that, nor expect anything else. There's been enough crying and enough trouble. I take the responsibility for it, and say it must end. If you do not agree I'll see that the rest of you live in trouble till you die. Do you understand?" He put it that way, the frank threat having its effect in their eyes. He realized it put them all farther away from him and ground their dislike deeper, and could not help it. Katherine showed him a glance dark and half-startled; and a quicker breath stirred her breasts.

Ketchum flung up his head, stung to sudden anger. "You're usin' the wrong tone," Majors."

"I'm speakin' to people who have been fools for fifteen years."

"Maybe we like our way better than yours," challenged Ketchum, definitely setting himself for a quarrel.

"You have a son. You want him killed?"

Ketchum flared up intolerantly. "I'll take care of my own."

But Buff Sultan suddenly said: "Be quiet, Jude."

Ketchum reared around. "Why, hell, Buff . . . !" He looked a long time at Buff Sultan, and finally shrugged his shoulders. He gave Majors a grudging answer. "I can't fight alone. I guess the valley's gone to pot."

Majors thought he saw relief loosen the corners of Dan Barr's lips. He watched all these people with a growing sharpness. He said, to Dan Barr: "Sultan is tired of trouble. So are you. We make our bargain on that. Your brother Fay won't change and your two relatives are thinking of ways to get even, right now. So all three of them leave the country."

Silence held the room. Fay Barr's mouth opened—and closed. Broderick, all the while in the background, hauled his vast frame around and gave the Barr family a speculating stare. Buff Sultan showed something like shock at the proposal; and in fact it had caught them all off guard—all but Dan Barr, whose attitude since the night before had been one of desperate resignation. Fay put his head near Dan's and started to whisper something. The first sound he let out of his lips was like the rasp of a file in this silence. He jerked back and kept still. Dan Barr turned his glance from Majors to Edith Sultan; and it was then that Majors saw the character of the man fully. Dan Barr had lost something that he couldn't recover, and he had no hope now. When he spoke it was as if he were announcing his decision for Edith Sultan to hear.

"All right. They'll go."

Majors said, to Fay and the two older ones: "You agree?"

But Dan Barr broke in with a grating voice: "I'll do the agreeing. They'll go."

"Tony," said Majors. "Tony, come here."

She had been in the dining room's doorway, silently looking on. She came forward, uncertain and disturbed. Majors smiled at her, his face growing smooth. Most of these people were watching Tony; but Katherine Barr's attention had never left the big man, and now she saw that expression which Tony seemed to draw out of him—so strangely sad and so kind; as though there was in Tony a quality that could break through the hardest temper in this man. There was a gentleness in him then she had never seen, and an affection she had never felt. Katherine's glance raced to the girl, and back to Majors. Afterwards she dropped her eyes and her lips pressed together to hold in the sudden cry that went through her—"Why to her? Why to her?"

Majors said: "Tony, that house up on the ridge is yours and the land around it is yours. Maybe it will help. These people, all of them, owe you something, but it is pretty late for them to make up for what they took away. It is a tough world, full of misery that men make for themselves. I have found it so. But once in a while I see somebody that reminds me of a light in the dark. You are like that." He looked at Sultan, and at Dan Barr. "That's the bargain—all of it. You agree?"

Sultan hadn't said much. All he had to offer now was, "I'm glad to have it over." Dan Barr nodded, without speaking. Broderick said: "How about Maffitt?"

Majors said: "I think he knows the good times are over. He'll run. Why should he stay, having no help from anybody in the valley? I'm through here."

Katherine Barr lifted her head. She turned to Edith Sultan and put out her hand, touching the other girl's shoulder. That was all, but afterwards, looking again to Majors, she saw a shading in his eyes, like relief or like pleasure. As though he was pleased with her . . . he went across the room to the door and turned there, and was smiling as he had smiled when he first entered Reservation, his long lips turned at the corners and with an expression in his eyes she never had understood. It was as though he knew something about life none of them knew—a knowledge which made him look at them rather wistfully, as though all that he felt and all that he believed brought him only to a hopeless answer. He was a tall, rugged shape against the door, his presence definitely influencing them. Katherine, no longer looking at him, knew that he was a bigger man than any of them had realized.

He said quietly, still smiling, "So long," and went out the door, closing it behind him.

Brand waited in the muffling drive of snow. Brand said, "Listen, friend, listen . . ."

He let it go like that. Majors shook his hand and went on to the stable. But then he changed his mind and trudged across the street to the jail office. The notice still fluttered on the bulletin board. He took it down and slid the badge into his pocket. This was something he would put to old Jeff White, leaving the answer to old Jeff. Retracing his steps, he observed that the saloon remained dark, and wondered about it, and dismissed the wonder as he entered the gloomy run of the stable. A lantern's light cut frigid, ineffectual lances of light through the pall. The hostler had gone.

Majors took his gear from a peg and walked into the gelding's stall. He saddled up, and spoke patiently when the gelding fiddled in the soft dirt. "Just save that for the mountain. You'll need it." He put his head against the gelding's side and waited for the horse to blow out its breath, and hauled in the latigo. The gelding grunted. It was all part of the game they had played through many another morning, leading back into the years. Never any change.

The hostler hadn't appeared. Majors went into the little office and calculated his bill, and laid five silver dollars on the table. He stepped out of the office and stopped there. His eyes came together, and he remained this way a long while. The job was done and it was a hard ride over the hill, but he was waiting for the old eagerness to possess him and the old impatience to call up the desire to be on the travel. It didn't come and he knew it wouldn't come. He had ridden out of many a town gaily, leaving nothing behind. This time would be different. When he crossed the bridge and turned up the Silver Lode he would leave something behind.

"Majors."

It came through his thinking. It came crashing through. And he turned, knowing the voice and what that voice meant, and saw Ben Maffitt's wide, short shape at the back end of the runway, half-merged with the gloom. He had made his mistake. Part of the job hadn't been done—the fire in the Pocket hadn't been enough; and he understood suddenly that he had made that most fatal of all mistakes: he had underestimated a man.

He saw Maffitt's face indistinctly through the muddy shadows. He had partially turned toward Maffitt, though he wasn't fully squared about and his position was bad for a clean draw. The gelding stood a little aside of a straight line between them.

Maffitt's voice was so easy, so slow and so certain that he had to admire it even while his thoughts began to race outward from his position and slam up against dead ends.

"Where'd you think I'd go, friend Jim?"

Majors said: "My mistake."

"Maybe. We got to find that out. It's what I'm here for, and I wouldn't leave till I know. If it's a mistake it's the first one you've made in this country."

"Ben," said Majors, "I thought you'd move on."

Maffitt showed his pride in the way he boosted his words down the runway. "You're a smarter man than that, friend. You're a wolf, like me. You crossed my trail. So I have got to find out. I'd go a thousand miles to find out. Hell, if we were ridin' together we'd lick the world. That's a thought, friend Jim. A thought."

The gelding's head turned toward Majors, its ears lifting and its eyes showing the luminous shine of the outthrown lantern light. It was a poor light but it made a deadly background for Majors, placing him definitely, targeting him for Maffitt's gun. Maffitt was an obscure shape, a motionless shape. The gelding blubbered and tossed his head, up and down; and looked toward Maffitt with a quick stiffening of muscles when the latter spoke again, as easy and as pulseless as before.

"A thought, friend Jim."

"Ben," said Majors. "I wish you'd kept on riding." His arms hung steady and without life. He watched the gelding's tail switch, and he was thinking. His fingers made one sudden sharp snap in the dull silence. "I wish you had."

The gelding's ears struck forward; it took one quick step backward, and then at once stood between them, blocking out Maffitt's fire. This was what Majors had been considering. Maffitt had started to speak. He had said, "I have got to find out—" but quit on that, just as the gelding blocked his aim. Majors' heard him grunt; and then Majors, spinning back on his heels, put a shot into the swinging lantern and knocked out the light. This runway dropped to a sightless, uneasy gray. The horse plunged by Majors, into the street. Majors rushed over the runway, toward the indeterminate mouth of a stall. The roar of his shot hadn't yet died—so fast was the run of all this—when Maffitt's gun began to rock the stable with long, hard beats of sound, one report upon another. Lead whined against the partition of the stable office, and struck low into the packed earth, the smell of that rank dirt beginning to rise at once. Turned by the edge of a stall, Majors saw the long flicker of Maffitt's gun muzzle and lifted his own gun and let go. He placed three shots at once, seeing the opposite muzzle light fade. There was a huge breath, dragged-out and broken, from the end of the runway, and a long, long pause, and afterwards the muted echo of Maffitt's body falling. The gun remained half-lifted in Majors' hand, shaped that way from its recoil. The yonder gloom was bottomless, nor could he hear any more breathing. Powder smell drifted across the stable. There was the quick tap of somebody running along the outer walk. Majors wheeled and walked on until the cross-supports of the stable's back door showed their faint seams in the muddy dusk. Maffitt's shape was a formless and sooty blur below him. He reached down and touched the man, and rose again. He thought: "So he found out, and I wonder if he remembers?"

Katherine's voice called, strong and swift: "Jim—Jim!"

He turned and went on until he saw her before him. Brand was behind her and Brand suddenly burst out: "Who—Soder? Maffitt? Who did that?" But he couldn't see Maffitt's shape at the runway's end, and Jim Majors didn't explain. For Majors, always a careful man with a gun, had stepped forward with the weapon still in his fist. And he was saying to Katherine Barr with tone that was hard and hungry and desperate:

"After all that's happened, Katherine? After all that?"

She was tall and slim against the gray race of snow. Her head was up and he saw her eyes, dark as it was here; and he saw her lips. He crossed the distance between and took her with his arms, forgetting the gun. Brand, absolutely shocked, saw those two great people standing together, with the big man's face changing and lighting and dropping down toward the girl's lips. Brand never spoke of it later, but at the moment, the big man's face dropped it was as though a flash of lightning struck him. Katherine's dark head was lifted and her body reached upward from the pressure of Jim Majors' arms.

Brand went down the street and waved at the other people standing outside the hotel. " 'Sall right," he said. " 'Sall right. Better ride home, Dan. She'll be along later."

Dan Barr knew. He said to the rest of the family. "So we ride," and swung to his saddle.

The Sultans were near the rig. Before he pulled away, Dan Barr looked back at Edith and met her glance. The darkness of the day seemed to grow worse and his own mind was darker still. He could remember how she had been at their meetings up in the ridge house—and he wondered if some of that old sweetness stirred her memory now, as it did his. He thought to himself: "There has been too much. Maybe time will soften it. Maybe a month, or maybe a year. Then I'll know. It is all I can hope for. Time." She had turned her head from him and was walking to the rig. So he rode out of Reservation with the other Barrs behind.

Matt Oldroyd remained in the lobby, awkwardly tall and very serious. Tony stood by the desk. She kept her glance on the street, on the departing people; she kept watching the stable's entrance. Her face was soft with its dreaming, and sad with the fading of those dreams. Matt recognized the reason and stood humbly by, waiting for her to see him.

She said, "Katherine is still there in the stable," in a small voice. "So it will be that way."

"I know," he said.

She looked at him, very near to crying. "Oh, Matt!"

"I know that, too," he told her. "But, Tony, here we are."

She said: "Me? I can't stand pity, Matt, and I'm not a very good woman."

"No, Tony. I've made my mistakes, but when a man wants a girl—"

She saw the way he looked at her, so stiff and humble, so terribly serious. It brought a curving sweetness to her lips. She dropped her glance, her breathing disturbed.

Long after she looked at him again, a glow in her eyes. "It is nice to be wanted, Matt. I have been alone so long."

Great Westerns from SIGNET

☐ **SIGNET DOUBLE WESTERN—APACHE HOSTAGE by Lewis B. Patten** and **LAW OF THE GUN by Lewis B. Patten.**
(#J9420—$1.95)

☐ **THE TRAIL OF THE APACHE KID by Lewis B. Patten.**
(#E9466—$1.75)

☐ **PURSUIT by Lewis B. Patten.** (#E9209—$1.75)

☐ **THE ANGRY HORSEMEN by Lewis B. Patten.**
(#E9309—$1.75)

☐ **POSSE FROM POISON CREEK by Lewis B. Patten.**
(#E9577—$1.75)*

☐ **DESPERATE RIDER by Frank O'Rourke.** (#E9534—$1.75)

☐ **AMBUSCADE by Frank O'Rourke.** (#E9490—$1.75)*

☐ **GUNS ALONG THE BRAZOS by Day Keene.** (#E9616—$1.75)*

☐ **LOBO GRAY by L. L. Foreman.** (#E9677—$1.75)*

☐ **THE TRAILSMAN #1: SEVEN WAGONS WEST by Jon Sharpe.**
(#E9307—$1.75)*

☐ **THE TRAILSMAN #2: THE HANGING TRAIL by Jon Sharpe.**
(#E9308—$1.75)*

☐ **THE TRAILSMAN #3: MOUNTAIN MAN KILL by Jon Sharpe.**
(#J9839—$1.95)

☐ **THE TRAILSMAN #4: THE SUNDOWN SEARCHERS by Jon Sharpe.**
(#E9533—$1.75)*

☐ **THE TRAILSMAN #5: THE RIVER RAIDERS by Jon Sharpe.**
(#E9615—$1.95)*

Buy them at your local
bookstore or use coupon
on next page for ordering.

Big Bestsellers from SIGNET

☐ **KEY WEST CONNECTION** by Randy Striker. (#J9567—$1.95)

☐ **THE DEEP SIX** by Randy Striker. (#J9568—$1.95)

☐ **THE DOUBLE-CROSS CIRCUIT** by Michael Dorland.
(#J9065—$1.95)

☐ **THE ENIGMA** by Michael Barak. (#J8920—$1.95)*

☐ **THE NIGHT LETTER** by Paul Spike. (#E8947—$2.50)

☐ **SALT MINE** by David Lippincott. (#E9158—$2.25)*

☐ **SAVAGE RANSOM** by David Lippincott. (#E8749—$2.25)*

☐ **ASTERISK DESTINY** by Campbell Black. (#E9246—$2.25)*

☐ **BRAINFIRE** by Campbell Black. (#E9481—$2.50)*

☐ **STALKING** by Tom Seligson. (#E9197—$2.25)*

☐ **THE 81st SITE** by Tony Kenrick. (#E9600—$2.75)*

☐ **THE NIGHTTIME GUY** by Tony Kenrick. (#E9111—$2.75)*

☐ **THE PHOENIX ASSAULT** by John Kerrigan. (#E9522—$2.50)

☐ **TRIPLE** by Ken Follett. (#E9447—$3.50)

☐ **EYE OF THE NEEDLE** by Ken Follett. (#E9550—$3.50)

* Price slightly higher in Canada